Project Unicorn
Volume 1

30 Young Adult Short Stories
Featuring Lesbian Heroines

PROJECT UNICORN
VOLUME 1

30 Young Adult Short Stories
Featuring Lesbian Heroines

Jennifer Diemer and S.E. Diemer

CONTENTS

By Jennifer Diemer:

UNCHARTED SKY

By S.E. Diemer:

By Jennifer Diemer:

EXTRAS

INTRODUCTION

There are countless young adult books in existence. And among those many stories, there are very few which contain lesbian main characters. If we were to look at YA books as a reflection of the teenage population, we'd have to assume that there were only a handful of lesbian teens in existence.

And that's simply *not true*.

There are so many amazing, vibrant, heroic young ladies who spend every single day living out their own stories. They go to school, hang out with their friends, get great or terrible grades, and they happen to date and fall in love with other girls. These ladies are not mythological figures or legendary creatures, but their virtual invisibility in young adult literature--the very genre meant for them-- renders them as rare as unicorns.

When you're invisible in your own cultural reflections, that suggests a few painful, though unstated, things: You *don't exist*. You're worthless, unimportant. You just don't matter enough to have your own story.

That's not true.

And we need to stop saying it's true by not telling these stories.

We grew up as invisible lesbians. We went to our libraries, desperately searching for stories that reflected us, and found none at all. If the Internet had existed back then, we may have had a bit more luck finding that ever- rare lesbian YA book, but, unfortunately, we didn't have that resource until S.E. was in her later teen years.

We know what it feels like to be relegated to invisibility.

It's 2012, almost 2013. We can make instant coffee with the push of a button. We can touch screens and talk to our phones and do all sorts of awesome, space-age things, and we *still* don't have lesbian main characters in young adult books. There's something woefully wrong with this situation, and, as storytellers (and YA authors), we decided to do our part to change the trend.

And Project Unicorn was born.

Project Unicorn: A Lesbian YA Extravaganza! is a fiction project that seeks to address the near nonexistence of lesbian main characters in young adult fiction by giving them their own stories. For an entire year, we've pledged to put out two short stories each week, each with a lesbian heroine, and each a genre story (science fiction, fantasy, dark fantasy, paranormal, etc.).

This first volume collects the first three months of the project's stories. Within these pages, you have girls who save themselves and each other, girls who rise up against terrible circumstances and find their own strength and courage, girls who deal with real-world problems and decidedly otherworldly ones...girls who live and love and create their own ever afters.

They are reflections of the real heroines who live and love today. Now. Everywhere. Lesbian girls who are not invisible at all, who matter deeply, who are cherished human beings.

This book is for every girl who has never found a story about someone like her.

These stories are for you.

With love,

Jennifer Diemer and S.E. Diemer
December 2012

THE DARK WOODS

WITCH GIRLS

by S.E. Diemer

If you're bad, the witch girls'll get you. Gran tells me that so often that I already know it's coming when she opens her mouth with that one eyebrow raised, already know that, yeah, they're gonna get me if I'm bad. I know. I know.

They come from the dark woods, she says, as she leans forward in her rocker, eyes narrowed at me, 'cause I'm staring at the sewing in my lap, and I'm not paying attention; I know this story. But she clears her throat and glares and won't stop glaring until I listen—so, *yes,* I'm listening. I know that they come from the dark woods, know that they're witch girls, wild girls. They dance in circles in the forest beneath the full moon, and they throw back their heads and howl at the night sky like wolves. Sometimes they even become wolves. Sometimes they make magic charms and sing the stars down to earth, and they're always looking to catch more bad girls. They watch for bad girls on the edges of town, wait in the shadows beneath the leaves, watchful for the bad girls, girls bad enough to snatch up and take away with them and turn into witch girls, too.

Be careful of the witch girls, Gran tells me for the thousandth time. *Don't be bad. Be good.*

She doesn't know I watch for the witch girls on the edges of town. It's only a story, but I still squint and peer beneath the trees, longing to see them with their lush, dark hair, their black skirts and pointed nails. I want to see their cherry-red mouths and their eyes flashing in the moonlight. They're wild, yeah, but powerful, fierce. And lovely, I think.

I want to see something lovely.

I'm not bad. Sometimes I trail the hem of my skirt in the mud, and sometimes I daydream and miss a stitch in my sewing, and I used to think too much about Anna from the village; I'd get all red when I thought about Anna, about wanting to kiss her. She's not like me: tall, gangly legs and arms, too-short sleeves. She's the merchant's daughter, and she's beautiful, wears her yellow hair in fine bonnets, lace-edged. Once I almost told her. I almost told her that I think she's pretty, almost told her that I want to kiss her when she smiles, when she opens her mouth to laugh, but then she started to laugh at me because I was stuttering, because I was red top to toe, and so I mostly stopped thinking about Anna.

I'm not bad, but I'm slow at feeding the cows, and I don't pick the lettuce fast enough, before the rabbits gnaw on the ends, and Gran's temper is short to begin with, so there's nothing but talk of the witch girls morning, noon, and night. But whenever Gran starts in about them, this little curl of *thrill* starts at the bottom of my spine and snakes upward, uncoiling. It isn't fear. It's something else.

It's late, later than I should be out, but the moon is so beautiful, and I feel like walking, so I skirt around the edges of town, holding out my hand to brush against the prickly branches.

And then I see a shadow under the leaves.

The woods are everywhere; we've carved out little places for houses, for gardens, but you can't borrow too much land from a thousand-year-old forest with trees tall enough to scrape against the stars. I'm used to the shadows of animals passing through, recognize them on sight—possum, squirrel, deer—but this shadow isn't an animal's, and the villagers never come this way, always take the path... This isn't the path.

On the edge of the town, beneath the prickling boughs of a broad-sweeping pine, she crouches. She's ducked back in the shadows, but I still see her, her dark outline; the long, frayed edges of her skirt; the mass of black curls that tumbles over her shoulders, some of the hair caught up in the green needles like strands of a spider's web.

She watches me with her head to the side, and her mouth is cherry red and smiling. There is a strange shock when our eyes meet, a spark of recognition, though I've never seen her before.

She is beautiful just as the crows are beautiful: not very, but in sharp, shining, curved ways.

I gasp and trip and blink, and she's gone without a rustle. But I know I saw her.

A witch girl.

When I come home, Gran tells me I was bad for staying out after dark, tells me the witch girls are going to come take me away, and my heart skips, and there is that *thrill* again, twirling around inside of me.

I want to see her again.

It's twilight, and I'm weeding a stubborn patch of potatoes, and when I look up and straighten with my hands at the small of my back, she's staring at me from beneath an evergreen, the witch girl, watching me, and she puts a finger up to her mouth, *shh*, but then she's gone before I can think or take a step.

Witch girls are wild girls, says Gran that night, shaking her head as she sits in her rocker, and she's rocking so hard over the floorboards, thump-thumping. *The witch girls*, she says, *spin charms and dance beneath the moon, and they do not obey the rules of anyone but themselves.*

I want to be a witch girl, Gran, I almost say then, but don't.

I'm finishing up my chores for the night, folding the clothes, five folds for shirts, three for skirts. The house is heavy with heat; sweat glides down my back, and my long braid beats against my breasts when I rise and lift the clothesbasket. I balance the basket on my hip and take it up to Gran's room, open the trunk at the foot of her bed. Humming a little to myself, I put away her things, and I'm about to close the lid when I spy a bit of dark lace, a garment I've not seen before, that Gran has never worn, buried beneath a pile of stockings. I tease it out, tease out the thing it's sewn to, stare at the impossible fabric in my hands.

It's a black gauzy skirt, just like the one the witch girl wears, the smiling girl I saw beneath the trees.

Gran's asleep in her rocker, and I tiptoe past her, go outside, and it's not dark because there's a full moon overhead, and the witch girl is there, under the pine. I worry that she'll vanish again, disappear before I've crossed the lawn and plodded through the garden, but I take slow, steady steps, and when my boots pad over needles, she's still watching me with a half-formed smile, chin tilted up.

Hello, I tell her, and my voice shakes, because it's fragile, this moment, could shatter with too many words.

She says nothing, just keeps watching me, and when I step forward toward her, carefully, silently, she moves forward, too, and then she reaches down, angling her face toward mine until her lips brush against my ear, until her chest is against my chest, and her hand presses five fingers against the base of my spine.

Come find me is what she whispers, and then, like smoke or dreams, she's gone.

Witch girls are wild girls, untamed girls, are powerful and strong girls.

Breathing deeply, I turn around, and I go back into the house, back upstairs and into Gran's room, and I kick off my skirt, brown and coarse-woven, let it fall into an untidy pile on the floor. Then I take out the skirt from Gran's trunk, step into it without a moment's pause, and the old, tattered thing flows around my legs, fits snug over my hips.

I don't think. I don't tiptoe. I just walk down the stairs and out the door, over the lawn and through the garden, and there beneath the trees is no witch girl, but Gran.

We can't hide what we are, I am, you are, she says, and she kisses my eyes with her lips, presses her palms against my cheeks, her eyes wet, weeping. *Witch girls are wild girls, and I thought...I hoped...I could save you from the wild.*

We can't hide what we are, I repeat to her, and she sighs and nods, stepping away, letting me go. I shiver at the absence of her nearness, but I lean forward, kiss her cheek, too, and I walk into the woods, because I must.

Come find me.

In a circle, they dance beneath the night-dark trees, hand in hand, laughing, charming, conjuring.

My witch girl stands apart from the others, her smile luminous under the moonbeams, and holds her hands out to me.

I kiss her cherry-red mouth, wild.

SURFACING

by S.E. Diemer

Sometimes, John drags the mermaids into the woods to die.

There are so many of them here at Port Luca, swimming around the hulls of the ships, sunning themselves on the rocks in the harbor, begging the throwaways of the day's catch. I know that out-of-towners seem to think they're magic, but they're as frequently spotted as a dolphin or a seagull, and they're not magic. Sometimes they're caught in nets, and it's the ones in Dad's nets, the ones on the rocks, that John targets.

He has to be in a particular mood. Angry, yes, but he's always angry, my brother. It takes a certain amount of planning to catch a mermaid on the rocks unaware, to grasp her by the hair or the flukes of her tail, and then use your cronies to lift her up while she's shrieking, screaming, because my brother has a reputation among the mermaids, just like he does at school: bully.

To-be-feared.

He brags about it. He always brags about it, that he took another one into the woods, saying the only way to get rid of their rat-like presence along the boats is to make them fear Port Luca. John's learning to be a fisherman. Dad's teaching him. John hates the mermaids and wants them gone.

Dad tries to talk to him about it, but Dad's gentle, quiet. Mom's gone, and Mom could never curb him, either, but at least John listened to Mom. Sometimes.

I never know about the mermaids until hours later. And it never matters how much later; my heart always goes up into my throat, and I find a way—any way—to leave, to run down to the woods, between the cool, dark pines, find the path I know he took, the easiest path, the only path he'd seek, and then move deep and deeper into the woods, until I find them. I always find them, laying still where they'd crawled back along the path, a shimmer of fish bones and scales and long green hair the only thing left of them.

Like fish, mermaids can't survive without the sea.

I hate him so much in those moments, picking up the handfuls of beautiful pearlescent scales, holding them in my hands so the moon shines over them, flashing in the dark.

The next day, at school, always the same. Like today:

"Got another one," he says, tipping up his nose, smirking at the boys seated around his chair, the desks creaking under them as they perch on the tops, the old wood groaning. "She gave me this," he says, and he holds up his wrist, shows the scratch across it, red and angry.

I sit at the desk furthest away from John, hiding my face behind my hair. I wish she'd bitten his wrist, instead of scratching, wish she'd thrashed enough to fall back into the cold water, safe from him. Alive. But she didn't.

Last night, I tucked one of the scales into my skirt pocket. I've never done that before. I don't know why I did it. I always hate him when I find them. I always pick up the scales and the bones, so light and soft, wrap them in the long, curling hair, and take it all back to the sea. It seems right to do this, but I don't know why, and I always whisper, "I'm sorry."

Last night, I cried. I tried to tell myself, "They're like fish, like dolphins, like seagulls," but I cry over them, too, when they're caught in nets, when I find their bodies broken along the harbor, castoffs from the boats, so wouldn't I cry over a girl who'd looked a little like me?

No. They don't look like me. Not really. But they have hair and eyes and pretty, curling mouths, and long fingers, and they look human, though even the babies here know they're not human. I know they're not human.

I know.

After school, we walk home, but never together. I walk alone, ahead of John, walking quickly, because as long as I'm out of sight, I'm out of mind. He walks with his *guys*, his cronies. We sweep through town and then up along the harbor, toward home.

But today I was running late. I'm behind John, and now John's stopped, and he's staring at something down among the rocks, and my stomach clenches, because he's motioning to the boys to be quiet, finger to his lips, mouth arched in a grin.

All the times he's done it, I've never seen; I've been too far ahead. I was delayed today because I dared to pick an apple from the churchyard. And I wouldn't have noticed that John stopped if I hadn't been so far behind, if I hadn't heard their loud laughter just…stop.

My stomach turns, and I turn with it, looking down the path.

They're moving onto the harbor's beach, skulking quietly, out of sight of the mermaid on the far rocks, the mermaid with her back to them, plaiting her hair, combing it with a fish's ribs.

I scream, but I'm too late. He has her. I stare in horror, sick, as he takes her hair and yanks it backwards, as the boys grab her slippery tail, flapping against the rock now, as they take her arms and hold them tight. They move as one unit, as if they've done this countless times, over the rocks and the sand and the beach, back up the path. Moving toward me.

They don't know I'm here. I panic, heart crushing against my bones, but then I push back into the trees. I'm not going to run, run *away*. This plan forms instantly, like blood spilled: I'm going to save her.

I don't know how. I'm trying not to think about the *how*, and, anyway, here they are, walking past my hiding place. She's struggling, kicking out with her tail, and when I look at my brother's face, everything in me drains away, cold. He looks...evil, his eyes *evil*.

After they've gone, after a few heartbeats, I follow along under the shadows of the trees. I move quietly, avoiding branches and large piles of last year's leaves. They don't see me; they don't hear me, and soon, soon, we reach the path that leads into the woods.

They take it. They take it farther than I've ever gone to find the mermaids, which means that the mermaids must crawl a very long way. As he goes along, John's laughing, tossing back things I can't hear to the boys, who also laugh.

I don't think he's ever going to stop, but he does, just then, startling me. He simply stops, and then they drop the mermaid onto the ground, drop her hard. She rolls away from them, hissing, spitting, tail coiled around herself protectively, and John grins, hands on his hips, before he turns, starts walking back down the path.

"Gotta wash the *fish* off my hands," I hear him say.

They're gone.

The sounds of the forest come back, the birdsong, the rustle of branches, of leaves in the wind. I stare, heart beating so fast it's pushing against my insides, demanding me to listen to its rhythm.

The mermaid stays coiled, panting for a long moment. I know they can breathe a little air—they sit out on the rocks for a long while—but their tails are always in the sea when they do it.

I don't have time.

I step out of the woods, onto the path.

She sees me. She's young, like me. Now that I can see her clearly, somewhat up close, I know she's maybe my age. Her hair is long and green, and her skin is the color of a dead gray fish. She stares up at me, tail wrapped around her, and then she lifts up her lips over her teeth, hissing long and low.

Her upper body may be like mine, but her tail is enormous. No wonder it takes four strong boys to carry one this far. I don't know what to do, but I don't want to make her upset. I put out my hands to her, palms up and open, fingers spread.

"Please don't be afraid," I whisper. "I'm so sorry. I want to help you. Easy, girl."

I usually use that last one on my pony, a headstrong, ill-tempered monster, and it often works on her, but I didn't even think to say it now—it just came. The mermaid stops, puts her lips down over her teeth, cocking her head to the side, like a bird.

She crawls across the space between us, her arms pulling herself along, her tail coiling around and around as she moves, and she comes so quickly that she startles me, but then she's seated before me, taking my hands in her own. She turns them over and over and drops them, rising up a little, looking into my eyes.

"You're not like him," she murmurs, like the shushing of the water. "I thought you were like him. You're not."

I take a step back, breathing out, shaking.

She…spoke.

She continues to watch me, mouth now closed, the end of her tail flopping against the pine needles—restless, like a cat's tail.

"I didn't know… I mean, you can *speak*," I'm saying, and I sound very stupid when I say it, but her face doesn't change. She keeps watching me, eyes wide, wet.

You're not like him.

I finally hear what she said. After the shock fades away, after all I thought I know of them, my lifelong knowledge of mermaids, as constant as a tide, has *changed*, and I *hear what she said.*

I surprise myself. I cry. Two big, fat tears squeeze past my eyes before I can think, sliding down my skin, and then my head is in my hands, and I wipe them away, and I feel strange, so strange, this turning in my heart, but the mermaid watches me, saying nothing.

"I wanted to help you…" I manage, pointing back toward the sea. She looks at my finger, at the path, back to me, but still she says nothing. I look at her, at her body, wonder how I can possibly, *possibly* do this, save her, and I feel the clock moving, like the great big clock in the town square, the arms swinging ever on, and I throw down my bag, my schoolbooks spilling out of the side, and I turn, my back to her.

"Can you…climb on?" I ask, and I peer over my shoulder at her. A long time ago, when we were very small, John and I would take turns carrying one another piggyback, and even though he was always so much bigger than me, I could still carry him that way, shrieking and laughing. It's a distant memory, covered in a haze, but I still have it.

I think she doesn't understand for a long moment, but then I brace myself, because she coils down and pushes herself off, scrabbling onto my back, hooking her arms over my shoulders.

I stagger under her weight, the weight of the tail resting against my back, over my hips, shifting restlessly there. She's as heavy as pails of water, but I can sort of, almost manage. I don't have any part of her to hold onto, and she's clinging to my shoulders without breaking my neck, so I start to move.

She doesn't speak, but her breath is against my neck, her skin against my skin, and I don't quite understand the shiver that moves over my shoulders, but it's there, and then I feel other things, softer things, pressing against me, and I've often *looked* at the mermaids, absently, and I always thought they were beautiful, and here's the truth: the fish tail is odd, and the green hair is unusual, but I think she's beautiful, too.

She chuckles a little. I don't know why she's laughing, but it's a strange little sound, like the clinking of the tiny bells on the bottom of a dress. I redden. I didn't say anything. Mermaids couldn't possibly tell what someone's thinking.

Probably.

The path goes on forever. I sweat beneath her, doing my best to avoid the bigger branches poking up and out of the greenery like broken ribs—I don't know how delicate her tail is. The birds overhead have gone silent, and normally, I would have noticed that, but I didn't, and I was concentrating so hard on the path before me that I didn't notice there's a shadow…

"What are you doing?"

John. He's angry, staring in disbelief at me carrying the mermaid on my back. She drops off me, hissing, backing up and down the path, and the sudden relief from the weight makes me stagger.

His boys are gone.

It's just me and John and the mermaid.

"I'm saving her," I tell him wearily, angrily. I can be just as angry as him. My hands are balled into fists, and I watch him at the head of the path. I hadn't realized exactly how close we are to the path, to the beach, to the rocks, to the sea. I shiver, my fingernails pressing against my palms.

No matter what, *it's close enough.*

"She's just a *fish*, Alice." He's laughing. Of course he's laughing. He puts his hands over his stomach, comically, heaving with laughter. "What did you think…that if you saved her, she'd give you a *kiss*? No girl, not even a *fish* girl, is *ever* going to want you," he mutters, suddenly dark, suddenly stalking toward me. "Why *would* they?"

I stand there. Normally, I shrink back. I agree—yes, why would they? But I don't today. I don't know why. *I don't know.* Maybe it's the ocean, so close. Maybe it's the mermaid cowering behind me. But whatever it is, suddenly I am not shrinking. I am not stepping back. I'm standing nose to nose with my brother, and for the first time, I realize that he's not so much bigger than me.

We're just as tall as each other now.

"Because, John," I hear, as if from far away. And then I know that I'm saying it: *"I'm not like you."*

He stares at me, eyes wide. He works his mouth, like he's going to say something, and then I take a step forward.

"I put her in the woods..." he says, then, childishly. "I put her there..."

"Go," I tell him, and the word is so low, it growls out of my throat.

For a single moment, I think that he's not going to go. But he looks over his shoulder, at the sea, and then he's moving back down the rest of the path, ducking out of the woods, walking quickly. Gone.

I don't think about it. I know I will later, often, turning it over and over in my hands like a treasure drawn up from the deep. But I don't now. I offer my back to the mermaid, and again she climbs on, and I stagger the rest of the way, out of the woods, across the shifting sand, and out onto the rocks, into the water.

When I'm up to my knees in the waves, that's when she lets me go; that's when she falls to the side, into the water. She stays under, just floating there for a long moment, and I'm so worried, I sink down, reaching out to her, but then she's reaching up, and I'm down and in the waves, tasting the salt, choking. She's embracing me and pulling me under the water.

She comes out of the waves upon her tail and helps me stand. *"Thank you,"* she whispers, and as the water runs out of my nose and mouth, as I cough a little, wiping away the salt water, she reaches up, putting her cold hands against my cheeks, angling my head down, and she kisses me.

She's soft and cold and strange, but her mouth is in a smile when she does it. It lasts a heartbeat, and then she's diving beneath the water, swimming away.

I stand alone, feeling the waves crash against my thighs, feeling my heart beat against my bones, feeling my world shift.

I turn, rising out of the sea, transformed.

CURSE CABIN CONFESSION

by S.E. Diemer

"So you're bringing me up to the cabin to chop me up into little bits and make pies out of my liver, right?"

It was a joke. *Why wouldn't it be a joke?* I was trying to make her smile, but she's been *so uptight*, ever since her parents dropped us off, and now her freckled nose goes white as cream as she stares at me with those big brown eyes.

"Robin, seriously," I tell her, when she pales even further. "Are you sick or something? You're *shaking*."

"Not sick," she tells me resolutely, yanking my hands out of hers.

I run my fingers through my hair, frown at her. A lot. She ignores me, wiggles her shoulders so her backpack shifts.

"I'm just…nervous…" she tells me, which, you know, I could never have determined. "This is the first time we're sleeping over…together…alone."

"Right," I say, hands on hips, my bullshit detector pinging. "Because the times we've done it in the locker room…"

"Doesn't count."

"The library restroom…"

"Nope."

"The church basement?"

She gives me a withering look, mouth sideways. "It's not about the sex, okay?"

"Because it's not like you're a stranger to—"

"Mal," she says, stopping on the trail. She rubs at her eyes with both hands, and when she looks away, the blood drains out of *my* face.

She's crying.

"Robin…" I'm suddenly afraid. I reach out, take her hands, and she lets me this time. "Did you bring me out to your family's cabin…" I can't swallow around the lump in my throat, but I try to, anyway. "Are you breaking up with me? Is that why we're here?"

"*What*?" She turns and looks at me and in a heartbeat has me gathered in her arms, rocking me back and forth. "God, baby, *no*. God. Just…*no.*"

"*Then what's the matter*?" I ask her, keeping my voice low and level, the words echoing among the silent pines. She sighs, clasping her hands around the small of my back, pressing her nose against my shoulder.

"I've got to tell you at the cabin." And then she's stepping away, rubbing at her eyes again. "God, I should have just told you from the start. I've been so freaking *stupid*. I just didn't think… I mean—"

"Okay, this is super weird, and you're kind of terrifying me. Just so you know," I tell her, and we continue walking down the path. "How far is this cabin? And why do you have to tell me there? Is it something terrible? Tell me you're not dying. Or that, God, I don't know…you're related to…"

"No, nothing like that," she says quickly, hitching the backpack straps up higher, moving faster, legs blurring in the almost dark. "I mean, I've completely psyched myself out for this, you know? I've dreaded telling you ever since we got together. I just know that when you find out, you're going to…" She gulps down air, won't look at me. "You're going to be the one to break up with *me*."

I stop in my tracks. "Did you sleep with Jenna?"

She stops, too, face hard to see in the twilight now.

Especially since she won't even look at me. "No. Can we just get to the cabin?"

"Did you let Jenna bite you?"

"God, no."

"I...don't know how I feel about vampires yet. But we could work through this if you were changing," I tell her, because when she said *no*, her voice shook.

She doesn't answer.

"I mean...I've done a little reading. They're doing a lot of campaigning now for equal rights and—"

"Let's just get to the cabin," she whispers, her voice strained.

Yup. She's a vampire.

As we walk along in the dark, a little thrill runs through me. I mean, it's not like I haven't watched the shows. I'm not immune to the oozing sex that's pumped out of the TVs. I know it's all PR; it's not really like that, but, yeah, I mean, it wouldn't be *terrible* to have a vampire for a girlfriend. I kind of wish she'd talked to me about it before she decided to turn, but maybe she'd already decided before I came into the picture. We've been dating a year, and a year is a long time, but we've never talked about vampires, which is kind of weird, now that I think about it.

And then we're there. The little building looms up out of the darkness pretty quickly, and Robin's clicked on the lantern. It looks like a camping cabin, not much better than the ones I used to stay in with my family when I was little. When Robin dusts off the latch and unlocks the bolt, the door creaks open, extra eerie because it rained earlier today, and there's a fine fog everywhere, eating up the lantern light.

We go inside, shut the door. There's a beautifully carved wooden bed frame, an ancient stove straight out of the old west (probably), really cute decorations, a la Smoky the Bear. It's nice. It's not my style, but it's nice. A vacation home, which is what Robin's parents have always used it for, she said.

And now we're here. Together. Alone.

I sidle up next to her, batting my eyes as she sets down the bright lantern on the stovetop, flicks the light switch. It's a low light overhead, but she clicks the lantern off as I put my arms about her neck, kiss her cheek.

"This is nice," I tell her, and press my head against her shoulder. "Now tell me what you were going to tell me so we can make the hotdogs."

"So romantic," she sighs, rolling her eyes, but her grin is only a little one, and she's pushing away from me, gently, pacing into the center of the room, running her hands through her hair. Again, she won't look at me.

"So you're a vampire," I tell her, shaking my head. "We'll get through it."

"Mal, I'm not a vampire," she tells me, face turned away.

I stare at her back, at her bent head. "Then what is it?" My voice wasn't as assured as I hoped it'd be. It comes out a little…weak.

"You know, it's kind of funny…" If *my* voice was weak, her voice is *shaking*. "My family always called this Curse Cabin. I never knew why when I was a kid…" She looks back at me, her eyes shining in the soft light. "Mal, I wanted to ask you if, whatever I tell you, would you still love me? But I can't," she says, shaking her head, biting her lip, looking up and at me. "Because that's stupidly unfair. You deserve someone not like me. Not a freak." She takes off her coat, folds it carefully, sets it on the back of the couch.

"A…freak…" I prompt her, my heart beating so fast, it's like a horror movie soundtrack.

"Okay, you know what? I'm just going to tell you, really fast, and then it'll be out there, and you can do whatever you want with it." She closes her eyes tightly, hands balled into fists. "Mal, I'm a werecat."

I blink. She said it so quietly, it takes a full minute before I've deconstructed it in my head and understood.

"A…werecat," I repeat, blinking again. "Like. A werewolf. But. A cat."

"Oh, *God*, I *knew* it," she wails, flopping down on the couch. "I'm ruined to you. Ruined forever—"

"Robin, would you just *shush*?" I tell her, kneeling down next to the couch, smooshing my palm over her mouth. "I'm just trying to understand, okay?"

Werecat. I'm picturing a cat like the one I used to have, a tabby with extra whiskers and a knowing expression, who would pee on my bookbag when he was pissed at me. Which was often. He was named Mr. Snuggles because I'd had him since I was two, and my parents were brave enough to ask a two-year-old what to name a kitten.

"I'm sorry," I tell her slowly, carefully, "I'm just surprised, because I thought there was only… I mean, I thought only were*wolves* existed."

"Werewolves," she says, lip raised, disgust dripping from her voice. "Everyone knows about werewolves. They're so *cool*. They're *sexy*. Not like werecats." She sighs for a very long time. "I will understand," she says coolly, "if you wish to break off our current arrangement."

"You idiot," I laugh, falling on top of her, tickling her stomach. And then I'm kissing her. She tastes of coffee and bubblegum, and she's kissing back, which is the most important thing. "Look, it doesn't matter to me," I tell her, firmly. "It's just an idea I have to get used to. I'm used to looking at Robin the human, and now I've got to get used to Robin the…werecat."

She looks relieved, breathing out, putting her arms around my neck. "Really? You don't think it's…God, I don't know…totally repulsive and weird?"

"Repulsive? Someone who's been watching too much *Secret Diaries of Hell Beasts*." I kiss her nose. "So…" I say, dragging out the word, lips arched. "Are you going to show me your kitty side?"

She shakes her head. "I can do it on the full

moon, and when I'm surprised or frightened…until I turn eighteen. Then I can do it at will. It's in the rulebook," she grins, and I half wonder if there is an *actual* werecat rulebook.

"Okay," I whisper to her, nodding. And then: "I'm glad you told me." I kiss her again.

And again.

We kind of forget about the hotdogs.

I'm having a nightmare. I know it's a nightmare—those are the most terrible dreams, where you *know* you're dreaming, but you can't do anything about it. You're trapped. There's a shadow moving along the wall, a shadow in sort of a body shape, a human, but with spikes coming out of its back, and its face, its hands, and everything is red and black, and I can taste metal.

It's crawling toward me.

I wake up, heart pounding, but there's still something wrong, the feeling of the dream remaining. Something's not right. There's Robin, arm wrapped around me, but I feel a chill breeze, and it's only then that I realize the cabin door is open, and a human form stands in the doorway.

Oh, my…God.

I poke backward. It's the only thing I know how to do in that moment, because the shadow is tall, and it's probably a guy who just broke into the cabin, and we're all alone out here, and *fuck*—why would be break into this cabin unless he saw us, unless he knows we're two girls? And I'm sweating, suddenly, cold, ice cold, and Robin moans a little and then breathes out in a rush, awake, and she's sitting up beside me, staring.

I'm not quite sure what happens. One moment, Robin's sitting there, but then everything sort of…shifts. Was it the cabin shifting, or my eyes, or Robin? I don't know, but where Robin was, there's something suddenly a lot bigger, a lot bulkier, a lot…animaly-er…and there's a deafening roar that rips through my body, and the shape hurls itself off the bed toward the form in the doorway, who's very suddenly no longer there.

The shadows tear off into the woods.

I turn on all the lights. Robin's not in the bed.

I suppose that was Robin.

Someone broke into our cabin. Oh, my God. Someone broke into our cabin. *Anything* could have happened. I run my hands through my hair, sit down in the middle of the floor, rock back and forth, get up, pace, go to the stove and take the heavy iron skillet and sit back down again, holding it.

I don't know how long it's been. An hour? Five minutes? But there's a *crunch* outside, of branches, of leaves, and then there in the doorway is… I mean, it's not a *cat*. It's like a *tiger* or a *panther*, the shape of it, but its fur is as red as Robin's hair.

As I watch, the cabin blurs, the beast blurs, everything blurs, and then Robin's standing before me, watching me with wide eyes, hands held out in front of her.

"Don't worry," she says, taking me into her arms, holding me close, squeezing me tightly. The skillet clangs to the floor, and I'm kissing her, holding her tightly, too, and she's telling me that the stranger's gone, that he's gone, that I'm safe.

Vampires. Werewolves. What the hell ever.

Give me a werecat *any* night.

WOLVES OF LEAVING

by S.E. Diemer

"Do you love me?"

I stare. Her eyes are downcast, mouth working but silent, fingers rubbing at her right shoulder, where the wound is healing—the ugly, jagged bite that Alpha gave her a few days ago.

Cadie should never have challenged her. She should have *known* better.

"Love…" My voice trails off, and I clear it. "I care about you."

She glances at me fast, eyes raking over me. "Not love."

"I need… I need time."

"Is it because I lost?"

I'm silent. No. It's not because she lost. Everyone loses against Alpha. Everyone *always* loses against Alpha. I curl my fingers tightly, nesting them into my palm, staring down at my hands.

"It's because we're fifteen," I finally tell her. "And Momma was fifteen when she made her decision, when she came to the woods. And I think that fifteen—"

"You're not brave." She's standing now, standing over me, lips up and covering her teeth. "If you were brave, you'd tell me you love me. You'd come with me."

Come with me.

I scrabble up, brushing the pine needles from my legs, staring at her. *Staring.*

"Got your attention." She's grinning.

"If we leave the woods, the pack, they'll find us, hunt us. They're *never* going to let us leave," I tell her in hushed, tight words, looking over my shoulder. What if Alpha is listening *right now*? She's everywhere, isn't she? "Cadie, you can't be serious." It's more of a plea than a statement, really. *Cadie, please don't be serious.*

"You say that because that's what they tell you. We don't really know, because *no one ever leaves*," she whispers, stepping closer, whispering into my ear, breath hot against my skin. "Juniper, we could be faster than them, cleverer. You know she'd send Danny, and he's an idiot. We can outwit Danny. We'll be wolves by day, and we're faster than him. We always outrun him on the hunts, anyway."

"The pack sticks together," I whisper—the same words I've whispered every day of my life. Every day. Always.

"We're a pack, aren't we?" She asks me then, and she steps back, searching my face. "You and me, baby. We're a pack…" Her eyes are bright, tear-filled.

Do you love me? is what she's asking.

We've been together for a moon. It's been intense. I always thought she was smart and courageous and pretty, and those three things are important, but Momma made her decisions too quickly, and I don't want to end up like Momma did. I won't. So I'm not going to promise Cadie anything. Not yet. Not now. I want to wait.

But I don't want to wait to leave.

I want to go, want to go so badly it eats me from the inside out, teeth sawing against my muscles in the dead of night when we run together, when Alpha snarls at us, at me, when I remember what she did to my mother.

How I have never, and will never, trust Alpha Wolf.

Cadie looks at me, breathing fast, chest rising and falling as she gathers my hands in hers. "We'll stay out of sight. By the time Alpha finds out, sends Danny after us, we'll be too far ahead. We can do this. Together, Juniper. Don't be like *them*, spending their whole lives in this forest. Come see the world with me."

What did Momma look like, still human then, when she stood at the entrance of the forest, Daddy's hand holding hers, trees ready to swallow her whole? Was she weeping? Was she smiling? Did she make the decision with all of her heart, or did she wonder if she should?

I gulp for air. I close my eyes.

I'm so tired of being afraid.

The decision is reached in silence: clasped hands; a small, tight squeeze. And then we're running, changing, and paws devour the earth as we aim for the edge of everything we've ever known.

Out from beneath the trees, I dare to look up.

There are stars, forever and ever.

DEVIL MAY CARE

by S.E. Diemer

I've never summoned a demon before, though I've read a lot about it. I've got *Miss Ramsey's Occult Compendium* and *The Darker Book of Darkness*, and they made it seem so easy that I thought I'd give it a try one day.

I never thought it'd be today, now.

But it's important. She's important.

My hands are clammy and cold, and when I flick the lighter for my candles, my fingers are shaking. I've cast the circle in salt, and I put up the "protective wards," which involved me reciting a lot of weird syllables that I hope I pronounced correctly, and now I guess it's time, because I can't really put it off anymore. The next step is clear:

Recite the name of the demon you wish to summon.

I've gone through the lists of demons at the back of the book, and I picked "Selimead," for no other reason than the fact that it was the shortest one. I lick my lips, clear my throat and say it as quietly as possible into the stillness.

"Selimead."

And, just like that, there's a girl standing in the center of the circle.

She doesn't...*look* very demony. She's wearing a black dress, and her hair is flowing black curls, and she, actually, looks practically *human*, though a touch emo, until she opens her eyes, and they're red, and nope, absolutely, she's a demon.

"Really," she says, eyebrow raised, staring me up and down, crossing her arms. "*You* summoned me?"

I clear my throat again. "I command you, demon," I tell her, desperately angling my chin up so that it doesn't appear I'm looking at the book too closely. I've tried to memorize the proper incantations for binding her to my will, but I hadn't had much time, and...

"You *command* me," she laughs a little, raising up her too-pale hand over her mouth. "Oh, that's *precious*. Who the hell are you?"

"It says...in the introduction," I tell her, flipping back to the beginning of the book, "that I shouldn't give you my name..."

She's suddenly at the edge of the circle, closest to me, her eyes blazing (no, literally...they're on fire), her teeth--which were so *human* a moment ago--distended and long, edging out and over her lips, dripping white poison out of their razor points. "*What is your name?*" she asks, her words making the floorboards shake and the windows rattle.

"Corrine," I tell her. I didn't *actually* tell her, because I didn't *want* to tell her, but I was suddenly speaking my name anyway.

Also in the introduction: *unless properly controlled, demons control* you.

"All right, *Corrine*," she says, and the sharpened teeth are gone, and she's back in the center of the circle, one hand on a hip, lips curving up in a smile. "Why did you summon me?"

I swallow. I rub at my eyes, and I breathe out very long and low. She watches me with interest, head cocked.

"I..." My mouth has gone dry. It suddenly seems so *stupid*. But she's been missing for a week, and they told me that after a week, the chances of finding her have been staggeringly reduced and...and I can't live without her.

42

There. I said it.

It's true.

"Demons have no patience," she says, grinning at me, lips arched much higher than they need to be, showing her incisors. "Did the book tell you that, too?"

I'm so angry in that moment, I forget to be afraid, I forget everything but the roiling ocean in my belly, crashing, roaring, and then suddenly I'm yelling at her: "I need you...I need you to help me find someone."

We stare at each other in the vast silence that descends when I stop shouting.

"Well," she glances down at her nails, darting her eyes back up to me, brow arched. "Now we're getting somewhere. Who's missing?"

I close my eyes. "Victoria."

How many times have I said that word this week, yelling it as I ran through the woods, through the parks, through the natural conservatory?

If we don't find her that first week, chances are we won't...

"Victoria," the demon repeats. "Vic-tor-eeh-uh." It's like she's *tasting* it. I watch her, arms folded in front of me as she tips her head to the side, blinking. "Important to you, is she?" I think she's laughing at me again, but she's not. She's just...watching me.

"Yes," I say. I choke on the word.

The demon knows, in that moment, what I'd give to find her.

She smiles.

"I think we both know that I am no good contained in this circle," Selimead whispers, her voice soft, soothing, candy-sweet. She takes one step toward me, and another, holding out a perfectly manicured hand, black nails flashing in the candlelight. "I can help you find her, but I need to be out of the circle."

"You must think I'm so stupid," I mutter, slamming the book shut. "I can't believe this...I can't believe I tried *this*." I'm crying. I hate that I'm crying, but I am. I crouch on the ground, and then I'm slumped down on it, sobbing, shoulders wracking as the tears that I thought I no longer contained come pouring out, plinking softly against the floor.

I close my eyes, take a deep breath, swallow down my tears. I'm going to extinguish the candle, and then it's over. Selimead will go back to whatever vile pit she sprang from, and the last hope I had is gone. That I even *had* the hope now seems so stupid. Laughable.

Dad was right.

I should just let her go.

"Wait." I scrub at my eyes fiercely, glancing up at the demon who hovers as close to the edge of the circle as she can get. Her eyes are round as planets, her mouth turned into an uncomfortable frown. "Why did you go to so much trouble if you're just going to dismiss me so quickly," she murmurs all in a rush, her tone soft, sweet again. "Just...*wait*. We can work this out."

"I *went* to so much trouble because I was *desperate*, and I was *stupid*," I tell her, snatching up the candle-snuffer (the book was very specific about this: *do not blow out the candles or the demon will steal your breath*). "Good night."

"She's still alive."

I stare at her. It's as if all the breath in my body is gone, and I gasp, stars pricking around the edges of my sight.

The demon watches me for a moment, then grins lazily, one corner of her mouth lifting. "She's only about a mile or so away."

"Does anyone have her...did anyone take her...is she *safe*..." I rush, but Selimead holds up one long, painfully-white finger. Except for the fact that she's chalkier than poster paint and about as evil as poison ivy, she's incredibly pretty, which is something that the book said they do to mask their inherent repulsiveness. *Think of what you are most attracted to, and the demon will become this*, the page stated in dire, pointy capital letters.

The fact that it--I suppose, for now, *she*--knows I'm attracted to emo girls with curly hair should be a slightly distressing thing.

Or the fact that she—so she says—knows where Victoria is.

And she's not telling me.

We watch one another again over the circle of chalk on the floor. Her arms are crossed and she's grinning smugly. I'm glaring at her, the tears drying on my face.

I need her.

She knows it.

God *damn* it.

(Kind of literally, in this case.)

"Let me out, Corrine," she practically purrs, stepping closer—as close as the chalk circle lets her. "Let me out, and—together—we'll get Victoria back for you." Her eyes are the color of drying blood, irreversibly spilled. I stare into them for a long moment, blink.

I'm many things. But I'm not stupid.

"Swear by the devils' code that you will honor your promise to me, and bring no harm to any living—or dead—thing," I say in one breath. "Swear it, and I'll let you out."

She opens and shuts her mouth. "I…"

I lift up the candle-snuffer.

Two can play at this game.

"I, Selimead, swear that it will be done as you say," she mutters sulkily, watching the candle-snuffer. "Now *let. Me. Out.*"

I flip to the back of the book and move my right hand in a circular motion, counter-clockwise, as illustrated. "I do lower this circle," I murmur, closing the book.

Selimead is gone.

"Fuck," I whisper as the candles gutter, as the room grows darker. I turn, glancing behind me, drop to my knees, even peer under my bed.

Nothing.

"Oh God, oh God," I breathe in and out, sitting back on my heels. But...

"You should *see* the look on your face!" She's gleeful when she appears beside me, legs stuck in front of her and crossed daintily at the ankles, her skirt tucked beneath her knees. She leans back, grinning, pointed incisors jutting over her lip. "Well?"

"I hate you," I hiss, feeling like I'm five years old again, my big brother keeping my stuffed pony out of reach.

"You know," she says, brow arched as she leans toward me, close enough to kiss. "I'm not terribly fond of you myself."

"Let's just get this over with." I'm standing, my heart pounding, but she stands, too, still far too close for comfort.

"Let's," she hisses, grinning like a tiger. We both turn and walk out of my room, down the hall and staircase, out the front door. My parents are both still at work—I have about an hour or so before they come home. I take a deep breath and exhale, realize how close to my ears my shoulders are. Everything about me is one big *stress*.

Just let me find Victoria. I would give anything to find Victoria. I don't believe in God, but hell—I didn't exactly believe in demons, either. And the prayer can't exactly *hurt*, but when I think it, tossing it up into the slate-gray clouds like a baseball pitch, Selimead veers a little away from me, pausing, placing her hands on her hips.

"What did you do that for?" she asks, nose wrinkled.

"What?"

"Pray." She shudders. "I can feel that, you know. Makes me iller than a keg party." She places a few fingers over her mouth, turns a little green. "Seriously, don't do it. It's not like it's going to work, anyway. The divine has a little more to worry about than one stupid dog."

46

I stare at this heartless creature for a full moment, my skin growing hotter and hotter until I feel that I might explode lava out of the top of my head. She was grinning in the beginning, but when another tear courses down my cheek, she stops smiling.

"Brimstone," she mutters, crossing her arms. "You look like a kicked puppy when you get like that. Just stop. Sorry. I didn't mean it. It's just the divine doesn't really care about people or people's problems. You're gonna have to trust me on that."

"I don't trust anything *about* you," I manage, swallowing. "Where the hell is my dog." I grit it out, teeth screeching together. Selimead runs a hand through her long, black curls, turning up her nose at me as she hops off my parents' porch.

"This way," she says over her shoulder, and I have no choice but to follow the demon into the twilight.

"She's not stupid." I can't believe I'm saying this, *especially* to a demon, but everything's under my skin at this point, and I've *got* to say it. "She's…she's everything to me." I swallow, stare down at the earth moving under my feet, at my hands balled into fists. Selimead doesn't even break stride, but glances at me sidelong.

"I said I was sorry. I don't think a demon's ever said that before in existence. I'm gonna get such hell when I get back." She sighs, reaches out, and then I can't *actually* believe she's doing it, but it's happening, so I suppose my brain catches up with my arm, because she's snatched up my hand and threaded my arm through hers. Like we're weird Victorian ladies or something, out for a twilit stroll.

Not desperately trying to find her. Victoria. The only creature in the world who gives a shit about me.

"Let me go," I mutter, trying to disengage from Selimead. And she lets me go, eyes wide in the darkness.

"Anyway." She flips her hair over her shoulder, putting her nose in the air, but her movements are jerky. "How long have you been summoning demons? You're terrible at it."

I fold my arms in front of me, duck under a branch as Selimead plows into the woods on the other side of the street from my parents' house. It's just light enough to see obstacles, but that's not going to be true for much longer.

"You're my first," I mutter, ducking again. Selimead doesn't duck—she just keeps walking, and somehow, impossibly, the branches aren't there when she moves through them.

She glances at me, rolling her eyes. "Okay, then, let me give you a few pointers…"

"No, really. Don't." I breathe out. "I think you're gonna be my last, thanks so much."

She looks a little hurt. A *demon* looks hurt, but I shake my head, move around a tree in the direction she was striding.

"Who the hell is interested in summoning demons these days anyway? What, you wanted a hobby that no one else had ever thought of? Don't they call people like you hipsters?" the demon snaps, but I ignore her, continue to move farther into the dark, silent wood until I realize she's not beside me. I glance over my shoulder, see her standing about ten feet away, arms crossed. I should be afraid—her eyes are actually *glowing* in the descending gloom. But I'm not. She's watching me with an expression I can't read, eyes hooded.

"She's on the move," says Selimead, then, shaking herself out of reverie. "She's heading more to the right, and she's about a half mile ahead in the woods." She steps past me, hitching her overly-lacey skirts up so that they don't get stuck on brambles. It's a very convincing form she's chosen—her stockings are even lace.

I blink, realizing I'm looking at her legs. And then I'm blushing, running my hand through my hair, fishing a ponytail holder out of my pocket.

"I'll have you know," says Selimead, calling it out huffily over her shoulder, "that you were *my* first, too."

I blink, trot to catch up and get hit in the mouth by

a whip-like branch for my efforts. I back up a step, reach up to my lips and take away my hand. Blood. I sigh.

She's suddenly in front of me. She was about ten feet ahead, but when I blinked, she was positioned close enough to kiss again, the red of her eyes so bright I can hardly see anything but the darkness and those two, glowing orbs. She reaches up with a finger and rubs it against the scratch on my lip. Staring steadily into my eyes, she brings her finger up to her own mouth and places it against her tongue, licking the blood off it.

I reach up and touch my lip. The pain is gone. The scratch is gone.

"Thanks," I manage, my heart pounding as she steps back, mouth curled up prettily at the corners.

We walk along in silence, feet snapping twigs and branches. Her eyes light the way, but just a little, and I keep moving from sheer euphoria that possibly, we might find Victoria, back to: she's dead and gone and I'll never see her again.

It's not that I want to feel this way, but I remember the feeling when the neighbor said he'd seen her. It was the first lead in days that I'd had, and screw my learner's permit, I'd sped my clunker to the street intersection he'd said he'd seen her at, and had spent hours combing the touching acres. Nothing. Not even a wisp of hair. I'd died, then. It had been too much hope, and then…nothing.

I can't *get* my hopes up again. I swallow, rub at my eyes as I pause for a moment, leaning against a pine tree. Selimead pauses, too, glancing at me.

"She's very close," she says, and am I absolutely crazy, or was it nice, the way she'd said it, the smooth way she'd annunciated the words, the way she stepped forward, holding up her hand to me as if she'd touch my elbow…

I close my eyes, breathe out, and then…

A bark.

"Oh my God," I whisper, and then I'm racing through the woods, branches whipping my arm that I hold up in front of my eyes, lashing against my legs, the back of my head. Another bark, a little ahead, and then I'm crashing through the barrier of trees, and out and into the meadow on the edge of route 217, and up the embankment. The stretch of pavement lies in front of me, and across it, in the median is *Victoria*.

Oh my God, it's Victoria.

"Wait, baby!" I cry out, sobbing, as she starts to wag her tail. She's thinner than when I saw her last. Her golden coat is caked with mud—she's almost unrecognizable because of it—and her tail is filled with burrs, but this great doggy *smile* comes over that beautiful, sweet face, and she bounds toward me, toward me across the pavement...

God, no. No.

A car. It's like a nightmare, moving through quicksand, panic, horror, a nightmare, it has to be a nightmare, because Victoria is outlined so perfectly, so vividly in the car's headlights, and when it hits her, she flies through the air like something in a dream. Not real. It couldn't possibly be real.

The car's gone.

She lays on the pavement, still warm to the touch.

I'm sobbing, pressing my forehead against her dirty, slick coat, can't breathe, can't breathe.

There is motion, beside me, as Selimead sinks down to her knees, so close that her thigh is against my thigh. I register that as if I was floating outside of my body, watching those motions like I'm no longer human, like I'll never feel or see or hear again. Selimead reaches down, hand hovering just over my shoulder, working her jaw, and then she doesn't touch me.

She reaches out, and she presses the palm of her hand against Victoria.

Everything's soft. I'm in bed. What...?

Like a strange half dream, I peel the covers back, and Victoria is here, sleeping on the edge of the bed. She's matted and muddy and dirty beyond belief, but when I press my fingers against her coat, she squirms under me, rolling over and licking away my tears as I crumple, sobbing into her fur.

She's *home*.

I lift my head, rubbing at my eyes as I stare at the chalk circle on the old floorboards of my bedroom.

At the candle burning.

Victoria presses her warm, golden body against my leg as I stare down at the circle.

From *Miss Ramsey's Occult Compendium*: *when a summoned demon's purpose is completed, the demon is returned.*

I reach up and touch my lip, my fingers cold and stiff. I breathe in, and I breathe out as my heart thunders.

I pat the floor as I sit down on the cool boards. Victoria *thumps* down next to me, wagging her tail and staring at the book in my hands with interest. "C'mon, baby," I whisper to her, turning the pages until I'm on the summoning ritual again. "We have a demon to thank."

A CRAVING

by Jennifer Diemer

Every day, she comes to the cottage door and knocks three times. Every day, I peer at her through the curtains, tell her that I can't let her in. They've warned me—a hundred times, a thousand—that I mustn't ever let her in.

And every day, she smiles at me and removes from the basket balanced on her hip one perfect red apple. So red, surprisingly red. She holds the fruit out to me, flat on her palm, just beneath my nose, and I breathe in its sweetness. My hand itches to enclose it; my teeth worry at my lips.

But, "No, thank you," I say—every day—even though I feel weak from my longing and must duck inside, must sit down and breathe and try to forget. The little men told me that the girl is a witch, that she means to steal me away from them for some dark purpose. Sometimes I believe them, when they speak in their low soft voices and pet my head and promise to keep me safe, to protect me from the dangers of the forest.

Sometimes...at night, before sleeping; or while I'm sweeping the floor with the ragged old broom; or while I'm setting the table—eight plates, eight cups—I remember the girl and her gleaming apple, and my hand itches again, and my eyes half-close, and I think, *Surely they're mistaken. Surely she intends me no mischief. Just one bite... What harm might one small bite of apple do?*

Irreparable harm, they say, when they come home

from the mountains and I ask them. They make me swear again that I will not let her in, that I will not accept her fruit, that I will stay here, where I am provided warmth and food and comfort and companionship. Where I am safe, where I belong.

And I swear. I always swear. But every day, my words taste less true, like a cake stirred with salt in place of sugar. I don't think they notice how I glance away when I make my promise, how my hands twist behind my back.

I'm waiting for her. The beds are unmade, and the washing has soaked too long in the tub, but I'm perched on my stool beneath the window, back against the wall, and I'm listening for the rustle of her skirt (having caught up dead leaves in its loose hem) and for her knock.

My feet scuff against the floor, impatient. I chew my nails.

Then it comes: *knock knock knock.*

And, "Apples," she calls. "Apples for sale or trade."

I close my eyes and open them—wide. Then I stand and draw the curtains aside.

"Good afternoon," she says, slipping the hood of her cloak back to fall upon her shoulders. Her hair is the color of honey and long enough to spill over her hips, to tangle with the rough straw of her basket.

"Good afternoon." I regard her coolly, though my heart tumbles and my skin warms as she watches me watching her and smiles gently. "You're late today. I thought you might not come."

"Were you hoping I would not?" She tilts her golden head, gripping the bottom of her basket with one hand and gesturing toward the woods with the other. "Did you hope that the forest had gobbled me up?"

"No," I whisper, startled by her words, because they—the little men—have used them often themselves. *If you disobey us, girl, the forest will gobble you up. We won't be able to protect you anymore, not if you disobey.* I shake my head and swallow. Perhaps it's a common expression. I've spoken with so few people; I know nothing but what the little men have told me. When they found me in the forest, I was only a child, lost and crying, waist deep in snow. I would have frozen if they had not taken me in. I owe them my life, my loyalty.

The girl—the witch—clears her throat, and my gaze is drawn to the fair skin of her neck, stretched pink over her collarbones. "I have fine ripe fruits today, still warm from the sun, plucked with my own fingers." Her eyes tease, tempt. "Tell me—would you like to buy an apple?"

"No—" I begin to say, out of habit, out of duty, but my tongue resists, falls slack, dead against my teeth. My fingers curl upon the windowsill and my mouth waters as she scoops from her basket an apple as red as hands chafed raw from too much scrubbing: my hands, reaching out now in accordance with their own secret pact. Disobeying me. Disobeying *them*.

The girl's green eyes shine. The apple hovers beneath my nose, near enough to bite. "Will you?" she breathes, and she looks so hopeful, so lovely, and the sweet scent of her—no, not of her; of the fruit—makes my head dizzy, my knees weak. "Will you?" she says again, moving nearer, trampling the hedge.

"I…"

But the beds are unmade. What will they have for dinner? And the washing… I must finish the washing. I must set the table and peel potatoes for soup and—

"Will you, Snow?"

"I… I promised." My hands are fists. I take them back, push them hard into the rough edge of the windowsill. "I promised that I would—"

"Obey?" She raises one honeyed brow.

I blush and bow my head.

Then she does an odd thing. I lift my eyes and watch her breathe upon the apple in her palm and, afterward, rub its surface against her bodice, over her heart.

"What are you doing?"

Again she holds out the apple to me, and its scent fills my nostrils, makes me shiver and crave.

"Look," she says.

I cock my head at her but peer at the fruit, and within its mirror-bright shine, I see…myself. My dark hair is piled loose atop my head, and my cheeks are flushed, my eyes black and wild.

"*There* is the one you must obey. Be fair to yourself, Snow. Obey your own heart."

I look up, startled. "No, I can't. I *can't*. They saved me. They take care of me—"

"And you have thanked them in kind. There is no debt owed."

"But…" I am standing on my stool, half out of the window, half in. "But they'll be angry. They'll never see me again if I…" The apple looms large before me, filling up my sky.

"If they love you, they will come to understand." She takes one step nearer; her body is pressed against the cottage wall. There are only bricks between us. Dull red bricks and one beautiful red apple.

This close, closer than we have ever been, she examines my face, and I examine hers. Blood quickens within me as my eyes rove the soft slope of her forehead and the place where her hair curls against her ear. She is a girl, like me, but there is a knowing, an ember in her eyes that melts the last drift of winter within me.

I lean out through the window, on tiptoes on my stool, and I bite the apple she holds in her hand.

My teeth break the skin easily. The flesh tastes like sugar. It tastes like the sun and the forest and the world. It tastes like… It tastes how I imagine…

I lean forward again, and the girl leans forward, too, and when our lips meet, I know why the little men warned me against letting her in. I know why they feared she would take me away from them.

And I know that she is not a witch, only a girl. A girl who has come to my door every day. She offered me her apples every day. And every day I refused—not because they told me not to let her in, but because I was afraid to let myself out.

I hoist myself onto the ledge, drag my skirts through the narrow opening, and fall into her arms. I feel her body fit against me, feel her sweetness slide into place at my core, in my heart.

"I shall pay you in trade," I say, breathless, my mouth pressed against her hair. "For the apple."

She draws back, grazing her lips against my eye, and smiles. "Oh? What will you trade?"

I kiss her again. And again, and again.

"I like your trade," she whispers. "Perhaps you would like another apple?" Her mouth moves in a sly curve as she slips her arm through mine.

We leave the cottage, and as it recedes behind us, then disappears between the trees, I wonder if my life there was real at all, if it was only a dream. Because I'm awake, deeply awake, and the forest does not look quite so dark anymore.

NATURAL

by Jennifer Diemer

She tells me her secrets, and they sink into my veins, some sweet as sap, some bitter, like wind through dying leaves.

"Everyone at school thinks I'm such a freak." I toss my backpack to the ground, and it lands with a smack and a squish—sinks into a perfectly backpack-sized patch of mud. I sigh. "Of *course.*" I collapse against the tree. "I've got the worst luck in the world. The worst life."

My gaze falls to the side, and I pick up a red leaf lying next to my hand, twirl it in my fingers, nestling my head into my favorite crook, between two big roots. "Okay, I don't have the *worst* life, obviously. I know that. I *know.* But that doesn't mean my problems are any less real, or important. They're very real. To me."

Overhead, the branches sigh. I look up and admire the arcing limbs' familiar sweep. Against the sky, the branches weave together in pretty patterns, like Gran's lacework. I don't know what kind of tree this is, but it's been *my* tree for as long as I can remember. No one else knows about it. No one knows this is where I come when I leave, when I *have* to leave. When I need someone to talk to.

Someone who won't judge me, or laugh at me, or

punish me.

Trees are great listeners, you know.

Especially my tree.

Okay, that sounds crazy. But right now, this tree is the best friend I've got.

"So today, in biology, Stacy thought it would be *hilarious* to ask Mr. Frank if homosexuality is natural or *un*natural, if there are gay lions and toucans and things, and of course he got all flustered and dropped his chalk and then gave us a stupid pop quiz, but everyone was staring at me, and Lucas threw a paper airplane onto my desk. I didn't unfold it, but one of the wings said 'unnatural' on it." I roll my eyes and gulp down a sob. "I just wish I'd never told Janet how I felt about her. That was the dumbest thing I've ever done. I knew she wasn't into girls, but…" The leaf flutters from my fingers. "I hoped. I wished."

I laugh a little, though nothing's funny. "Have you ever wished?" I ask, gazing up again at the branches overhead. "Do trees wish? I guess you don't really have any reason to. I mean, you've got everything you need— earth, water, sun." I trace a hand over the rough bark of the trunk. "It must be nice to be a tree. So simple."

When she curls up on the ground and rests her head against my roots, I imagine my branches cradling her—no, I imagine arms, not branches. I imagine arms and legs and eyes, a mouth, a voice…

She's right: it is simple to be a tree. It's simple and dull, and perhaps I was never meant to be a tree at all, because I want to move, *I want to* feel, *I want to speak and laugh and sing. But my roots are too deep, and I have no tongue.*

All I have is the sky, the stars, and my wish, the same wish I wish every night.

I hate that I'm crying—*again*—but at least I was able to hold back my tears until I got here, safe beneath my tree. Sometimes, when I'm feeling this low, this alone, I wish a crazy thing: I wish that this tree was not a tree at all...but a person. A girl, even. A girl like me. And I wish that we met here every day in the forest, far from home, from school. I wish this was *our* place, our special, secret, safe place.

We could listen to each other, and make fun of the idiots in class, and she would tell me that, in time, Gran will get used to the idea of me being a lesbian, that she'll ask to see me again, that she'll tell the nurses I'm allowed in her room. Or even if she doesn't, even if she really has disowned me forever, my tree-friend would give me a hug and promise that *she* would always be with me, no matter what, that she didn't think I was unnatural at all—because if I was unnatural, that would make her unnatural, too.

I sit down on a root and cradle my head in my hands. It's stupid to wish for something so weird, so impossible. But I wish it, anyway. I wish it hard, pressing my hand into the bark until it makes imprints in my skin. When I pull away, I gaze at the tree veins on my palm and feel a little dizzy. I've given myself a headache, I think, from crying, but I'm not crying anymore.

I rub the tears from my face and sigh, stand up. Somehow I always feel a little better after I spend time with my tree.

I'm afraid.
Afraid?
I think I'm...changing.

There's a girl standing next to my tree.

I gasp when I see her, and I feel silly for gasping, but I still want to turn around and go back the way I came, because I come out here to be alone, not to be bothered by…

Well, I don't recognize her. She's about my age, but she doesn't go to my school. Maybe she's new?

She's staring at me. She looks kind of…confused. Or worried.

Maybe she's lost.

I swallow and stuff my hands in my pockets. My backpack falls to the crook of my elbow, so I just let it slide to the ground.

"Hi," I say, and my heart does a little flip, because I *never* say hi first, to anyone, but this girl looks even less likely to say hi than me, and… Okay, she's kind of cute. Pretty.

Yeah, she's really pretty.

Her hair's a bit messy, tangled, and she's wearing a plain brown dress, no shoes. But somehow the simplicity suits her. She looks natural. Sweet.

"Hi?" she whispers, and then clamps a hand over her mouth, as if she's mortified that she spoke the word out loud.

I can't help myself; I laugh, but then I take a few steps closer, approaching her like I approach the feral cats on our street: slow and patient. "Did you just move here?" I ask. "Because I don't think I've seen you at school."

The girl shakes her head, one arm wrapped tight around the tree. My tree. With her free hand, she points up at the interlaced branches. "I…" She clears her throat, eyes on the ground. "I have been here…for a long time. But not at school, no."

"Oh, homeschooled, then?" I wrinkle my brows

and come up on the other side of the trunk. "I always wanted to be homeschooled, you know? But my mom's working a double shift, and my dad is hardly around. And Gran..." I sigh and tilt my head against the bark. "Gran's sick, and she doesn't want me near her, anyway."

"I know," the girl whispers, which makes me peer at her closely, eyes narrowed. "I mean..." she stammers, visibly swallowing. "I mean, I know..." She bites her lip, sighs.

I circle around the trunk to face her. "What's your name?"

"Oh. Um..." Her eyes dart about; she picks at the bark with her nails. "Fern?"

"Fern? Really? Like in that book about the pig?"

"What?" she asks, looking more worried than ever. "Isn't Fern a good name? What about...Leaf? Or Sky? Rain?"

"Hold on a second." I jam my hands into my pockets again and sigh. I have no idea what's bothering this girl, but I can't stand seeing her so nervous, especially not because of me. "Let's start over. Hi." I wave. "I'm Terra. What's your name?"

She looks panicked for a moment, but then her eyes fall upon the tree, rest there, and she runs her hand over its bark, lids closed. "I'm Ash," she whispers, certain. "My name is Ash. I've lived here all my life. I have no family. I'm alone. But I...I've seen you before." She says the last part shyly, like a secret, and blushes.

"Here? You've seen me here?" I cross my arms over my chest, suddenly anxious. If she's seen me here, then... Has she heard me talking to the tree?

"Yes. Here."

"Were you hiding? Were you spying?"

"No. You came to me. There was nowhere for me to go. And you wanted me to listen. Didn't you?

"Wait. What?" My head is reeling. I've never come to the forest to see *anyone*. No one but...my tree.

"I made a wish," Ash goes on, and now she's

staring at me again, green eyes gleaming bright. "I wished to be a girl like you, and I am." She gestures down at herself, rests a hand against her cheek. "I think I always was…inside."

I take a step back. "No, I don't—This makes no sense." Have I lost it? Is this girl even real? I mean, I had a good day today, actually, so I don't know why I'd start hallucinating now.

Impulsively, I reach out a hand and intend to tap her on the head—just to make sure she's solid, not a mirage—but instead I lay my hand on her hand, the one she's pressed against her cheek, and she doesn't pull away, doesn't even look surprised.

She's smiling. A soft, sweet smile.

She's beautiful when she smiles.

But that doesn't change the fact that she seems to be suggesting that she is—or was—my *tree*?

"Please explain what's happening here," I whisper.

She sighs, and her expression takes on a dreamy glow. "I made a wish, and I think…*you* made a wish. And that changed things. Changed me." Her eyes trail up the length of the trunk at her side. "It pushed me out. The wish. It set me free."

I stagger on my feet a little, remembering the wish I made yesterday. I wished that my tree were…a person.

I wished it, and now—

"I hoped that we could be friends?" Ash blinks at me, taking a step nearer.

"Friends?" I shake my head, overwhelmed, baffled. I've never had a friend, not really. And the butterflies in my stomach are fluttering like crazy—*not* because I'm excited about having a friend, but because I think I have a major crush on this tree-girl. Just like that. The way she's looking at me…

I swallow. "Okay, this is all really weird, and I'm still not entirely convinced that I haven't lost my mind, but you *feel* real enough, and, if you *are* real, we'll have to find you a place to live, and then you can go to school—

with me. I mean, if that's what you want to do."

"It is," she smiles, and she takes my hand between both of hers, presses it against her heart. "Thank you for wishing for me, Terra." And she kisses the back of my hand.

My heart nearly bursts out of my chest.

I'm pretty sure she's real.

Ash turns away a little, presses her palm against the trunk for a long, silent moment. Then she looks at me with a big, blue-sky smile.

I can't help it; I give her a giant, goofy smile back.

"Tell me about your day, like you always do," she says. "How did your Spanish test go?"

"Oh…right. Muy mal," I laugh, and it's so easy to talk to her that I go on to describe the Incident at lunch—Stacy tripped and got spaghetti all over her frilly white shirt—and Ash giggles and squeezes my hand, and we're so busy laughing and chatting—and, okay, gazing at each other with wide, sappy eyes—that I fail to notice the moment we step out of the forest, onto the road, but Ash lags behind, peering over her shoulder, between the trees.

"We'll come back," I promise. Then I wag my finger at her in mock reproach. "But only after we get you some shoes, young lady. Your poor feet!"

Ash takes a deep breath, gives me a grateful smile and nods her head.

Hand in hand, we move in sync beneath the open sky.

I'm free.
And me.

HAUNT

by Jennifer Diemer

When our lips touch, bits of myself float away, like iron shavings drawn to some kiss-activated magnet. There goes my fretting about next week's chemistry test, drifting off, up, fragmented and forgotten. There goes my stress over the upcoming family reunion, where I'll have to see Aunt Peg for the first time since she found out I was gay and posted that Bible verse (something about being "detestable") on my Facebook wall. *Floating, floating...* And there go all of my worries about not being smart enough, pretty enough, *normal* enough to ever make my parents proud.

All of my brain junk vanishes, just like that, and what remains is only *this*, this moment, her mouth pressed against mine, her arms curved around my waist, her heart beating against my chest. (It beats, really beats.) The nearness of her—aligning, allaying, quenching.

What else matters? Nothing else matters. Because I know, *now*, right now, that what we have is beautiful, that *we* are beautiful, that the whole world is *beautiful*.

The beauty is so palpable: I taste its sweetness, smell its roses, feel its velvet settle over me like a fitted cloak.

I lean back against the tree and sigh into Ailsa's hair. It moves with my breath, her baby-fine hair, moves just like my hair, like anyone's hair, and she feels warm, vital against the length of my body, but I know—we both know—that the moon is yawning, the sun is waking, and we are running out of time. Again.

"I don't want to go," she whispers, lips brushing my neck, hot tears sliding over my shoulder. "I want to be with you. I want to leave this place. I want to—"

"Shh," I whisper, holding her close, because I'm near tears myself, and we only have a few minutes more. Tears are best saved for later, shed in a locked room and muffled into a pillow. I overlooked the pillow once, and my mother heard me, knocked on my door—*What's wrong, Tam? Why are you crying? Is it a boy?*—and I couldn't help it: I laughed. She thought I was hysterical (I was) and jiggled the knob until I leapt out of bed and swung the door open, said, "No, it's definitely not a boy."

And then I told her. I finally *told* her, and she said she didn't believe me, that I was just *going through a phase,* but now she was the one crying, and she called Aunt Peg while I fell back on my bed and stared at my ceiling and left through the window when purple light filtered through the curtains, when twilight came.

"There must be a way," Ailsa insists, and she pulls me in and kisses me hard, desperate. It's like this every night. We hold on to each second, hold on to each other, afraid to let go, because when we let go, we disappear, both of us. She evaporates. I watch her trickle away. She fades, and then I go back to my faded, half-alive life. But at least it's a life.

For Ailsa…there's just the dark.

We're on the ground now, lying curled together on our mossy bed, and she's bending over me, still crying, but softly, valiant, trying to smile. *You're a miracle*, I think, because she is, because somehow we found each other, despite impossibility, despite time and physics, and she loves me. I never knew I could love someone so much.

Her eyes—grey, like the stones surrounding us—gleam in the dreaded, rising light. "If only," she says.

"Yes," I sigh, and we kiss again, and her weight presses upon me, grounds me, anchors me to the moss, to the earth, deeper.

And then the pressure's gone, and I open my eyes, squint at the yellow rays filtering through the leaves, and my arms, holding nothing, drop to my sides.

Alone, I rise and walk between the gravestones, my hands dangling, scraping against the names of people no one remembers, people buried in this forgotten place to be forgotten. The cemetery surrendered to the green invasion of the forest decades ago, and a network of vines trails from grave to grave.

I crouch in the pine needles, and my fingers trace the eye of the peacock feather chiseled crudely into the headstone before me, but my gaze is fastened to the name, her name: *Ailsa Merrick.* There's no date, no epitaph. Just those two words. My heart stops every time I read them, every time she leaves me.

I never meant to fall in love with a ghost. I never meant to fall in love. But when I found this place, when I saw her standing beside her headstone, beneath the moon, hands clasped, patient, as if she were waiting for me, as if she'd always known I'd come, I knew that I was already changed, just by the sight of her.

She was so *real*, more real than anyone or anything I'd ever encountered. And in this wild, neglected place—with her, my Ailsa—I feel alive, truly alive. Only here.

In cemetery lore, peacocks symbolize eternity, immortality. I looked it up on the Internet once. Maybe that's why Ailsa wakes every night, why her sleep is splintered. Maybe the person who engraved her headstone knew her sad story, wished her more time, another chance. Love.

But I'm greedy: I want to watch a sunrise by her side; I want to watch the newborn light play over her skin, paint her golden. Someday, I'll unbind her from this grave, this forest, from the darkness that takes her away from me, dawn after dawn.

For now, though, the stars are kind to us, and they

keep our secret safe.

I press two fingers to my lips, touch my fingers to the headstone.

Then I run away from the woods, keep to the shadows on the streets, and climb in my bedroom window, shower and dress for school. I'll sleepwalk through class, nap before dinner, and when the sun dips below the trees, I'll find Ailsa, silver-eyed, waiting at the cemetery's edge. Beautiful. Mouth to mouth, we'll resurrect by moonlight.

DREAMING GREEN

by Jennifer Diemer

I catch the seed in my hands. It grazes over my gloves, weightless, roughly round—and green, like the trees in Zavi's book. I'm not certain that it *is* a seed; I've never seen one this close. Only the Verdis are permitted to plant and propagate. Besides, I haven't been earthside in five years, not since my parents signed me up for this flight. There wasn't a lot of green in Lumino, anyway.

And there is none at all here. My eyes have gone dull from all of the silver and black, white and grey-blue.

Sometimes I ache for green. When I'm not aching for Zavi.

The seed begins to lift from my palm; I cover it with my other hand, enclosing it completely. I peek between my gloves, marvel again at the living green.

I never realized that I dreamed in color until I boarded this ship. It's normal, Zavi promised me, to have strange dreams when you're skyside, but my dreams aren't strange so much as tragic. They make me long for impossible things: green grass under my bare feet, green forests so thick with trees that I have to turn sideways to brush between the trunks.

Once I saw a willow in Zavi's book and cried myself to sleep, because there are no more willow trees, not even in the Garden Museum at Capital City. *It's not a priority*, my father told me, when I asked him why we were letting the trees die. *They're fragile, and they claim too much space, and we have all the trees we need at the oxygen farms. The trees' time, the Green Time, is past.*

I can't help thinking that I was born out of sequence, misplaced, too late.

I close my fingers over the seed and turn, slowly, toward the entry chute. Zavi—floating on her tether a hundred feet to my right—peers over her shoulder at me and propels herself in my direction.

What's up? she think-speaks.

I found something. Let's go inside. I want to show you, I tell her, and she nods, brown eyes curious behind her helmet shield.

Side by side, we boost into the chute, and when we burst through the tube and insert our boots into the metal traps, Zavi punches the combination on the containment keypad. Doors slide out, cut off the tube, and another door clangs down to seal up the space top to bottom. The lights snap on, and the grav sinks until we're heavy enough to undo the traps and remove our helmets.

I fling off my gloves and unstrap my neck belt with one hand, then flip back the helmet. My sweaty hair clings to my forehead; I push it away with my wrist.

"Look," I whisper, as Zavi—already stripped down to her black boardsuit—comes near, resting her chin upon my shoulder.

"What is it?" she whispers back. "A rock?"

"No, I don't think so." I take a deep breath and catch Zavi's scent: hot and loamy, like the Verdis' greenhouse back in Lumino. My mom took me there once on a water delivery, and I've never forgotten the way the humid, glass-walled place smelled—or felt. A wet heat upon my skin. There's little to feel here on the ship, shut up and controlled as it is.

Except when Zavi's close—like she is now. Then I feel…too much.

"I think," I say, turning the green sphere in my fingers, quirking an eyebrow, "that it might be a seed."

Zavi narrows her gaze for a moment, then slants a smile at me, stepping around to take the seed in her own hand. "Mir, a seed? Seeds don't just float around in space." She holds the thing near her eye, squinting. "You're right, though. It's definitely not a rock. And I admit—I've never seen a seed in my life." Her shoulders rise and fall in a shrug.

Zavi grew up on this ship; she's never been earthside, not ever. Her mom gave birth to her on board, then died. Her dad, the flight commander, keeps to the command module and only speaks when he has to. He's said about fifteen words to me since my parents committed me to the Youth Study program and I joined his team. He doesn't talk to Zavi much, either. She thinks her mother's death took the life out of him.

I bite my lip as I remove my remaining gear, letting it fall to the floor. My boardsuit always feels so thin, barely there, when I lose the heavy helmet and equipment. I tug at the zipper on my chest—it slid down when I stripped—and regard Zavi with a small smile. "Should we show it to your dad?"

"*Give* it to my dad, you mean." She closes her hand over the seed. "No, he'd just take it, put it in a capsule and forget about it. I say…" Her eyes capture mine, glittering. "Let's plant it."

"What?" I take a step back, shake my head. "No, we can't—"

"Why can't we? It's probably not even a seed, only some space junk. Nothing will happen. Nothing will grow." She stares at me for a heady moment. Then a grin slinks over her face. "Probably."

"Zavi—"

She rolls the seed into my palm.

"It's your call," she smiles, resting her hands against my hips. Electric sparks zing all throughout my body. Her black, short-cropped hair shines as she tilts her head near. "You found it." She taps my forehead with her own. "You choose."

My heart is beating so hard, I'm sure she can see its outline through my boardsuit. A sudden courage—and my longing, my verdant dream—compels me to whisper, "Yes. We'll plant it."

Zavi gapes, then laughs. "Well, this will be an adventure."

We've broken at least five hundred rules. We stole the door code for Storage Unit T—Zavi distracted her father while I hacked his system—snuck into the unit and are now snooping in every crate, agonizing over the time passing by, searching for—

"Dirt!" Zavi exclaims, and I slap a hand over her mouth, even as I scoop out a handful of the brown stuff and grin. Our eyes lock, and I hold my breath.

"Are we really going to do this?" I watch the soil slide between my fingers. "If we're caught, I'll be kicked off, dropped who knows where. And I'll never see..." I swallow. My mouth is so dry.

"Hey, Mir," Zavi says, sliding her arm over my shoulder. "If you're kicked off, I'm coming with you."

I look at her quickly, startled. "Are you serious?"

She doesn't answer, just holds my gaze. Then she moves close, slides her cheek against mine, and I feel her lips against my ear: "Promise." Her mouth moves into a smile. "Now let's find a bowl or something and see what that baby's made of!"

It's growing. It's *growing*.

It really was a seed. I snatched it from space; who knows where it came from? Who knows what it's going to *do*, to *be*?

I can't breathe.

Zavi crouches beside me, leans forward on her knees until she's face to face with the not-possible-but-somehow-growing sprout. "When did this happen?"

"I don't know. I don't know." I sit down on the floor beside her, cross-legged. "Sometime during the night? I woke up and opened my closet door to change and—I mean, it's not…It *can't* be growing. It's only been one day. Don't plants take a long time to grow?"

She shrugs and touches the newborn leaf with her fingertip. "Depends on the plant. My mom's book doesn't go into much detail. Can't, I guess. Only the Verdis are supposed to know that stuff."

"Yeah," I breathe, leaning back. "Only the Verdis are supposed to grow plants, and we're growing a plant, and I think we should just take it out on our next recreation drift and…let it go. Then no one will know. They'll never know. We'll be safe."

Zavi's face stills, and her mouth draws into a thin line. She stares down at her hands in her lap and speaks very softly. "Is that what you want, Mir?" Her shoulders slump, and she turns to face me. Her eyes move over my face, restless. "To be safe?"

"Zavi, I want…" My nerves falter. *I want you*, I think-speak, but she can't hear me, isn't wearing her helmet, and, anyway, that's beside the point. We have to deal with this plant, this terrible, miraculous, lovely green thing straining to live. In my closet.

My earth-starved eyes water at the sight of it. I blink and swallow, and I know: I can't let it go. I can't give it up. It'll die if I release it back into space. It'll die like the trees, like the willows.

I sigh and, summoning the last trace of bravery within me, put my hand on Zavi's knee. "We need light," I say. "Lots of light."

I wake to a dream.
Green.

I'm not sleeping—I know I'm not—but there's green all around me, above me, trailing over my bunk, twining around my wrists, my ankles. I'm curled on my side, and the bed is tilted, pushed up by the undergrowth, nudged half off the ground by the trees—

By the *trees*.

I sit upright, tearing leaves with the sudden movement, and open my eyes wide.

A forest. I'm in a forest.

I'm dreaming.

No, I'm awake.

Frantic, I pinch myself, dig my nails into my palm, and I stare at the red welts on my skin, stunned, because I'm definitely not asleep, not dreaming, and there are trees in my room.

Except…this isn't my room. It's bigger, wider; I can't make out its boundaries, can't even see the ceiling overhead because of the trees, the leaves. The green.

The plant, I think. The plant did this. It couldn't have; this is *impossible*. But it's happened, anyway. And Zavi needs to see—

I crawl over the vines on my mattress and lower my feet to the mossy floor…or ground, I guess. Dirt. Earth. I can't think about it, can't let myself try to figure it out, because I'm this close to hyperventilating as it is, so I plunge into the forest and aim toward the door, where the door *should* be…

Where the door still is. I scrabble for the latch, drag the door open.

And I see silver and black: the long, narrow corridor of the ship. And Zavi. She walks toward me, teases—"Morning, sleepyhead"—smiling her warm, sly smile, but her face changes as her eyes examine me, as she comes near and stops, leaning against the wall, looming.

"What's wrong, Mir?" Her hand smoothes my hair back and comes away with a bit of leaf. She lays it flat in her palm, shaking her head. "The plant? Did it die? Should we have watered it more, stolen more lamps—"

I put a finger to her lips, and she cocks an amused brow, puckers her mouth against my skin. A kiss.

I swallow and take a few deep breaths. "Zavi, promise not to scream, okay?"

Her brow arches higher, but she nods her head and takes my hand, squeezes into my room behind me.

And screams.

"Shh." I pull her further in and follow the trodden path back to my bed. We sit down awkwardly on the leaning frame.

"What—"

"I don't know."

"But it's—"

"Yeah. A forest."

"Mirelle! A forest?!" She faces me, eyes wild and shining. "Trees? Real trees? I've never seen... I never *knew*..."

It's then that I realize Zavi hasn't ever seen a tree before, besides the ones in her book. A sort of giddy excitement bubbles up in me, watching her gaze all around us, watching her hand trace over the bark of the trunks, watching her fingers slide over the glossy leaves.

"It's too beautiful," she breathes. "I want to live here forever."

Tears stand in her eyes. She's staring at the trees—numinous, aglow—but I'm staring at her. Even amidst all of the green, at the center of my dream-come-true, I'm longing. For her. I breathe in the lush air, and the words come naturally. I'm dauntless, unafraid. "I want to live here with *you* forever," I say simply. I smile a little to myself, feeling silly, bow my head and toy with a curling vine in my lap.

"Mir." Zavi tilts up my chin. The awe in her eyes has been replaced by something new, something that makes my heart forget to beat, something that makes me feel as if I, too, am a green thing, a sprouted thing, growing, leaning toward the promise of her sun.

"Oh, Mir," she sighs, and a tear glides over her

cheek as she reaches out to catch my own tears on her finger. "I've wanted… For *so long*, years, I've wanted— Can I kiss you?"

I don't answer, can't answer, because I'm already kissing her, and the contact is electric, *fire*. I pull back, stunned. But Zavi grins and reaches for me, claims my mouth with her own. She's so soft, and her hands entwine with mine, and then her arms enclose me, pull me close— not close enough—and I'm breathing Zavi, breathing green, and I feel like I could float away, I'm so light, so *free*.

"Let's stay," she whispers in my ear, her finger tracing stars over my bared shoulder. "Let's stay here. Let's never go back. That's not our world. It never was."

I shudder beneath her touch and open my eyes to find her staring at me—eager, solemn, awaiting my reply.

I lay my hand against her cheek, and she leans in to me. "We planted a seed," I whisper, "and it grew us a world."

"Yes," she smiles, kissing my hand.

"We'll make our own rules." I laugh. "Or no rules. We'll take turns naming the trees. We'll care for them and kiss"—I take her lips, savor them—"in their shadows."

Zavi grins, slips my arm through the space between her elbow and her hip, begins to rise, but I hold her back. "What about your father?" I ask.

"He would make the same choice." She smiles at me softly, pressing a hand to my heart. My lashes flutter. "He would run toward love, if he had a second chance. He'd never let it go if it was in his arms."

I hug her close, and then we're hand in hand, turning sideways to brush between the thick trunks. We run and run. There's no ending to the forest, to our world, in this dream-that's-not-a-dream. I caught the seed because my hand was open; we planted the seed together, and it *grew*. There's no logic to it—a forest on a spaceship?—no method, no way to predict what's to come.

It's like drifting into space without a tether and hoping that you'll somehow float home. I can only wonder. And trust. And love Zavi.

"I love you," I say, and she sweeps me off my feet. I squeal and laugh and wrap my arms around her shoulders, arching down to kiss her.

"I love you, Mir." She grins up at me. "Before you came, all I knew was black sky, stars. I fell in love with the earth when I fell in love with you."

I melt against her.

When we find the willow tree, I tilt my head back and smile and whirl around, and Zavi holds me beneath the dripping green, and everything's new—*I'm* new.

At nightfall, we'll learn the new stars together and dream beneath our own sky.

MIRRORS

by Jennifer Diemer

There's a girl in the mirror who isn't me.

I snap the compact shut with a click and flip it over in my hand, trace the inscription on the back with a shaking finger. It's not English; I don't even know if it's words. The lines engraved into the silver are fine and curving, like filigree... But they aren't symmetric, and there are breaks, stops and starts, so I don't think they're just a decorative design.

The lady at the pawn shop said she'd had the compact in her window display for years, that no one had ever shown interest in it before. It was dusty when she brought it out for me, and so tarnished that it felt oily in my hands.

I don't know why I bought it. I've never had a compact, don't bother much with hair or makeup. I don't even carry a purse. I was supposed to use that money on new shoes for school, but I hate going to the mall, and my old shoes aren't so bad, just a little scuffed at the toes. Plus...I saw Lucy and her friends hanging out at the food court, and if they'd seen me, even glimpsed me, they would have started fake-kissing each other and chanting *gay McCray, gay McCray* in their stupid cheerleader voices. So I turned around and left, ran until I was out of the mall parking lot. I get enough of that torment at school.

I've walked past the pawn shop hundreds of times. I guess I never paid it attention before—I usually walk with my eyes down, so I don't make any accidental eye contact—and I wasn't trying to pay it attention today, but I was huffing past on my way home, and the compact kind of…twinkled at me. I couldn't help but stop to take a closer look. It was open, little round mirror facing upward, toward the ceiling, but even from the street, I could see that the reflection was *moving*.

I take a deep breath and reopen the compact now, and the girl's still there, looking out from the mirror, staring back at me with one hand pressed to the surface, as if she wants to come out. As if she's some sort of genie in a bottle—or a compact, I guess.

Maybe I haven't been getting enough sleep. I do have nightmares a lot, especially lately. My mom thinks that I'm stressed out, that the dreams would stop if I just did yoga and drank her herbal tea, but even if those things *could* help me relax, I'd still have to go to school in the morning and face the chanting, the spitballs tangled in my hair.

The girl in the mirror is beautiful—though not in the way Lucy and her friends are beautiful. She looks more…open, somehow. Her brows are up, not narrowed, and she's wide-eyed and sort of smiling, or—no, I think her lips naturally curl upward like that; she has the kind of mouth that probably always looks amused. I've never seen eyes quite so green before. Or…I don't know. They remind me of something. I can't remember.

Now the girl's waving her hand. She's waving her hand and sort of motioning with her head, looking straight into my eyes.

I think she *sees* me.

But how is that possible? How is any of this possible?

I lift up my free hand and wave it in front of the mirror, just to find out if she really *can* see me, and I guess she can, because she starts waving her own hand even faster and then kind of bounces up and down and smiles. And now I know that she wasn't actually smiling before, because this smile is like Christmas and summer vacation and that expensive dark chocolate Mom always buys me for Easter all rolled into one. It's like...*joy*. I don't think I ever knew what "joy" meant before, not really, not until now.

I can't look away from her smile, and when she pushes her face closer to the surface and tucks her hair behind her ears, I stare even harder, eyes so wide they hurt, because her ears are decorated with swirls of metal, pierced through over and over, silver spiraling in complex patterns all along her lobe, so similar to...

I flip the compact over and shake my head. I don't understand any of this. But the girl's ear jewelry looks as if it's from the same alphabet as the scrollwork on the compact.

She's still there when I turn the compact back over, and she looks worried at first, forehead wrinkled, but then her face smoothes out, and she smiles her joy-smile again.

I swallow and try to smile back.

But silver filigree isn't the only strange thing about her ears. They're *pointed* at the tips. Pointed like elves' ears. Or fairies'. They look very convincing; I can't find the seams where the stuck-on pieces join up with her skin. But, granted, the mirror is tiny, about the size of my palm. I can't expect to make out every detail.

The girl keeps staring and smiling, and I blink at her, blink and think, and then—very carefully, very slowly, I click the compact shut and place it upon my bedside table, and I sit still for a moment before I fall back on my pillow and close my eyes. Behind my lids, I see a shining tracery of the word-like forms engraved on the compact's surface.

Maybe I should have just braved Lucy and her gang and bought the shoes. Shoes are a lot less complicated than compacts. Or, at least, *this* compact.

It's all so strange, so surreal. I don't understand why she smiled at me like that. No one's ever smiled at me like that before.

It was a joke, a game, but I'd wanted it to be true so deeply that I overlooked the obvious, ignored the anxious flip-flop in the pit of my stomach. Because there was another sort of flip-flop in my stomach, and it had nothing to do with teenage pranks.

Abby Wingrove was a new girl, a transfer from Syracuse, but already she occupied a seat at the popular girls' lunch table. Lucy's table.

Abby wasn't just pretty but *lovely*, in the way that Jane Austen heroines are lovely: rosy-cheeked, charming, spirited. Her hair was long and black, her eyes midnight blue, and she always wore a rhinestone kitten pin on the collar of her sweaters—a tribute, she told me, to her beloved cat, Whisky Whiskerson, who had died a short while before she and her family moved to Rochester.

I wonder now if that was true.

For a couple of weeks, I'd noticed her noticing me. She wasn't sly about it. She gave me sweet smiles and little waves during Chemistry every time I glanced her way, and whenever we had to work with partners in Spanish class, she fell into the habit of sliding into the desk next to me, pushing it up against mine so that our elbows and hips were touching.

We were working out the conjugation for *ver* when she told me she had a crush on me. She wrote it on my notebook paper, leaning over the desk so that her arm brushed against my chest: *I like you, Mai. I REALLY like you.* I blushed and stared at the letters for a long time before I took up my pen, scrawled a spindly *seriously?* beneath her neat cursive.

I swear on my Whisky pin, she wrote back, tapping the top of her pen against my hand and winking at me. "Want to come over tonight?"

And that's when I felt my first warning flip-flop,

but I ignored it, blamed it on the cafeteria's canned spaghetti.

Si, I wrote, and she giggled, and I blushed again.

I felt like a pauper at Abby's house, with its Grecian-style columns and four-car garage. Neither of her parents was home, so Abby led me straight up to her bedroom—full of unpacked cardboard boxes—and closed the door.

She wasted no time.

"Do you want to kiss me?" she asked, breathless. Her eyes were wide, shining.

"W-what?" I edged back toward the bed and sat down. "I..." My mouth was dry all of the sudden. On the walk to Abby's house, I had daydreamed, wondered if we might kiss at the end of the night, but to be confronted with the possibility so barely, so quickly, froze my tongue—and my body—in place.

"Come on, Maisy. I thought you liked me, too. Don't you?"

Her lower lip started to tremble very prettily. I swallowed hard.

I'd always known I was a lesbian, and somehow, this year, all of the kids at school had figured it out, too. Maybe it was a lucky guess, but when I didn't deny it, when I looked all wide-eyed and flushed at the accusation, they ran with it, made an art of it with their back-of-the-bus taunts and captioned stick people in pornographic positions on the classroom chalkboards.

But I'd never kissed a girl before.

I'd imagined it hundreds of times... Maybe thousands. And now, it seemed, it was about to happen. I, Maisy McCray, was about to kiss the prettiest girl in school.

My stomach flip-flopped insistently. It wasn't the

nice kind of flip-flip. Still, I rose from the bed and took a tentative step in Abby's direction. Her eyes darted away, toward the closet, and I saw something strange flit over her expression, something like fear. But the next moment, she moved nearer to me, reached out for my waist and rested her hands comfortably upon my hips.

Then she closed her eyes, tilted her chin forward ever so slightly.

I leaned in, licked my lips—

And the closet burst open, and a white flash blinded me, and all I could hear was laughter, laughter so sharp it must have punctured my chest, because I couldn't breathe, couldn't *see*, and then Abby said, "Told you I'd prove she was a lesbian," to the shadowy hyenas amassed around her, waving cell phones and cameras in the air, and I fell toward the door, stumbled out into the hallway and tripped down the steps.

Somehow I made it home. To her credit, my mom never asked me what happened. She met me at the door, took one look at me and gathered me into her arms. Then she filled the tub neck-deep with hot water and my favorite pineapple bubble bath, and she left a mug of lavender-chamomile tea on my nightstand, perfectly steeped.

I can't really say things got worse at school after that, because they'd already been the stuff of nightmares. But I failed my Spanish test and stopped caring about studying altogether. Some part of me went Novocain-numb. A large part. I felt like half a person, or a zombie, or an understuffed doll.

Abby tried to talk to me in the hallway once. We were alone, and I think she was going to apologize, but I couldn't look into her midnight blue eyes again, because then I would feel, and then I would fall. So I just ran.

Many prey animals survive by running. The mouse runs from the cat; the rabbit runs from the fox. But it's hard to know which way to run when the foxes are everywhere and there's a cat hissing at every turn.

I almost leave the compact at home the next morning, but something makes me grab it, stuff it into the bottom of my backpack. It seems wrong, somehow, to shove it in amongst all of the ordinary things: notebooks and textbooks and pencils with broken tips. But during lunch period, I find a deserted stairwell and root it out, lay it flat on my palm. I feel a little thrill of—what? hope, anxiety?—when I flip open the top. I'm worried that the girl won't appear again. I'm worried that the girl *will* appear again. Because what does it mean, to see a girl with pointy ears inside of an old compact's mirror? Does it mean I'm crazy? Sick? Desperate? I want to see her smile again…

She's not there.

I gape.

Neither is my reflection.

Stupidly, I shake the compact as if it's a vending machine, as if the girl will tumble out of the sky like an unstuck bag of potato chips. She doesn't, but I peer closely, because instead of the girl, I *do* see a sky, or bits of sky between the tops of trees. Willow trees, I think.

And I wonder, then, if the girl isn't actually trapped in my mirror but loose somewhere in the world and had been gazing at me through her *own* magical compact. Maybe she dropped her compact on the ground, in a park or a forest, and lost it.

Then I remind myself that this is real life, not *Sailor Moon*, and I have American History in two minutes. Sighing—I'm more disappointed than I would like to admit—I drop the compact into my backpack and shuffle off to class.

After last period, I don't want to ride the bus, can't

bear the thought of it. Even when I sit at the front, right behind the bus driver, Millie, Lucy and her friends still throw spitballs at me, and Millie never says a word to them about it. She's always too busy grumbling about her cold coffee and the kids hanging their arms out of the windows, making rude gestures at the cars beside us.

I sling my backpack over both of my shoulders and keep to the shady sidewalks. When I drag myself away from my thoughts and look around, I realize that I'm standing at the entrance to the nature trail, the one my dad and I used to walk on weekends when he was still around. I haven't been back since the divorce, though I didn't keep away because of bad memories. I just kind of forgot the place existed. It belongs to a different time in my life, when I had friends and a father, when there were slumber parties and midnight bowling, when I smiled at other people and they smiled back.

It all seems made-up now, like a lonely person's fantasy.

But I walk the trail and find the tree where my dad and I carved our initials. It was his idea. He chiseled a heart around my blocky *M.M. was here.* I don't feel much when I look at the carvings now. Maybe there's a sort of dull ache somewhere deep in my chest, but I just cough into my hand and continue along the path.

Mom won't be home for hours, and I don't have any homework—at least, none that I intend to do—so I take my time, pausing to brush my palms over bark and shiny leaves.

There's a boulder off the path, big and smooth with a flattened spot at the top, a perfect place for sitting. It's an easy climb, even though my old shoes have no tread, and I like being so high and half-hidden behind the shaggy pines.

I let my backpack fall from my shoulders to rest on the rock beside me, and then I pull out the compact.

I take a deep breath and open it.

She's there.

She's *there*, and I smile without thinking, really smile, and she smiles back, smiles with her whole face, and I can see her ears again with their pointed tips and silver swirls, and her eyes gleam so green that I gasp, because I remember... I remember where I saw that shade of green before.

It was here. It was here, on a walk with my dad.

I'd forgotten. How did I forget?

I was in kindergarten, or maybe first grade. We'd just bought cupcakes from the bakery downtown, and I was carrying the white, sweet-smelling bag in one hand, gripping Dad's fingers with the other.

"We'll have a picnic!" Dad announced, and we walked the trail, wandered off into the woods, and found a lake. It was a beautiful lake, startlingly blue. I dropped Dad's hand and the cupcake bag and ran up to the edge of the water, where I crouched down to watch a pair of ducks skimming over the surface.

I looked down at my reflection, fascinated by the way it moved and shone in time to the heartbeat of the water...

And then, suddenly, my reflection wasn't there anymore. Someone else was.

A girl, about my age, stared up at me from beneath the water, and then she rose up and, laughing, shook her wet head of hair, just like my puppy Moss shook his head after Mom gave him a bath.

She wasn't an ordinary girl. There was something shining about her; she shone all over. And her eyes were so green that they seemed to have a light behind them, beaming out.

I glanced back over my shoulder, but Dad wasn't watching. He was chatting on his cell phone with someone, speaking in a low voice behind the willow trees.

I turned back to the dripping, smiling girl. "Do

you like cupcakes?" I whispered.

She tilted her head at me, laughed again.

I crawled over to the pastry bag and, trying not to snap any twigs beneath my knees, crawled back. We only had two cupcakes, and I thought Dad might not like it if he knew I'd given mine away. But I wanted to give it away. So I dug it out and presented it to the girl on the palm of my icing-smeared hand.

She licked her lips, took the chocolate cupcake, and had it gone—paper and all—in three bites.

Her eyes seemed to glow even greener, and her wide smile revealed little chocolate-stained teeth.

"Where's your mom?" I whispered then, but the girl didn't hear me, or didn't seem to hear me. She stepped out of the water and knelt on the ground beside me.

And then she kissed me.

It was a little kiss, a baby's kiss, and we both giggled behind our hands afterward, and suddenly I wanted to introduce her to my dad, wanted to ask him if she could come home with us for dinner, but when I called for him, she shook her head hard—once, twice—and then leapt back into the water, sticking her hand up in a little wave before she disappeared completely.

"No, come back!" I called, and Dad walked up beside me, stuffing his phone into his pocket.

"I'm right here, honey. I was just talking to a friend."

"So was I," I whispered, but he didn't hear me, and when he asked me what had happened to my cupcake, I told him that I ate it already, that I couldn't wait.

I blink down at the compact, shaking my head. The girl stares back at me, and it's unmistakable: she has the same eyes as the little girl from the lake.

But that… That couldn't be true. I'm not sure if that encounter really happened. I was an imaginative child, prone to fantasies about dragons and unicorns. For years during my childhood, I was convinced that a gnome not only lived in my closet but stole my single socks for his mismatched sock collection. He even had a name: Footman.

The girl in the lake was probably just like Footman, another childhood daydream, *had* to be that, because what sort of parent allows their child to swim alone in a hidden lake in the forest? And how could she stay underwater for so long?

I don't know.

I don't know.

Nothing makes sense, and I want to shut the compact and never open it again. My life is problematic enough without...this. Whatever this is.

But the girl is gesturing to me, trying to regain my attention. I gaze at her sullenly, accusingly, and she holds up a finger, as if to say, *Wait*.

And then she disappears, and the compact shows me blue slivers of sky framed by draping green branches. Did she drop her compact again?

I sigh and rest my head on my knees. I should talk to my mom about this. She would listen. She would try to help me. When I came out to her, she reacted in the best way possible—by shoving me into the car to go get banana splits. To celebrate.

But the truth is, I haven't even told Mom about the kids at school, about the things they say, how they treat me. I don't want to upset her, or embarrass her. I don't want to be one more disappointment in her life.

And I can handle it. I've handled it up until now. For the most part. Whenever it's too much to bear, I spend a period in the bathroom or eat lunch in the library, where I can be alone.

I'm tired of being alone.

Somewhere beside me, a branch rustles, and I wipe my face, glance over, expecting to see a bird fluffing up its feathers. But instead I see her.

Her.

It's really her.

I mean, I think she's real. She's climbing onto the rock beside me, all long-limbed and sure-footed. When she reaches the top, I edge back a little, because how are you supposed to react to a daydream, a hallucination, a *reflection* come to life?

But then she crouches beside me, peers at my face with something like wonder, and she almost touches me; her fingers hover inches from my cheek. She lets her hand fall, though, fall right into my hand on my lap, and I jump a little.

She's smiling. It's that smile, that joy-smile, and she's smiling at *me*, definitely at me, because no one else is here. We're alone, and we're together.

I swallow. "Hi," I whisper, because I'm lost in her green, green eyes and can't think of words, thoughts, right now. So, "Hi," I say again, and she squeezes my hand.

Her hair is wavy, long, autumnal red and gold, and she's wearing something shimmering, a dress that gleams like copper. I feel very plain in my t-shirt and jeans, but she's not paying any attention to my clothes. She's staring at me, smiling at me, as if she's waiting for me to do something, say something.

"Um…" I stammer, watching her hand in my hand. Her skin is so soft; I've never felt anything so soft.

I'm really nervous.

"How did you—I think… Do you know if—" I shake my head, try again. "Have we met before?"

And I don't know if she understood me—she still hasn't spoken a word—but she tugs on my hand a little and begins to slide down the side of the boulder. Quickly, I slip my backpack onto my shoulder, tossing the compact in its open front compartment, and follow her down to the ground.

She's taller than me, though only by a few inches, and when she gazes down at me, her smile softer now, my stomach flip-flops—or, no, it *flutters*, like wing beats.

92

I know you, I think. Except...I didn't think that at all. That wasn't my thought. It came into my head, filled the same space as a thought would fill, but it feels different, *sounds* different than the familiar whispers of my own brain.

It kind of had an accent.

I shake my head, confused, but the thought comes again: *I* know *you.*

And the girl bows her chin at me, expectantly, hopefully. Because it was her thought. I know it as surely as I know that none of this is possible, and yet it's somehow real.

We're running. I don't know where we're running to, but it doesn't matter, because she's still holding my hand; she hasn't left me, hasn't made fun of me, has done nothing but *smile* at me, and I really hope she doesn't turn around, doesn't see the tears in my eyes. I never cry, not anymore, but this is different. These tears are different.

Do you remember? I hear then, and when I look up, I see that we're standing before a lake, the lake with the willow trees, with the cupcakes, with the girl. And I'm here with the girl, and she's...

Who is she? Or...*what* is she?

I don't think she's...

I don't know what I think.

She guides me to the edge of the water, and we kneel down together, just as we did all those years ago.

Do you remember? she asks again.

I spread my hands over my lap, sighing. "I don't—How do I—" Her cool hand presses against my lips for a long, lovely moment. And then she removes it, taps a finger against my brow, then against her own brow.

I take a deep breath, close my eyes, and think as hard as I can. *Yes, I remember you. I mean, I think I do. I was never sure if I made you up, because... Because that kind of stuff just doesn't happen. And so I kind of forgot, and I'm sorry that I forgot. But I still don't understand. How did you get into my compact? How did you...find me?*

I feel her hand again, this time grazing my eyes. I open them, gaze at her.

She's so beautiful.

Her smile changes then, slants to one side, and I watch, amazed, as she bows her head and blushes.

Can she hear my thoughts? All of my thoughts? The notion makes me blush, too, because now I can't *help* thinking about her, how lovely she is in this strange, unexpected moment.

She points to the lake, then leans over it and gestures for me to do the same. I prop myself up on my hands and knees and look into the water beside her.

I feel dizzy at first, think my eyes are playing tricks on me, because in place of my own reflection, I see her smiling face, and where her own reflection should be, my face gazes out with a shocked expression.

Our reflections are reversed, mixed up.

The girl gently takes my backpack into her hands and removes the compact. She opens it and hands it to me, but all I see is the sky, the branches. Then she makes another *wait* hand motion, and she leans over the lake again.

And she appears in the compact.

All this time, she's been watching me in the lake.

Do you understand now? she think-speaks, and I sort of nod and shake my head at the same time. Her fingers trace over the symbols engraved on the compact's surface. *They are a spell*, she explains, looking a bit sheepish. *To bring you back to me. But it took such a long time! I am not a skilled caster. I know only what my dreams have taught me, because there are none like me here.*

You're alone? I ask her, and her face falls, but she doesn't glance away.

Yes.

Oh. I take the compact from her, place it on the ground, and then, quickly, before I can lose my nerve, reach for her hands. Her fingers slide easily between mine. *So am I.*

But she shakes her head, smiling softly. *No. Not anymore.*

I swallow.

It happens slowly but suddenly. I see every moment, like frames in a film, and I also see nothing, because I'm too surprised, too amazed, too…*everything.* She's kissing me.

I, Maisy McCray, am being kissed—thoroughly kissed—by the prettiest girl in… the forest. In all the forests in the whole world.

She tastes like sunlight.

When she pulls away, resting a hand upon my knee and smiling coyly, I feel the strangest flip-flop in my stomach, and I know it's not a warning, but it's not that fluttering, either. It's something else.

I think it's joy. I've felt it before, when I was younger, but it's been so long that I hardly recognize it. I welcome it like a stranger—tentative, distrusting.

She notices my expression, and her smile fades a little. *Was that all right? Did I offend you?*

Offend me? I shake my head and blush. *No,* I think, *it was…perfect. Thank you.*

She ducks her head, blushing, too, and sidles next to me, wraps an arm around my waist. *I have missed you.*

And I realize, then, that I have missed her, too, without knowing who I was missing, or why. I missed her like you miss air when you're underwater, or earth when you're in a plane. I missed her like something essential and irreplaceable that I had, in my distraction, in my despair, forgotten.

I'll never forget her again.

I kiss her, and her lips are so soft beneath mine, so warm. Her body curves against me, fits against me as if we made for this moment.

I think we were.

*Are you…*I begin, hesitant. *Are you a—I don't*

know. An elf? A fairy? Your ears—

She grins and pushes her hair behind her pointy ears, showing them off to me proudly. *I am Fia, and I am what I am,* she says, with a little shrug. *I am different from you, but...* She presses a gentle kiss to my brow. *We are the same.*

I'm standing at my locker, shoving all of my textbooks inside—except for my English book. We have a test on *Julius Caesar* tomorrow, so I'll have to study a little at home tonight—after I visit Fia in the forest.

"Hey, Mai?"

I freeze, book in hand. Then I take a deep breath and force myself to turn around, force my legs to remain still, command my feet to *not run.*

"Mai, I just wanted to tell you something." Abby's dark hair falls over her eyes as she sighs and stares down at the floor. "Look, I just—I just wanted them to like me, you know? I mean, I was new, and I thought it would be easy to—I don't know—win them over if I did something really epic and really..." She pauses, lifts her midnight blue gaze to meet mine. "Really mean."

I stare at her steadily but keep my expression cool, unmoved.

"It was awful, what I did to you, and... Can you forgive me, Mai? Please?"

I slip a hand into my jacket pocket, feel the compact's cool, comforting shape. "I forgive you," I say, and Abby looks surprised, as if she got off too easy, so I add, "It doesn't matter anymore. I know who I am. I'm not a mouse, and I'm not ashamed." Then I turn my back on her and walk away.

Because Fia's waiting for me, and I promised I'd bring her a cupcake today.

THE MONSTROUS SEA

A HISTORY OF DROWNING

by S.E. Diemer

1

I'm six, the first time. I swallow the blue water in mouthfuls, feel the heaviness in my gut, filling me. Everything is weighty, solid, and I'm floating in the water, surrounded by it, suspended. My eyes are closed. My lungs are full of an alien thing, but I don't feel it anymore.

Just relax. It'll all be over soon.

There's screaming, distantly, and a great splash. Mom says that when the lifeguard drags me out of the pool, pounding against my belly and squeezing my nose with his big hands, she sees an angel hovering over us both, silver and glowing and perfect.

I don't die that day.

I wish I had.

2

I'm sixteen, the second time. At the school's pool, the sharp stench of chlorine clings to my skin as I slice through the water, parting molecules.

Annie's at the side of the pool, her long white legs dangling in the water, and she's drawing her hair up into a ponytail. Her fingers move through the brown waves with precision, eyes downcast, rubber band between her teeth.

I love her so much, I can't breathe, can't think. All I am is that love, a beating pulse that runs through my muscles, electric, as I dive below the surface. Her feet are there, kicking back and forth, a froth of white bubbles obscuring her bubble-gum pink toenail polish, the bright scar that runs over her heel, the way her second left toe is a tiny bit crooked. I don't need to see the details—I have her memorized now, every line of her.

I erupt out of the water beside her, lean on the edge of the pool, looking up, sputtering the water out of my mouth as she grins down at me, face glowing, lips wet. I reach out to touch her leg, devouring the distance between us, but she looks up, eyes darting to the girls on the other side. Lana is watching us.

"Not here," she whispers, and sidles a little away, but I move closer, mouth down-turned.

"You told me it didn't matter anymore," I whisper, because she's whispering. The words echo around us, anyway, the pool a shell of sound.

She rolls her eyes, draws the band across her hair, and she slices into the water beside me, moving away from my touch with quick and easy strokes.

She promised it wouldn't be like this anymore. She's promised many times.

I'm left in her wake, swallowing water.

Alone.

3

At the ocean's edge, my lips taste like salt, my skin coated in a thin sheen of spray as I stand in the water, feeling the roll of sand beneath the balls of my feet.

I'm seventeen.

I feel a hundred.

Annie left me today.

I knew she would. It was a long trail of inevitabilities, but she's gone now. She's too afraid. Too afraid of what the others think, of the rumors, of the whispers behind hands, and when I left school a few hours ago, the backpack on my shoulder weighing more than the moon, she was grinning up at Pierce, safe Pierce, Pierce who happens to have the necessary hardware to make life safe. A boy.

Not like me.

The girl who loved her.

I'm drowning. The water is only up to my knees, but it's so heavy, so calming as it rushes and roars and speaks: *Come in. Relax. It could all be over soon.*

I'm a good swimmer, but the storm last night made the riptide harsh. I can feel it sucking, pulling beneath me. If I went out, if I kept walking... The waves are enormous, like the curling fingers of God.

It's so easy to drown.

I breathe out, feeling the hot saltwater slide down my face to splash into the ocean below. It would almost be poetic if I didn't feel so *angry*.

I didn't ask for this. I didn't ask to fall in love with her, didn't ask for her laughter, her smile, the softness of her mouth and fingers. I loved her, and I never asked for it. I wish, in a thousand ways, that I'd never had it. Life would be so much easier if I'd never had it. I wouldn't know what it was like to kiss a girl's mouth, swallowing her laughter. I wouldn't know what it was like to hold the curve at her hips, the perfect compliment to my fingers, like a puzzle piece, shaped true.

But because I know, I'm ruined. I can't turn back. I can't be something that I'm not. And the pain is a swallow too great for me. I loved her with a fierceness I didn't fully understand. Not until now that I've lost her.

I take a step into the water. And another. I'm past my knees now, my jeans chafing my legs as the water licks my fingers, reaching up for me as I reach down to it. I take another step, and the sand shifts beneath my feet, dragging me closer to the gray water that crashes and sings. Another step, and I stumble, taking a mouthful of bitter cold.

Out of the water, someone takes my hand.

It's a full heartbeat before I feel the warmth of skin against mine. I turn, the roar of the ocean in my ears, pounding in my blood.

The girl stands in the water beside me, staring out to sea. Her eyes are dark, shadowed, but when she turns and glances at me, I see a flash of light there, a spark.

"I was afraid," she says, licking her lips. "I didn't want the water to take you. She's very angry today."

"She," I whisper.

The girl points out to the crashing waves, points down to the water that curls around our thighs, rushing and cold and what I wanted. The ocean. The sea.

We stumble back to shore. I still feel the water, even when I'm standing on the shifting beach, even when the girl lets go of my fingers, stepping back from me. She's wearing a strange white dress. It drips from the hemline, soaking the sands.

"It's not time" is what she tells me.

Later, I will say that I walked, numb and cold, to my car, and when I turned back, she was gone.

The truth is, she kissed my cheek and disappeared.

Her lips were like ice, searing.

I remember that.

4

I am almost eighteen when my car hits the patch of black ice. There is gravity pressing me against the seat of the car, and then a great roar of nothingness as it propels me off the bridge and into the water.

Somewhere, I'm scrabbling at my seatbelt, pressing the palms of my hands against the glass, sobbing as everything becomes a nothingness of black.

Until she comes, like I knew she would: strange white dress floating in the darkness like spun silver.

It's over, she tells me, when she presses her lips to

mine. I breathe her in, like light, like oxygen.
   The water carries us both, quiet as the dark.

MELUSINE

by S.E. Diemer

It's the oldest thing I know: don't go into the water if someone is watching.

That would ruin *everything*.

It makes me sick with fear, pricking at the back of my throat at school. Mom spoke with the principal: "Mel can *never* go swimming." There were doctors' notes, and they didn't fully convince him, but then Mom...*did* something. And the principal agreed with a glassy look in his eyes, smiling at me, head to the side like an agreeable dog.

I go home every day, comb out my colorful mohawk, tape the curtains closed, flush to the wall. I stuff a towel under the door, making certain every crack is sealed. Then and only then I take off my clothes and step into the shower.

The water hits me like a kiss, hot and soothing and soft, and I throw my head back, let the deluge pelt my neck, my chest, my skin...

My scales.

My wings.

I press my palms to the glass door, wipe the water off my face, let the stream propel over my back as I stare down at the coiled green beneath me, the gigantic feathered wings that press around me, against the enclosing walls.

I breathe out, and for a perfect moment, I'm not a fucked-up freak.

I'm just…Melusine.

"The omens," says my mother. "The omens have been especially bad this week." She's sitting on my bed, tapping her nails against my algebra book. "You must be doubly careful."

"Yeah," I grunt at her. Like I'm not careful all the time. I move my algebra book out of her reach and prop it open on the desk.

"Mel," she says, and the world grows quiet between us.

It's not her fault. None of this is her fault. A family curse. Genetics. Mom didn't make this happen to us, to me, but I get so *angry* just the same. Like I'm *stupid*, like I don't know that someone seeing me…like *that*…could ruin everything forever.

I stay silent until she leaves the room, and then I lean over, press my cheek against the cool page of the textbook.

The next day at school, I duck out after first period. What's the point? My blood's hot, angry, my breath coming out in excited puffs. I grab my bike, peddle until my legs scream in protest. I wander all the way down to the beach, the shushing sand, the dangerous waters.

I ditch my bike in its practiced place behind the scrub brush, dig my hands deep in my pockets as I make my way down the dunes. The *hiss* of the water on the sand almost sounds like music, and the gulls overhead punctuate the rhythm with chaos. There's a French fry wrapper on a bank of seashells that the gulls are harassing each other over. I watch, let my eyes unfocus until the birds are a mass of gray and white and nothing more.

A strange pricking on the back of my neck makes me stand a little straighter, makes me blink. Something's wrong. I shiver, though it's not cold, and I'm peering at the ocean waves as if they can answer an unasked question.

And they do. Because out on the sea, there's a splash of purple. I stare at it, heart pounding, and then I'm racing across the sand, not even thinking.

It's a jacket. Brown hands. Black hair. Flailing. Drowning.

There's no one else on the beach. I stand perched at the edge of the water, in agony.

Don't go into the water.

Every memory I've ever had, every promise I've ever made comes pounding back, like the rush of the sea.

Don't go into the water.

God. I put my hands to my forehead, rip off my jacket, kick off my sneakers, and I'm in the short waves, peeling off my pants, moving as the salt water licks me.

I'm in the waves, swimming toward the girl.

And I'm a monster.

My wings propel me, my serpent's coil slicing through the blue like it was always meant to do. I take a deep breath, and then I'm beneath the surface, where the girl is now. It's so quiet here, the roar of the waves muted as I hook my hands beneath her armpits, moving as if through sand or smoke, so slow, too slow. I drag her up, gulping in the air as we break the surface, and then I'm angling back toward the shore, holding her head up and out.

When I toss her onto the sand, flop her over onto her back, terror grips me, closing my throat. She's blue. I press on her stomach, and then I press harder, against her stomach, her chest, and then her eyes are open somehow; she's rolling over onto her side, coughing and spitting. I slump back, the serpent's tail twitching in agitation, my wings drooping wet on the ground.

She doesn't see me yet. Still spitting up water, she slumps to the side, breathing in and out a ragged gasp that makes my own lungs hurt.

"Thank you" is what she's whispering, over and over again. "Thank you."

I'm crying. Hot tears are coursing down my cheeks as I push my hair out of my eyes, try to make myself smaller. Less.

It's over. The damage is done. She saw what I am, what the water makes of me. I stand balanced as my wings shake out, the salt dripping from my eyes, my feathers, my scales. I can feel the creaking wheels of fate turn, the curse growing and deepening and becoming.

She looks up at me before she loses consciousness. Her eyes grow wide as she sees me, truly *sees* me, but she reaches out, and then she's smiling.

"Angel" is the one word she whispers to me. She crumples to the sand.

She'll live. I bend down, brush my lips over hers.
I rise.

My mother stands at the edge of the dunes, serpent tailed, wings outstretched, waiting.

Hand in hand, we come together. Cursed, wave-held, we sink below the surface, where the curse compels us to go.

She does not blame me. I don't blame her.

But someday, I'm coming back.

NO BIGGER THAN THE MOON

by S.E. Diemer

What if you were *meant* to be with someone?

I don't know how the world works. Hell, I don't even believe in god, and I don't think there's angels or some shit watching over us. But I think that when I was born, something happened, something I can't explain. That I was meant to be with Kylie.

It's this thing that I feel in my gut whenever I'm around her. Like a line, stretching from me to her. I can *feel* it. A gravity, maybe. She's my star, and I'm just a planet, revolving. Someday, when it's legal, I'm gonna marry her, and it's going to be the sappiest wedding *ever*. And I'm totally okay with that. Sophie—that's my stepma—says I got it real bad, which I guess is as good an explanation as any. Kylie knows I love her, would fly to the moon and back for her, would do anything to make her happy.

But I never expected this.

She's white as a sheet, like all the blood's drained down to her legs, and she's standing at the back door, leaning against the frame as if it's the only thing keeping her upright. She's breathing hard from running the three blocks from her house to mine, and she can't quite get the words out, but she straightens after a moment, pushes the hair out of her eyes, stares at me.

"Ted needs help," she tells me.

Ted's her older brother, by a year—he just turned eighteen two days ago. He looks a lot like Kylie—long straight black hair, long nose, dancing green eyes. But unlike Kylie, he's a *fucking bastard*. I've never liked Ted.

"What's wrong?" I'm asking her, but she's shaking her head, tears bright in her eyes.

"You've gotta come with me, Anne. I can't explain it…" She's already halfway off the back porch, hands shoved deep into the pockets of her hoodie. "Are you coming?"

"Geez, yeah, yeah, I'm coming," I mutter, grabbing my jacket off the peg. "Sophie!" I holler. "I'm going to Kylie's to…study!"

"Yeah, right, you are," she hollers back from the living room. "Use protection."

"Very funny," I return, but I'm blushing when I shut the door behind me. Kylie doesn't think it's funny or embarrassing or anything. She's already off the porch and trotting across the lawn, back to the sidewalk. I follow as fast as I can, catch up, run beside her.

"What the hell's the matter?" I'm asking, already breathing hard as we slog down the block.

"Ted's sick," she huffs, turning the corner. "I don't know what to do, and Mom and Dad… I don't think they're going to be much help."

"Whoa…" I slow down, stop. "Look, if he's sick, why don't you just take him to the doctor—"

"It's not like that." She's grabbing my arm, pricking me with her long nails. "*Christ*, Anne, it's not…" She runs her hand through her hair, starts to cry, great choking sobs that wrack her body. I'm speechless, but eventually neurons fire, and I gather her into a hug.

"He's so sick," she whispers, over and over. "I don't know what to *do*."

"It's all right," I tell her, but now I'm afraid. I don't *know* if it's all right. Kylie never cries. I'm shaking. Something's *very* wrong.

"C'mon," she says, wiping at her eyes, her runny

nose, with the sleeve of her hoodie. *"C'mon.* He's all alone. He's probably so scared." She hiccups a great sob but trudges down the sidewalk again.

It really only takes eight minutes to get to Kylie's house, but it's the longest, quietest walk of my life. My heart's racing as we get closer. A million scenarios have played through my head, and I keep sneaking glances at Kylie, her hood pulled up and over her face so I can't really see her. The bright afternoon, the sharp sunlight filtering through the towering clouds—it's taken on a much more sinister color.

Kylie's parents work late, so of course there's no car in the driveway or garage. We go in through the garage door and up into the kitchen.

A crash comes from the living room as we shut the door behind us.

"Ted, it's just us!" Kylie's voice comes out in a panic. She rushes into the living room, and I'm right behind her. But in the doorway, I stop as if I've hit a wall.

"It's all right," she soothes, arms held out, up and open, like she's going to receive a message from god.

She's holding her arms out to a gigantic white horse.

It's massive, head almost scraping the eight-foot ceiling. Its nose flares, and its nostrils are blood red. When it lifts up its head, opens its mouth to scream, I step back so quickly, my foot comes out from under me, and I skid on the tile floor of the kitchen.

Its teeth are pointed like knives, and it has a whole mouthful of them.

"No, no, don't be afraid," says Kylie, turning to look back at me, tears cascading down her cheeks. *"Please,* Anne, don't be afraid…"

"What…the *fuck*…" I manage.

"It's Ted."

"This is the *sickest* fucking *joke*…" I start, but she puts her face in her hands, her shoulders shaking with sobs. The horse stops pressing itself into the corner and steps forward, nostrils *whuffing*. It clops tentatively behind Kylie, pushes the small of her back with its gigantic nose.

"I don't know what to do," says Kylie, voice tiny. "I came home from school, and Ted was really sick on the couch, and then he just...began to change. I wouldn't have believed it, either, but I *watched it happen*. Grandma Lorrie always ranted and raved about how we had kelpie blood, and that 'the change is gonna happen at the eighteenth birthday,' but...I mean..." She's looking up at me with tear-filled eyes. "Why would we have *believed* something like that? And now when Grandma Lorrie's gone, it actually happened. I mean, *what the fuck?* My brother became a kelpie." She sits down on the floor miserably, puts her face in her hands again. "I don't know why I brought you here," she whispers. "I just thought that... I just needed you."

"What the hell's a kelpie?" is the first semi-intelligent thing out of my mouth. Kylie looks up at me, eyes wide.

"You believe me?"

"I don't know. I don't *know*," I mutter, leaning against the butcher's block, staring at the dejected horse, its nose almost brushing the ground. It gazes at me with one mournful eye. "Are you Ted?" I ask it, and it raises its head, nods like a ridiculous pantomime of that really weird show with the talking horse. What was it...*Mr. Ed*?

"This is fucked up," I say then, to no one in particular, but I cross to Kylie, sit down next to her.

"What do we *do*, Anne?" she whispers, voice shaking.

"What's a kelpie?" I repeat.

"Well." She picks at the frayed edge of her jeans. "It's a...water horse. Supposedly, they live in water, have sharp teeth, lure people to their deaths and eat them."

Ted shakes his head vehemently, rolling his eyes.

"But I don't *think* Ted wants to eat people," says Kylie slowly. "I just... I don't know. Grandma Lorrie said kelpies lived in the ocean, and we'd have to go back someday. Oh, god, Anne. She said the same thing would happen to me…" Kylie takes a great huffing sob, leans forward, is crying again.

"Let's just… Let's just deal with this one step at a time," I offer, putting my arm around her shoulders, pulling her toward me. "So…"

"I'm worried that if we don't take him to the beach, he's going to die," she says, voice so soft, I can hardly hear her. "We have to get him there."

"Great." I look up. And up. And *up* at him. Ted shakes his head again, sighs. "He's going to look right at home in the *suburbs*."

Kylie shrugs, stands, brushes off the bottom of her jeans. "I don't know what else to do."

"How are we going to get him out the *door*?"

Turns out that he could just squeeze through the back door, out onto the lawn. Kylie crawls onto the picnic table, stands up, angles her finger to me. "C'mon, we gotta go."

"I'm not riding that. I've never even ridden a merry-go-round," I'm muttering, not that that matters. She crooks her finger again, and I climb onto the picnic table, too, then sort of hop up and slide my leg over Ted's back. He's wider than a barrel. Maybe wider than a Smart car.

I help Kylie up, and Ted doesn't waste a second— he's already moving. "Whoa!" I grab great chunkfuls of his mane. I manage to not slide off in the first five steps or so and congratulate myself on this fact. The ground is *awfully* far away.

"Don't go faster than this, okay, Ted?" Kylie says around my shoulder.

He tosses his head in the air, nods again.

So, this gigantic white horse is walking down the sidewalk. And we're both riding it like a magical, mystical unicorn—sans bridle and saddle. But it's *not* a magical, mystical unicorn but a bloodthirsty kelpie.

I rub one hand over my face, then grasp at Ted's

mane again.

This is the strangest day…

A car drives past very slowly, man almost veering onto the sidewalk in his attempt to stare at our freak show. I scowl at him, and he rights the wheel, but Ted's head gets a little higher, and he sort of skitters in place for a moment.

"Don't lose your cool, big guy," I mutter, patting his neck like they used to do on the old black-and-white westerns. "Don't you think people are going to find this a little strange?" I ask Kylie over my shoulder. She shrugs against me, tightens her hold around my waist.

And then I hear the blaring siren.

"Oh, shit," Kylie whispers, angling back. "Oh, *shit.*"

I glance to my left. A cop car has pulled up on the side of the street, the guy hopping out, kind of staring for a long moment, his shades not masking the what-the-fuckness happening on his face.

"What…" he says, then shakes his head, comes up onto the sidewalk, peering at the two of us. "Is that a draft horse?" he's asking. I sort of stare at him blankly, and he shakes his head. "What are you two up to? You can't ride a horse on the sidewalk without proper… I mean, you can't ride a horse in—"

Ted turns around, angling his massive head back. The cop stares as Ted flattens his ears and—oh, god, Ted, *don't do it*—bares his teeth.

The razor-edged, pointed monstrosities flash in the lowering sun, and the cop lifts up his sunglasses, staring.

"Go, go, go!" Kylie yells, and kicks her brother in the sides—hard. I think Ted was surprised more than goaded, but he takes off down the sidewalk at a dead run. Luckily, my hands were tangled up in his mane, which is the only reason I'm not a splat beside some garden gnome.

I bounce up and down, up and down and *sideways*, but Kylie jerks me back, yells in my ear, "Hold on with your legs!" Normally I'd have all sorts of things to retort to that, but I don't quite have it in me right now. I do try to hold on—I think that's what Kylie's doing—but it's much easier said than done.

I don't know how I manage to stay upright, and as the houses whiz by, there are clattering, terrifying moments when Ted dashes across intersections, and I feel for certain that we're probably dead, but then we aren't dead, and behind all of this is the constant, droning blare of a siren.

"Ted, take the alley!" Kylie shouts, and Ted manages to slow down enough to thunder into an alleyway. We're out of the suburbs now, drawing closer to the shopping district, and just beyond it lays the beach.

Ted's slowed down, sides heaving, snorting as his breathing increases. "You're doing fine," says Kylie, but her voice is shaking.

The sirens are softer now in the alley. Maybe they went the wrong way. Yeah. I'll just keep thinking that. We cross back parking lots and side streets, and eventually the tang of saltwater assaults my nose. We're almost there.

Kylie directs Ted over to a Dumpster, and we both slide off onto it. I don't think I'm ever going to be able to walk in a straight line again. Everything aches.

We three walk together now. Kylie keeps her hand on Ted's shoulder, and I try not to panic about the cops. We get out from between the buildings, and the dying sun behind us sets the beach in a long shadow. There's a guy playing Frisbee with his dog, and a jogger, and, yes, they totally stare at us, but the place is pretty deserted now, nothing like the usual crush of people, so I'm not complaining.

We get to the shoreline, and Kylie's throwing her arms around Ted's neck. "I don't know if this is the right thing to do," she's telling him, "but I really hope it is…"

He shakes his head, eyes the sea. I think he's worried. But he places a hoof tentatively in the receding water and shudders, sighing for a long moment. I think it felt…good.

"This so fucked up. This is *so fucked up*," Kylie whispers as Ted walks into the surf. He keeps walking, and we keep staring, because when the waves hit him, he doesn't float or rise up… He just keeps plunging into the water, walking down and in until he disappears from sight in a matter of heartbeats.

"Oh, my god. Oh, my god, Anne…" Kylie clutches my arm. "Did he drown?"

"I don't…think so," I manage, my heart in my throat. I don't know. I haven't even brought up the Wikipedia page for *kelpies* yet on my phone. I don't know anything about them. About this. *I don't know*.

"He's just gone," says Kylie, swallowing a sob. "Oh, my god. Anne, what if he's drowning? Anne, please…" She's staring at me, eyes wide.

"Oh, well, *fuck*," I mutter, taking off my sneakers, peeling off my jacket. And then I'm trudging into the waves, too.

I'd fly to the moon and back for her, wouldn't I? Swimming out to see if I can spot her brother, the weird monster, is really not that high on the List of Impossible Things I'd Do For Her.

The water is ice cold, dashes against my jeans like a thousand needles. I grit my teeth, huff out, and step in further, eyes peeled on the incoming waves, on the outer water. Nothing.

"Do you see him?" Kylie calls. I shake my head, wade in deeper.

Something white flashes on the incoming wave that's rising much too fast. It hits me in the chest, pushes me back toward land.

I trudge deeper.

Another wave. Another flash. This time, I get water in my mouth and nose. I wasn't expecting how ferocious that wave was. I wasn't expecting—

There's a piercing tear in my arm. I feel…strange. There's water everywhere now, a twist of it that's holding me down, and I see a glinting eye rolling in the blue.

...Ted?

More piercing pain, and numbness. Red mingles with the white.

He looks beautiful, suspended in the water. A mystical, magical unicorn.

With teeth.

Kylie told me once that our love was bigger than the moon.

I think she was lying.

IN THE GARDEN I DID NOT SIN

by S.E. Diemer

In the beginning, my mother was immortal.

When she puts her hands to the small of her back, when her pained, pinched expression makes her tongue sharp, I watch her in small, risked glances, trying not to stare. Trying to imagine what she must have looked like, been like, once.

Before the fall.

My mother is not beautiful. Her body sags and arches in the wrong places, and she never stops frowning. Her long black hair lies tangled about her face, and her eyes are red and puffy from always crying. There is dirt beneath her fingernails and blood on the edges of the skins wrapped around her waist, from when she drags them through the fire where the men leave the bones.

Sometimes, when I am alone with her, she cups my cheeks in both hands, pressing hard enough against me that I breathe out. She watches my eyes, her own blurred with tears, and she tells me, "It wasn't always like this. It's getting worse."

And then she tells me about the garden.

"There was *no pain* there," she whispers, words so soft I can scarcely hear them. I lean forward, not daring to breathe. "It was beautiful. So beautiful. Fruit fell off the tree into your hands. The animals spoke to you, would never harm you. It was perfect," she says, closing her

119

eyes, rocking herself back and forth.

She'll stay like that until the sun sets, in the corner of the cave, face against the wall, rocking back and forth, eyes tightly shut against…everything.

She used to talk more about the garden, until father demanded she cease. My brothers and father mimic her, laughing, when she brings it up now in those rare moments she's forgotten his order.

Mother is with child again. She is always with child, because she must always be with child. She's sick this time, and Bidia stays with her constantly, rubbing her back, placing wet leaves on her forehead.

I'm angry. Mother has always told me I have the same spark in me that made her do it. That I must be careful, must never let the spark ignite, for there are always consequences.

I mustn't say it aloud, but I think it, fiercely:

God was wrong.

One of Mother's punishments was that bearing children would be excruciating. And it is. It always is. But one of her "gifts" was that she would be the mother of all people. It is not a gift to watch her stomach's contents spatter against the rocks. It is not a gift to watch her retch and moan, day in and out. It is not a gift when she turns white as a doe's belly, when she shakes and trembles when it's hot.

Bidia says she might become like the still ones, if it gets much worse.

The still ones never rise again.

Another of the punishments.

It isn't fair. It's pitiful, that thought, but as constant as the thrum of life moving through me. My mother's punishment isn't fair.

The moon is full and white and cold, far away, when Bidia wakes me in the firelight. I am sick, immediately, watching her face in the shadows. She is weeping.

"I think Mother will not make it until morning."

I gulp down air, rise, stumble through the caves until I am at her side. Mother grips my hand tightly in her own white knuckled one. She is so thin, so frail, her lips almost blue.

"Meno," she says so softly, I must lean down until her mouth is almost against my ear. "Meno," she repeats my name, drawing it out, and my breath catches. A single tear falls from me, dashing against the skin of her wrist. "Meno, you must believe me," she whispers, "In the garden, *I did not sin.*"

"I believe you," I gulp, closing my eyes tightly. "Mother, I've always believed you."

There is such a terrible pain within me, erupting, pricking. I stand suddenly, staring down at the husk of my mother, this poor, pitiful creature who plucked a fruit. *This*, all of *this*, for something so simple as reaching up and taking an apple from a branch. I am so angry, I cannot speak, can only stare down at her writhing, panting, my fists clenched at my sides.

She closes her eyes, and she does not open them again.

I am one of so many, they do not notice when I leave the caves in the early morning. I take nothing to protect myself with, because to touch one of the men's weapons would be a sin—according to our father. I run out into the woods, and I do not look back.

I am not afraid.

I am raging.

My mother was the first woman. She was beautiful once. She was strong once. She chose once. She did not sin. I run until I collapse beneath a tree, head in my hands, sobbing. She's gone. My mother is gone forever.

I take great, heaving breaths, lean back against the trunk, feel everything in me breaking. It's so big, this feeling of despair; it's going to swallow me whole. I can't go back there. I can't, not into that putrid, stinking mess of a cave. It makes me feel so small, so meaningless, one of so many girls who will grow up to be one of so many women, rutting with one of the boys who will become one of the men, because we were told to do so. I press my fingers against my face, run them through my hair, stare at the dirt beneath me.

I can't go back.

I won't be like my mother.

In the garden, I did not sin. I stay very still, listening to the forest around me, the harsh squeal of a boar as it quarrels with its siblings, the cry of birds overhead, the countless insects that buzz and whir.

In the garden...

"Why can't we go back there?" I'd asked my mother once. Only once. She pressed her finger against my lips, shaking.

"There is an angel," she whispered, her eyes bright with fear. "He guards it. He would destroy us. We cannot go back."

I don't know what an angel is, but the way my mother spoke the word brooked no argument.

But any place is better than the caves.

Isn't it?

I stand shakily, pressing my hand against the bark of the tree to steady myself. I close my eyes, and I listen. There is a riot of song, of chaos, around me. There are no predators nearby.

It is forbidden (as so many things are forbidden) to go near the edge of the great blue waters. I have always thought that the garden must be there, green and beautiful on the cusp of blue. I breathe in, and I breathe out, and I gaze up at the sun, slowing the beat of my heart. I make my decision in that heartbeat.

I turn and begin walking west, through the trees.

Toward the waters.

"God used to walk among men," she tells me, voice softer than a whisper. "But he doesn't walk among us anymore because of..." She blinks, breathes out. "Because of my sin."

I stare at her, gritting my teeth, when she says it. "You took an apple..." I begin, as I've begun a hundred, a thousand, times before.

Sometimes, my mother will look up at me with fear in her eyes. Sometimes, she will say, "I should not have," or, "I broke a promise," or, "God said not to do it, and yet I did."

Today, she does not repeat these excuses. She murmurs only, "I hate that word, *sin.*" She scrubs her hands against the rocks for a while, then, so hard that her palms bleed as red as apples.

The sun is overhead when I reach the garden.

And it is the garden. There is a great wall, as rock makes a wall, but built of bush and tree, branches interwoven so tightly, I cannot fit a finger between them. Mother told me that the garden was surrounded by a wall. I walk along it for a long while, heart beating so strongly inside of me, it makes my breath come short.

I do not think that I am afraid of the angel. I've seen nothing that makes me think another person is here. Only animals. I stop every few steps to listen, listen closely, but the predators have left me blessedly alone. It is strange, but I do not question it.

Staring up at the wall, I wonder what Mother could have seen in it. I cannot see over the wall, cannot see through the wall, but it is as green and lush as every other part of the forest, does not look different, better.

I walk along the wall until the sun begins to set, until my feet cry out in protest, my stomach joining in that wail with a desperation of its own.

I find the opening then.

Where the wall was, it is no longer, but replaced by an opening wider than the mouth of the cave. The wall continues along after the opening, but this is the way into the garden.

I can see into the garden.

I breathe out.

It is not beautiful. It is nothing like my mother told me, not glorious or perfect or lovely. It is only the forest, overgrown and wild and dangerous.

Is this truly the garden? It must be; the wall is here. But there is no angel, whoever an angel may be.

It is ordinary.

Something in me cracks. I kneel down, and I weep. Hot salt tears course down my cheeks, pattering upon the earth. What did I want? I don't know. I wanted a glimpse of what my mother loved, when she loved something. Once, she loved the garden, and it is no longer what she loved.

My mother is gone, and her garden with her.

A sound—in the forest beyond the opening, within the walls. Within the garden. I raise my head, leaning back on my heels, because after all of this, if I am hunted... I don't want to become still this way. I hold my breath, stop my tears, run a quick hand over my cheeks, gulping.

A snap of branch, a movement of leaves, and she walks out of the shadows, pausing.

In the dying light, I wonder if my eyes play tricks on me.

There is Father, and there was Mother, and there are now their many children and grandchildren. There are no other people in the world, only our family.

But this girl is not of our family. Her skin is brown like ours, but it seems to glow with starlight. Her hair is black like ours, but shiny, not tangled. She wears something white and soft, not an animal skin. I've never seen anything like it. And she's holding an elaborate spear, what is forbidden for a woman to touch.

She stands with her feet apart, watching me, and when my gaze stops lingering on her form, I gaze up at her face and fall back onto my bottom.

Her eyes are red.

She takes a step toward me, and another, and I crawl backward, falling down onto my shoulders.

"Who are you?" she asks, her voice a deep hiss. I shudder, closing my eyes, waiting for a blow.

It does not come.

My eyes open, and she's standing over me. She doesn't look angry. She looks...excited, mouth opening and closing as she drops down to her knees beside me, setting the spear down upon the earth.

"Who are you?" she repeats, leaning forward. She is close enough to touch, and I...do. I touch her. I reach up, and I brush my finger along her arm. She cocks her head, stares down at my hand inquisitively before she picks it up, threading her fingers through mine.

"I am Meno, daughter of Eve," I whisper.

She stops breathing, glances into my eyes with her own, flashing red ones.

"Eve," she whispers, mouth open. "It cannot be..."

"Who are you?" I ask, finally forming the words burning in me.

"Lysys," she says, breathing the name between us. "Daughter of Lilith."

I stare at her for a heartbeat more, and I shake my head slowly. "I know no Lilith. There is only my father, Adam, and my mother, Eve, and all their get."

"No," says Lysys, leaning toward me, close enough to touch, close enough to smell the sweetness of her. "I am the daughter of Lilith. She knew your mother. She knew Eve." She works her jaw for a moment before she stares at the ground. "Why are you here? Why did you come to the garden of Eden?"

The garden of Eden. My mother never called it

that, but when Lysys speaks the word, a thrill runs through me. I shudder.

"I came…" I breathe out, close my mouth. "I came," I try again, "because my mother has gone still. And I…" I run out of words. I don't know why I came. I wanted to leave the cave. I wanted to leave all the pain behind me. But there is only family, and there is only the cave, and that is my only future.

But Lysys watches me curiously. She does not look afraid of anything. I doubt she has bent her head to anyone in her life. She has a proud tilt to her chin, and she smiles easily.

We don't smile often in the cave.

"It's just so strange that you would come…now." She rises in one easy motion, offers her hand down to me. I stare at it before I take it, but her grip is tight, fierce, and she helps me up to my feet before I can even think that I'm rising. We stand close, my heart thundering. She steps back once, turning away from me. "You must come see," she says over her shoulder, hefting up her spear. Her arm muscles flex, and I know the spear must be heavy, but she lifts it easily. "Come, Meno," she says, and I'm following her into the garden.

Only my mother ever spoke my name. But in this stranger's mouth, it sounds as warm.

"How are there other people? I don't understand," I say as I follow her. She tosses a smile back over her shoulder, shakes her head.

"I'm not human," she answers easily, holding aside a branch in the overgrown path. I duck around it before I stop, staring at her.

"Not human? You look like no animal I know," I mutter, perplexed.

Lysys bites her lip, shrugs a little. "Your mother, Eve—she never mentioned Lilith?"

I shake my head.

"Did she mention the snake?"

I shake my head.

"Well," says Lysys slowly, carefully. "My mother certainly talked a lot about your mother." There is pain in those words. I don't know why, but they make my heart ache. "This way," she says, clearing her throat, and we walk further into the forest.

I hear it then, a sort of rushing, a sighing, a great breathing. "What is it?" I whisper, heart pounding against me, but Lysys reaches back and gently plucks at my elbow with her warm fingers.

"It's only the sea. It's all right," she says, voice still a hiss, but kind.

Through the trees comes the blue.

My mother told me about the sea, about the endless waters that go farther than your eye can follow. I'd tried to imagine it, there in the muddy grip of the cave, but it seemed like something from a dream.

There is a bluff of earth overlooking the water, which we stand on now. The water seems dangerous, angry. The garden simply...ends. The trees beyond, in the water, are teetering dangerously toward the sea. As I watch, the water draws closer, closer, climbing up the wall of the bluff beneath us.

"The sea is taking the garden back," says Lysys quietly. "It won't survive the night."

I stare, speechless, at the swirling, dirty waters.

"Why?" is all I can manage.

"I don't know," says Lysys quietly. "Because God wants it to be so, I suppose." Her tone is sharp, biting. "But I'm glad," she whispers then, "that I got to see it before it went. My mother spoke of this place often. I needed to see it."

"It isn't beautiful," I tell her, in a rush. "I thought it would be beautiful." A single tear runs from my eye, splashing down and down, eaten up by the waters.

Lysys glances at me sidelong, hefts the spear up and over her shoulder, staring out at the horizon. "No," she agrees. "It isn't beautiful. But I think it was once. I think it could have been again."

I stare at her. "Nothing *becomes* beautiful." I whisper. "Everything becomes ugly. From beauty to ugliness. That is part of the curse..." I trail off, staring down at the swirling waters.

She takes my hand. It surprises me, my breath quickening, heart thundering. She squeezes my fingers tightly.

"It's a lie, Meno," she says. "I promise you."

The water curls long blue fingers over the earth, tearing it apart. We watch wordlessly as the garden of Eden is claimed by the never-ending sea.

"Endings are beginnings," is what Lysys tells me, promises me.

I don't know why, but I believe her.

TWO SALT FEET

by S.E. Diemer

You can buy anything at the city's meat market.
Even a mermaid.

Mom wanted me to pick up salmon. I'm a vegetarian, I tell her. She says that doesn't matter and to be a good girl and go get the fish. I tell her I'll spend the money on candy cigarettes and pistols, and she just waves me away, which proves she wasn't listening. Whatever. She knows I'm going to get her the salmon because she's my mom, and for whatever reason, I love her, *even though* she makes food that is completely incompatible with my morals, ethics and awesomeness.

So I'm trudging through the meat market with a really deep frown on my face, throwing judgey looks at every single meat vendor until I end up throwing my judgiest look at the mermaid seller.

"What?" he asks, crossing his arms, glaring down at me. I have spiked green hair; a lot of people give me his look, so I stick my tongue out at him and blow a bubble with my gum. I stop and look at his tanks, though, because the mermaids are always so beautiful, they make my bones ache.

The tanks are big and round and gross. The mermaid seller is set up at a corner of the market, because it's the only place large enough to hold the three gigantic vats of water. Two of the vats are empty. It's late on a

Saturday afternoon. I guess two of the mermaids were already spoken for and taken. The thought makes me feel a little sick, and I stop chewing my gum.

But the third tank, with its brackish green water and slimy glass, still contains its occupant.

She looks out through the thick glass, webbed fingers pressed against the sides, eyes wide in the murky depth of the vat. Her hair—I can't possibly tell what color it is through the grime, though it's probably green—floats around her like a halo. Her tail is long and sinuous and flops halfheartedly against the bottom of the tank. Her little pointed teeth stick out over her full greenish lips, and her bare boobs rise and fall as she turns this way and that.

But she stops moving when she looks at me.

We stare at one another. The mermaids don't usually *do* that, *look* at me, and it makes me feel weird, like my skin is burning. I turn away from her as I hear a man step up to the vendor, ask, "How much?" The vendor's voice drops down to a hushed whisper, and I look back at the mermaid again.

She mouths something behind the glass. I stop, my heart thundering.

Words. She's mouthing words.

Help me.

I take a step back.

That's totally ridiculous, Sam. Get it together. Mermaids don't speak. They're fish. Really weird, pretty fish that strange people cook up all fancy like lobster, but that's it. You *know* that. *Everyone* knows that.

But as I watch her, my blood thundering through my veins, her mouth moves again. *Help me*, she begs, her forehead crinkled, both hands pressed flat against the tank. She's staring at me with an expression of pure fear and desperation. Even as the vendor and the man move nearer to the vat of water. Even as I see the guy take out his wallet.

"Hey," I say, shoving my hands in my pockets. The vendor ignores me until I say it again, "*Hey*." He rolls the little ladder over to the tank, pauses with one elbow leaning on a rung, staring down at me with a frown.

"I got no time for deadbeats today, chick. Run along," he mutters with a growl. Normally I'd retort with something about misogyny, using words he'd have to look up in a dictionary, but I don't have time for that kind of shit today.

"How much is the mermaid?" I say, swallowing my feminist rage.

The vendor stares at me, and then he laughs a little. The man who was interested in purchasing her himself glances down at his watch, taps his shiny toe, frowning at me.

"No, seriously," I say, stepping forward, jutting my chin out.

"Seriously too much for you," says the vendor, placing the ladder against the tank. The mermaid looks up at the surface of the water, cringing and backing away until she's at the opposite corner of the vat as the vendor begins to climb up the little metal rungs. They squeak in protest beneath him. I've never seen a mermaid get fished out, but watching this, I'm speechless.

She's afraid. I've never seen a *fish* look so afraid.

There's a small crowd gathered now, because—like me—they've probably never seen anything like this happen. The vendor has a pair of tongs as long as his forearm that are rusted, dripping. He reaches down into the water with them and, quick as a shark, pinches the mermaid's tail in the tongs. She thrashes, the water getting murkier and muddier as she heaves against the side of the tank.

The mermaid's head clears the water, mouth gasping as she flies through the air into the vendor's arms.

He carries her down, thrashing, squirming, and he stands beside the tank, waiting a moment to catch his breath.

The mermaid's movements become softer, slower, and then she simply lies in the vendor's arms like a movie starlet from the '50s, bosom heaving, eyes half-closed.

"They can't breathe the air so well," the vendor tells the man. "She'll be dead before you get home. Easy."

I'm gonna be sick. The man gives the vendor a stack of bills, and the vendor gives the man the still-as-death mermaid—her lashes still fluttering, but just a little, her fingertips dripping salt water with a steady *plink, plink* on the pavement.

There's no warning for what happens next. If I hadn't been staring, eyes wide, at the mermaid, I never would have seen it. The change was instantaneous, a heartbeat: where the shining, opalescent scales of her tail had been, there is only bare skin now. Human skin.

Two legs.

My breath catches, and I almost trip, taking a step forward. But the mermaid girl opens her eyes, no longer a mermaid, just a girl now, a *girl*, completely naked, resting in the man's arms against his tailored suit.

She looks up at him, and she screams.

I would laugh if it wasn't so weird. His mouth makes that round O of supreme confusion, and he drops her like she's poisonous. She falls against the pavement, still screaming, and then there's a dense press of bodies around all of us, precluding a riot or a panic-driven crowd, and I don't even know I'm doing it, but I guess raw instincts take over or *something*, because I scoop up that mermaid—I don't even *think* about it—and I'm pushing back through the crowd so quickly that, even if I wanted to stop, I don't think I could.

I don't want to stop.

We duck into an alley and around a Dumpster. I don't think anyone saw me run, and even if they did...what could they possibly do? Because she isn't a mermaid, not anymore.

I help the girl to her feet. She wobbles a little, pressing a hand against the slimy bricks behind her, and I can't help staring, then internally yelling a lot at myself for staring. I peel off my jacket, hand it to her, which she gapes at with big green eyes, like she's never seen one before.

"Put it on," I say, clearing my throat, but the girl looks from the jacket in her hand up to me. She's shaking a little, and I notice her hands aren't webbed anymore; her teeth aren't pointed. She's blonde-haired, not green-haired now, and her skin's as pale as mine.

Shouts are coming from the market behind us. I hear a whistle blow.

"Here," I mutter, taking the jacket from her, holding it out by the shoulders. She sort of shrugs one arm into one sleeve, and then into the other, and I pull it over her back, grabbing her hand. "We've gotta go," I say, glancing over my shoulder at the milling crowd behind us.

She doesn't take a step. She stares down at her feet as if hypnotized or something, as if she can't move, and then I hear, *"There she is!"* and I just pick her up again, my heart hammering. I turn down the alley and run, carrying her.

She isn't light. I'm not strong. But I dash through alley after street after alley, and I stop eventually by another Dumpster and set her down as gently as I can, my whole body shaking, my stomach heaving from running eleventy billion miles while carrying someone close to my weight and size. I press my hands against my legs, but I can't make the heaving stop, so I finally just go and vomit up my Starbucks no-water, non-fat soy chai against the wall.

The mermaid stares at me, eyebrows furrowed, and eventually she puts a hand on my arm when I stop retching.

"I'm sorry," she says, voice soft and small and sweet. She stands up on tiptoes and kisses my cheek.

I rub the back of my hand over my lips, swallowing. "What the hell," I say then. "What. The. Hell."

She stares at me, cocking her head.

"Are you a mermaid?" I ask her. She nods, smiling a little, drawing the coat closer around her.

"Yes." She looks down at her toes, peering at them as if mystified. "I know I don't look like one right now. But I am. Too many of my kind have been eaten by yours. We've been evolving. It had just never happened to me before." She gestures to her feet. We both stare at them.

"But you talk… And you look human now…" I trail off, watching her, reaching up to touch my cheek where she'd kissed me. I feel warm and light.

"Don't look so surprised," she whispers, smiling secretly. "You were all once fish, too."

"Yeah, well." I shove my hands into the pockets of my jeans, shiver a little. "It was a while ago when we got legs."

She laughs at this, tips up her nose and laughs loudly and clearly, and she's so pretty when she laughs that I kind of have to shake myself to stop staring at her neck thrown back, the curve of her chin, her mouth. I bite my lip, look away.

"So, uh. I guess I have to…take you back to the ocean?" I ask her. I don't know what else to do. She's a mermaid. She belongs in the sea, not in the green vats of putrid water she came from, not about to be sold to be eaten. She stares at me, though, eyes wide, as if she'd rather be back there.

"I'm actually hungry," she says, glancing up at me sidelong. Hopefully.

"Hungry." I have no idea how to respond to this. This isn't really how I thought my day was going to go. "So, what do mermaids eat?"

"Anything!" she answers blithely, smile wide.

I glance down at her legs, how my jacket is just long enough to cover the special parts, but really…*just* long enough. "You can't be seen like this." I run my hands through my hair, stare up at the slash of sky I can see between the buildings towering above us. "We're close to the McKay Thrift Store," I tell her then. "Just…just wait here." I eye her up and down, totally not for any other reason that an ogling of measurements, and I'm there and back in a tiny amount of time, because while I'm running to the thrift store, dashing through the aisles, paying the clerk with shaking hands and running all the way back to the alley, I keep thinking that this must be a dream. It has to be.

But no. Mermaid-girl is still there, leaning against the wall, her hands in my jacket pockets like she's done all of this before.

She's smiling.

At me.

"Here," I mutter, handing her a knee-length paisley skirt and some flip-flops. She stares at them like she's never seen such things…and she probably hasn't. So I pantomime putting a skirt on, and I help her into the flip-flops not totally unlike Prince Charming when he's fitting Cinderella's shoe.

"There," I say, buttoning the jacket and taking a step back to check out her outfit. It works. Barely.

"I'm so excited!" says mermaid-girl, grabbing my hand when I'm done and squeezing it tightly. "Nothing like this has ever happened to me before!"

"Yeah," I manage, swallowing. "Me, either." We walk out of the alley, taking small steps, which she overexaggerates—but not enough for anyone to notice, really.

The meat market is close… We could go back, buy food from one of the vendors, but what if the mermaid vendor sees us, recognizes me? I don't think he'd recognize her, but I know he'd spot my green hair. We stand on the sidewalk, out of the alley, and it starts to drizzle while I contemplate if I should take her to McDonald's for her first human food experience, and I realize that would kind of suck, but then I hear someone calling my name, breaking me out of my reverie with cold dread.

Mom…

"Sammie!" she calls, paper bag in hand, and she's sort of staring at me from across the street, mouth open. She's actually not staring at *me*, though. She's staring at the girl clinging to my arm.

Mom looks both ways, then darts across the street to stand beside us, eyeing the mermaid-girl up and down, down and up.

"Sammie…" Mom murmurs beatifically, then looks at me, grinning hugely. "Who's this?"

"Uh," I mutter, breathing out, but that's enough for my mom, apparently, because she steps forward, shifting the bag to her other hip, and envelops mermaid-girl in a tight squeeze.

"It's so nice to meet you! Sammie didn't tell me she was dating anyone right now!" She rolls her eyes and chuckles the conspiratorial chuckle of, "Oh, you know how girls are." Mermaid-girl obviously *doesn't* know how girls are, doesn't have any *clue* what my mother is talking about, but laughs because Mom is laughing.

"My name's Eveline," my mom gushes. "I'm Sammie's *mom*! And you are?"

"Mom, we've gotta be going," I mutter, tugging on mermaid-girl to start walking down the sidewalk, *away* from my mother, but she's not budging.

"My name's Mer…"

"…na," I finish for her, gulping. "Merna. This is Merna, Mom." Mom stares at me, eyes narrowed, but grins fetchingly at newly named mermaid-girl when "Merna" grins hopefully at my mom.

"So nice to meet you, Merna," says my mother, not even skipping a beat. "Sammie, why haven't you told me about her?"

"Because it's just so gosh darn new!" I say, grinning widely, too, but pretty much dying on the inside. "*Anywho*, we were on our way to get Merna something to eat, because she's *famished…*"

"Oh, no. I know I'm probably embarrassing the

irony out of you, my darling girl, but I've never even met one of your girlfriends, and I'm just so tickled *pink* to meet this one! I insist on taking you both out to lunch—my treat!" My mother is grinning so hugely, she looks like a shark. Merna glances from me to my mother, back to me again, smiling, too.

"That sounds nice," says Merna.

Nice. Right. This couldn't possibly go terribly, *terribly* awry.

"*Moooooooom*," I manage, as she ushers the two of us down the sidewalk.

"*Yes*, darling?" she practically coos, hooking her arm around my shoulders.

"Mom, why do you have to be so invested in your child's business? Why can't you be aloof and disinterested?" I groan. "You know, like all my friends' parents."

"You're just lucky," my mom coos, squeezing me. "And a brat that you don't tell me when you're dating someone so *sweet*! She's just *darling*, honey. Seriously, next time tell me."

"Oh, I will," I breathe out, watching Merna out of the corner of my eye. She's trying to take in the window displays and cars and the people walking by us. Her eyes are wide, her mouth open in astonishment. She looks so *happy*.

And so beautiful.

We eat at Mike's Crab House, because nothing screams *classy* like a restaurant with a dancing crab for its logo.

Mom slides into the booth across from us, putting her chin in her hands, staring at us all doe-eyed.

"So, tell me, you two, how did you meet?" she asks what I was praying and hoping she wouldn't ask. I swallow, glance sidelong at Merna. Does she understand what my mom assumes yet?

No clue. Merna is staring down at the fork and spoon and knife on her napkin. I say a quick prayer to any god listening that she doesn't pull an Ariel and test the utensils on her hair.

"We've…not known each other very long." I try, desperate to avoid lying.

"Just this morning!" Merna pipes up, reaching for the fork. I snatch her hand, cradling it in what I hope is a loving manner in mine.

"Yes! It was…fate," I try. My mother's brows are quirked that way she gets when things aren't adding up for her. "She just moved here?" I try, and that seems to mollify her. For the moment.

I really don't need to explain that the girl clinging to my arm happens to be a mermaid. And that—surprise, Mom!—they're evolving creatures! They can totally grow legs now when in crisis-saturated situations! And lose their webbed fingers! And their green skin!

Yeah, I mean, *I* don't even believe it, and I *saw it happen*.

"I think you should get something with fish in it," I tell Merna when she opens her menu. She stares at all of the choices with wide eyes, then shakes her head at me, mouth quirking sideways in a truly adorable grin.

(Get yourself *together*, Sam. She's a *mermaid* who's going back to the ocean *right after lunch*. This is not going to end well if your stomach gets all knotty and tied up over some girl you can't possibly have.)

(*Too late.*)

"Gosh, Sam, I eat fish all the time." She stares at me with dancing eyes, holding back a laugh. "I think I want something that I don't have to eat all day every day."

"Oh, you live in a coastal town?" my mother asks, all-at-once super interested. Of course.

"Something like that," says Merna, grinning at me.

Under the table, she squeezes my hand.

And just like that, I'm not thinking about anything other than the fact that her fingers are threaded through mine. And she's *not letting go*.

It's the nicest thing.

After a lunch consisting in three salads, three fries, three Cokes and a brownie sundae (for Merna), we're out on the sidewalk again, and Mom's cradling the brown paper bag in front of her and grinning so widely, her face is in danger of cracking.

"We've really gotta go," I tell Mom. "We're going to…the ocean now." Merna glances at me quickly, frowning, but Mom's shaking her head.

"That's a long walk! Ten blocks, at least," she says, hitching her thumb in the direction of the water. "I'm parked super close. I can drive you two!"

"You don't have to," I mutter, but she's already saying what my mother always says: "Don't worry about it! My pleasure!"

I really think she likes Merna. That's the thing. She's not usually this pushy, and never this pushy when it comes to my friends. Or my girlfriends. The grand total of two girlfriends I had before this she's-not-my-girlfriend day.

So we pile into the back of the car and sit in silence while Mom drives the really not-that-far distance to the people beach. Which is next to the dog beach, where a Labrador retriever is currently giving hell to a piece of driftwood.

"I'll pick you up in an hour, Sammie," says Mom, gushing out of her window at the two of us, once we get out. "And don't even *worry* about the salmon, honey. I got it covered." And then she winks at me. Actually *winks* at me. And drives off.

My mom. She's weird. And I love her.

"Your mother's really nice," says Merna distractedly, staring over her shoulder at the water.

"Look, it was really…" I stare at her, gulping, and then *I can't actually believe this*, but there are tears in my eyes that I absolutely, positively, refuse to let spill.

One runs down my cheek past my nose.

Sam. You knew this would happen. I mean, you *helped* her. This isn't like the ending to *Old Yeller* or anything. It's happy. She's going to go back to the sea, and she'll be safe and not in someone's stupid stomach. It's good. It's *good*.

But she stares up at me with those bright green eyes, and I breathe in, and I breathe out, and I feel hollow.

"What's the matter?" she asks me, distraught. I shake my head, sniffle a little.

"I like you," I manage, then. "Do you... Do you know what that means?"

Her smile is instant. Surprising. Beautiful. "Yes. I know what that means." And then, before I can do anything, she's standing up on tiptoe in her flip-flops that are two sizes two big, and she's kissing me.

She tastes sweet. Like a brownie sundae.

"Look," I say, when she stops, when I wake up from my shock, when we stand facing one another, her hands in mine. "I know that this can't work out, but..."

She wrinkles her nose, blinks. "What are you talking about?"

I stare.

"Sam," she says, mouth quirked up on one side, grinning at me. "I can grow legs now. I think that I could work out seeing you again."

I continue to stare.

"That is...if you'd like to see me again," she says, leaning forward, breathless. Her eyes are wide, her smile is electric, and when she kisses me again, it moves through me like a wave. Like a tide.

Like gravity.

I have no idea how this is going to work. But I think we're going to try it.

Weirder things have happened.

Right?

DAUGHTER OF BLUE

by S.E. Diemer

She never thought she would go this far.
I'm afraid. It's cold. I can't swim.
I'm afraid.

Leila gripped the edge of the rock, feeling it cut into her palm, glad for the vivid red that trailed down the side of the boulder, color in this monochrome heartbeat. And everything was heartbeat, this great rushing that filled her ears, nose, mouth, throat. The ocean pounded relentlessly at her feet, hissing and dragging, curling white fingers of foam toward her boots.

It wanted her.

"For the spell to work, it *has* to be thrown into the sea, at twilight, the day of the full moon," Jess had told her, pressing the notebook paper into her hand, the same hand cut by the boulder now.

"That's stupid," Leila had muttered, glancing down at the carefully folded paper before shoving it into the zippered front of her backpack. "You know spells can be done whenever you need them."

"Not this one." Jess's eyes had gotten all big, like they did when she told Leila about the first time David kissed her. But Jess was dramatic all the time, really. The spell didn't need to be perfect to work. If Leila knew anything about Wicca, she knew that much.

But none of that explained why she was here now,

edging out onto the slippery rocks as the tide came in, tiny bottle filled with carefully ground and measured ingredients hanging from a thong around her neck.

She sighed, reached up, touched the cold glass with a frozen fingertip.

Stupidity would explain it. She rolled her eyes, glanced at the turbulent heavens above. Or desperation.

"By my will," she began, closing her hand around the bottle, "and charmed by one, this spell is marked and cast and done. An' it harm none and blessed by sea, as I will, so mote it be." Her teeth chattered on the last line, but she didn't really think it mattered. With a vicious tug, she yanked the bottle off her neck and flung it as hard as she could over the water. The waves crashed and roared, and the bottle disappeared from view, swallowed and gone.

Leila almost fell as she made her way back across the boulders. She cut her other palm as she scrabbled for a grasp, the water sucking at one sneakered foot.

The wave was cold as death.

"Well?" Jess's face always looked super distorted through the web cam. The lighting in her room consisted of one string of Christmas lights and a glow-in-the-dark My Little Pony. She was grinning, though. That much Leila could make out.

"It's done," said Leila heavily, bringing up a browser window and minimizing Jess. "Look, I've got a lot of homework—"

"That's ridiculous! Tell me how you did—"

"Tomorrow, Jess."

She could hear the pout rather than see it.

"Well, fine. See if I ever give you super awesome spell knowledge again."

Leila couldn't keep from grinning as she rolled her

eyes. "Good night, Jess."

"Good night, Ms. Brooding."

The chat blinked off, and Leila closed her laptop, glancing sidelong at the crinkled piece of paper on her desk.

Wicca 101: Do Not Under Any Circumstances Ever Cast a Love Spell on Anyone. Do Not Pass Go. Do Not Collect Love Potions.

Wicca 201: It's Totally Okay To Cast a Spell for Love, In General.

The notebook paper had a list of herbs, crystals and ephemera scrawled out in Jess's blocky writing. Instructions. Not a single mention of the word "love." But still. Leila folded it, carefully and small, and put it in the Altoids tin in the top drawer of her desk.

She still got sick to her stomach every time she cast a spell. It was silly, really. It's not like her mom was religious or anything, but there was always this undercurrent of dread... How do you explain Wicca?

How do you explain how lonely you are?

Leila rubbed at her forehead, her temples, squeezing her eyes shut so tightly that she couldn't see Tamra's laughing face anymore. It had really seemed like she was into girls. Totally. Even Jess had thought so. But then Leila had become friends with Tamra, and they'd gotten close, and then Leila had come out to her and asked her out to a stupid fucking movie, and Tamra had *laughed*.

And the next day at school:

Dyke.

Dyke.

Dyke.

Everyone sang the same chorus: *Dyke*.

Leila sat back, pressing her palms against the cool surface of the desk. She breathed in, and she breathed out, and then—with a shaking hand—she turned out the light.

"What would you do for her?"

Leila opened her eyes.

Blue. Everywhere. Crashing, roaring waves. Her lips tasted of salt, and she was the coldest she'd ever been. But everything else disappeared, falling away, as she stared.

It was vaguely human-shaped but towered over her, its giant-sized beard blue and white and dripping water down its massive chest. It held a silver trident in one powerful, fridge-sized hand, and it seemed to be made entirely of water. As if water were trapped in a massive bag and vaguely shaped like a man.

It was monstrous and beautiful, and it was staring at Leila with two wide, baleful eyes.

Leila blinked.

"What would you do for her?" it repeated.

"Her?" Leila managed, and the great being shook its head in disgust.

"To whom much is given, much is required," it said, its voice a cross between a wave pounding against rocks and the roar of a sea squall. "You asked for love. You desire it. I do not give freely."

Leila dropped to her knees, staring up and up at the watery being.

Ocean, she realized.

She was staring at the spirit of Ocean.

It raised its trident and pointed it down at her. "What would do you for her?" it repeated, staring, staring. Leila swallowed, breathed out, tried to stop shaking.

"I don't...I..."

The Being cocked its head as Leila stammered, biting out syllables that meant nothing.

Between them, a strange blue mist began to form in the air. It writhed and twisted and turned, almost at the longest point of the trident. A sphere of water began to spin, suspended.

And in the water, there was a girl.

"You asked for this," said the being, its voice thunderous. "Now, what will you do to deserve it?"

Leila stared at the suspended girl, her features blurred by the water that moved around her. She was curving and rounded, blue-tinted by the water, and—if Leila could judge—the most beautiful sight she'd ever seen. Her heart hammered as she stared, as she longed.

As she wished, with all her heart.

"I would love her," she whispered, gulping air. "So much. I would love her with all my heart."

"You must do better than that," the being roared.

"I would protect her from assholes," said Leila, biting out the words. "I would..." She thought of her mother, before her father left. "I would listen to her. I would comfort her when it was hard. I would be kind to her. Gentle." Her mother flashed before her eyes, sobbing in the kitchen when she thought Leila couldn't hear. "I'd protect her from the shit in the world," she said.

"No being can do this," said Ocean gravely.

"I would try," Leila whispered.

It stared down at her, the sphere of water spinning, suspended.

Glorious.

And a wave of blue crashed down on Leila, absolute.

And cold as death.

Leila gasped, thrashing, opening her eyes to the blurry dark of her room, her sheets tangled around her legs.

Fuck. *Fuck.* She pounded against the mattress with her fists, shoving her wrist against her mouth so her mother wouldn't hear her sobbing.

What did you expect, Leila?
It was just a fucking dream.

"Wooooooow," said Jess, not unkindly, as she slid next to Leila at their table. "Jesus Christ, who died?"

"Shut up," said Leila, pushing the sunglasses farther up her nose to hide her eyes. Jess stared down at her lunch tray, then back up at her best friend.

"So...the spell..." she began, but Leila crossed her arms, slouched against the table.

"I don't want to talk about it."

"Leila..."

"Seriously, Jess. No."

Jess shut up.

They ate their lunches in silence, Leila breathing in and out around gulps of turkey sandwich that tasted like dust in her mouth. It was so stupid, really. Why had she thought it would work? She got up, balancing the tray on her hip while she hoisted the backpack up on her shoulder.

Then she stopped and stared across the room.

The girl who'd just walked in was dressed all in blue. That's why Leila noticed her, really, her eyes drawn to her as if by gravity.

She was curvy and tall and walked with confidence through a group of boys who were jeering at her for wearing a hippie skirt. She ignored them. Her warm black skin at the plunging V in her blouse hypnotized Leila's eyes, and when Leila was able to wrest her gaze away, she was captivated by the stranger's face, this girl who came toward her like a tidal pull.

"Hey," said the girl, smiling, the most beautiful smile Leila had ever seen. "I'm Shay. I'm new here."

"Leila," Leila muttered, when Jess punched her in the leg.

"Jess!" said Jess, grinning so widely she might have been mistaken for a Cheshire Cat.

"I know this might sound ridiculous," said Shay,

leaning closer, voice dropping to a stage whisper, "but I feel like I've seen you before, Leila. Have we met?"

"No," said Leila, mouth moving of its own accord. "I would remember you."

But she *had* seen Shay's shape before. She was certain she had. If only in a dream.

"I'm sorry for being so forward," said Shay, flashing her stunning smile again, "but I'm not one to sit by and not talk to people. I'm trying to make friends here, and it's hard for me not to say hello to beautiful girls."

Jess blushed the brightest shade of red Leila had ever seen.

And Leila stared at Shay, spellbound.

Shay reached out, took Leila's hand. "Would you go see a movie with me?" she asked. "Sometime?"

Somewhere, the ocean hissed and roared and came and went.

Here and now, Leila breathed out and simply said, "Yes."

And the spell was done.

THE MERMAID CIRCUS

by S.E. Diemer

Some people say that writers lie to people for money. They make up stories, don't they? That's lying, and people actually pay for those lies. So it's fair, yeah?

That's how Ma justifies the Mermaid Circus.

"Annalee, your guilt is gonna be the death of us," she says, pinching my skin so that it fits into the rubber. Then she yanks on the zipper (I don't know why it hasn't broken yet).

"Ma, reading a book and promising 'real life mermaids' when there's no such thing is another kettle of fish," I begin, as I always begin whenever she starts. But, as usual, she's not listening today.

"That's right, honey. But lots of people paid today to see a 'real live mermaid,' and that's just what we'll give them, yeah?" She pats my cheek absentmindedly, and then hooks her hands under my arms, dragging me across the floor to the pool entrance. It's a hole I drop into, falling ten feet before the water. It covers my head, swallowing me.

The crawlspace is tiny, dark, and I have to hold my breath and swim without being able to see anything for a good minute. Then the little corridor branches to the right, and there's the pool.

"Pool" is kind of a nice word for what it is: a gigantic vat of water dirtier than sewage.

Through the grimy, algae-coated glass, I can see the kids, peering into the depths, their eyes round, their mouths open in glee. I sigh out a little, bubbles escaping my lips and move toward the surface.

I twitch my fins, smile widely.

They paid to see a real live mermaid. That's not exactly what they're seeing, but I should at least *try*.

No one ever asks why the mermaid has to come to the surface once a minute or so. They watch my tail twist and spin, they watch my tricks, my "dancing" underwater. The music, pumped in through underwater speakers, is sickeningly sappy, but it's the same music that they had when Ma was the mermaid, and why change a good thing? I go through my entire routine, keeping the smile pasted on my face, and when I can hear the thumping of what I always hope and assume is the applause, I blow a kiss to the glass, and turn and crawl back into the hole, swimming as fast as I can for the back room.

"You did great, baby girl," is what Ma tells me when she hauls me up herself, cranking the lift. I flop onto the concrete floor, shaking, until she puts a towel around my shoulders. "*Great*," she repeats, with a big grin. "I like that little kick you added at the end! It's not in the choreography, but…"

"Ma, *listen*," I start, trying to catch my breath, but she's yanking on the zipper of the tail.

"I'm listening," she grunts, pushing her knee against my thighs. "I think we're gonna have to make you a new one someday soon…it's being ornery lately…" she groans, hauling on the zipper.

I fold my arms, waiting.

The zipper stays stuck.

"Well," she says, wiping off her forehead with a tissue, "we'll just have to get your father to do it. You can come up and say hi to the kiddies."

"Ma, I don't *wanna* say hi to the kiddies." I sigh for so long, I don't have any air left in my lungs. "I really want to talk to you about the Mermaid Circus…"

Ma stands up, lifting me into a chair. From that, she hauls me over her shoulder, so I'm carried like a sack of potatoes. It's terribly uncomfortable and a really crappy position to have this talk in, but I can't stop now. I've started it.

"Ma, I think I want to go to college," I mutter into her back.

That's what gets her to pause, her hand on the doorknob.

"Annalee, we'll discuss it later." Her tone is brisk. I clear my throat.

"'Later' means 'never,'" I say, poking her in the kidney. "I picked out a school and everything, Ma."

"You can't leave," is what she's saying. She opens the door into the cacophony of the midway, the carnival rides of the Mermaid Circus in full swing. The merry-go-round plays the same song it's been playing since before I was born: cheerful, out of tune and never ending.

"You could get one of the local girls to do it," I'm muttering to her lower back. "It's not as if someone couldn't keep a secret."

"Mermaid!" I hear the squeals. We've been spotted.

"We will discuss this *later*, Annalee," says my mother through gritted teeth. And then I'm plunked down onto the folding chair in front of the stand that does the deep fried cheesecake. The sickening wave of grease and deliciousness encases me, and then the children attack.

"*I* wanna sit in her lap!"

"No, *I* wanna!"

"Momma, make her wait her turn!"

I keep the same smile pasted on my face as the kids climb all over me like I'm a jungle gym with a tail, and, mercifully and eventually, the crowd dies off, and I'm left alone. It's getting close to closing time on a Tuesday, and not many people are usually here on Tuesday, anyway, but I'll have to stay here until we close.

I never mind the sitting and talking to the kids and taking pictures. They're always so excited to see me, and it means that Ma is usually off tending to something else, and we're not arguing. I know it's weird, but those are some of my most peaceful times.

I'm woken from my daydreaming—I *was* staring a little too fiercely at the merry-go-round--by a cleared throat. I breathe out, straighten up, forcing myself not to crick my back, and smile up at the person standing over me.

And stop.

No one local comes to the Mermaid Circus—why would they? Everyone thinks we're scam artists (not that they're wrong), because, really? A "real live mermaid?" Not so much. We *exist* to be a tourist trap. So it's kind of shocking that, standing over me in all of her plaid-wearing, skinny-jean adoring glory is Maggie…the girl I've been crushing since…well. Since I knew what a crush was.

"Hey, Annalee," she says grinning, hooking her thumbs in her belt loops. I hope that my mom's makeup job is hiding the fact that I'm blushing so hard I can almost see the heat waves rise off me.

"Hey, Maggie," I breathe out, grinning up at her.

"It's been a long summer," she says, leaning down, blowing her carefully-swept-over-one-eye hair up with a puff of bubblegum breath. "How've you been?"

OhmyGodohmyGodohmyGod. I swallow, try to remember how to breathe.

Pretty much it's known, school over, that Maggie's gay. And pretty much everyone assumes that I'm weird enough, so yeah, why not like girls, too. And they'd be right, by the way. But Maggie and I have never really talked or done much of anything outside of that one time Maggie borrowed my phone because hers was dead, and she had to call her step-dad for a ride. Not that I totally remember that day or conversation or how she smiled at me, and how I'd *hoped* that when she returned my phone back to me, her fingers had lingered on mine just a *touch* longer than only-an-acquaintance would.

"So, I have kind of a weird question," says Maggie, tilting her head to the side in a way that makes my heart beat faster. "Can I ask you?"

Oh my God, Annalee, do not *screw this up.*

"I might have a weird answer," I say, doing my best to smile fetchingly, and trying not to leap to an instant *yes.* "What is it?"

Please say a date, please say a date…

"Well, my uncle found this kind of weird thing when he drew his paddleboard up on the beach the other day." She puts her hands in her pockets, frowns a little. "And I said that you'd be the only one who knew about strange ocean stuff, on account of your job and all, and that—if it'd be all right with you—I could bring you by to take a look at it?"

I hope I don't look as crestfallen as I feel. Why did I think she'd ask me out on a date? I'm hopeless. "Yeah, I could come look at it," I smile up at her.

"How about when you get off?" asks Maggie, glancing at her watch. "Fifteen minutes?"

"Sure," I promise. Then my heart starts beating fast again, because Maggie drops on one knee beside me, bringing her down to my level where I sit in the folding lawn chair, useless tail flopping.

"Thanks, Annalee—I really appreciate it." She leans forward, and then she envelopes me in a hug. She smells like boy cologne and hair gel and sun-warmed skin. I breathe in and out and melt under her hug, weakly patting her arm (it's hard to lean forward in this stupid tail). "See you soon!" Maggie practically purrs, breaking away from me and bounding away.

I stare after her, cartoon hearts dancing around her receding form.

"College?" asks my mother, viciously ripping down on the zipper. I sigh, roll my eyes as she tries, for the eight millionth time, to get it unstuck.

"Ma, I need a new tail," I try to switch the subject. I'm no longer brave enough to tackle this today. "It's too old. This gives an entirely new meaning to 'wardrobe malfunction.'"

"Yes, well, it was good enough in my day," says Ma huffily, squatting back on her heels. "Really, honey, I think your dad's gonna have to get you out of this."

My pulse quickens. "Ma, I can't wait—I gotta…go help a friend. I promised her."

"Okay, once more…" I grab onto the post and Ma tugs with all her might, and then suddenly, blessedly, the zipper gives, and I spill out of the mermaid tail.

"It's just…" she starts up, as I knew she would, as I pull on my jeans over my bikini bottom. "I thought you'd carry on, you know? We've tried to build a legacy for you here."

"Ma, I'm not cut out to run the Circus my whole life. You've known that. I wanna do awesome things, I wanna go to weird places. I want to not be a mermaid forever." I laugh a little at my own joke, but Ma doesn't think it funny, screws up her mouth into a sad little frown that cuts my heart into small, aching pieces.

"Who would take over the Circus?" she asks, and I shake my head. I don't have that answer.

"I'll try to be home by dinner," I tell her, and kiss her cheek. She smells of deep fried cheesecake and hard work, and as I turn to grab my socks and sneakers, I can't help but see the way she pushes her jaw to the side, her downcast face, the tears in her eyes.

I'm cut to the quick, but swallow it down.

"Hey!" says Maggie, straightening up from her

oh-so-cool leaning against the front gate of the Mermaid Circus. Everything she does is so hot, so effortless. Even the boys, knowing full well what she is, watch her when she moves through the halls at school. I grin up at her now, still hoping I'm not blushing.

"So what did your uncle find?" I ask her as we start down the road toward the coast. Her uncle, Harry, lives in a little shack every summer that he fishes out of.

"It's kind of weird," she shrugs, grins a little. "I dunno—I think you'll have to see it."

"My curiosity is piqued," I reply, grinning too, praying to the universe that I don't sound as lame as I think I do.

It's such a gorgeous afternoon, the breeze whispering through the salt grasses and sea grape bushes. We leave the road behind and walk along one of the white-as-snow sand paths, down the dunes and toward her uncle's shack.

"Huh, that's weird," Maggie says, after hulloing her uncle and getting no response. She knocks on his door and pushes it in, but in the one room dwelling there's no sight of Harry. "He said he'd be here," she frowns, shoving her hands into her pockets. "Wanna walk down to the water, see if he took his boat out?"

"Sure," I tell her, and we stroll down to the water's edge. The boat's gone, and Harry with it.

Maggie plops down on the sand, the sea breeze rifling her hair. "That's the last time I ever do a favor for my uncle," she says, smiling up at me and patting the sand beside her. "What a bum."

I plop down beside her, too, drawing my knees up and clasping them tightly against my ribs and chest, hoping the solidity will make my heart stop racing.

"So," says Maggie, drawing out the word and leaning back on her hands in the sand. "Have you always been a mermaid?" We're both laughing at that, the sunshine spilling over us like water, the sound of the surf loud and pleasant all around us.

"Yeah, I was born into it," I roll my eyes, place my cheek against my knees as I turn and look at her. "Ma was a mermaid, and her ma, Gramma, was the lady who built the Mermaid Circus. So I'm third generation mermaid."

"Do people actually believe you're a real mermaid?" asks Maggie. There's no judgment in her words—she genuinely wonders about that. I shrug.

"I mean, they made that one mockumentary about the Mermaid Circus, and the director made it seem it was real, so lots of people believe it is, and that's enough for them. But yeah, two internet searches, and you'd know it wasn't. But that doesn't keep people from wanting to believe."

"Wanting to believe…" Maggie repeats, looking out across the ocean. "Huh."

"What?" I ask, furrowing my brow. She looks so far away, in that moment, as if she can see across the horizon to another place. She shakes her head, blinks.

"I've never told anyone but my dad this," she says, looking down at her lap. "I mean, it's really stupid."

"I won't think it's stupid," I tell her, voice soft. She sighs.

"Yeah. I believe you." She's staring at me so intensely that my heart is in danger of hammering itself out of my ribs. "Well. When I was a little kid—I thought I saw a mermaid." I cock my head, waiting for her to finish. But she just shakes hers, smiles a little. "See? It's ridiculous."

"No, wait," I tell her, shaking my head. "So what happened?"

"I was on Uncle Harry's boat, and I was helping him fish. My parents had dumped me there for the day. So I'm holding his bucket of fish bits, and I peer over the edge of the boat, and there she is. She's a mermaid. Tail, boobs, the whole nine yards. She had a dolphin tail. I remember that, I remember thinking it was weird, but that it made sense, because mermaids are mammals, right?

156

They're not fish. And she grinned at me, and she blew me a kiss, and then she swam away."

"Wow," I breathe out, looking out at the ocean.

"You think it's stupid."

I shake my head. "No I don't."

"So do you think I actually saw a mermaid?" She's looking at me, eyes wide, brow furrowed...almost pleading. I swallow, breathe out, try to think.

"I mean, maybe." I tell her, though it falls flat, even to me. She deflates a little, so I keep talking. "I mean, no one knows about the ocean, right? It's the most unexplored thing. There could be thousands of species that we've never even seen. Why *not* mermaids?"

"You believe me," she says flatly, staring at me. I wait a second, questioning myself...do I?

And then I'm nodding.

"Why not," I grin at her. "I believe you."

The distance between us is so small. Small enough that, when Maggie leans toward me, all I have to do is lean a little, too. And then we're kissing. She's so soft, her lips so soft that a shiver of delight runs through me. I'd imagined it, oh my God, how often I imagined it...but she's warm and soft and gentle and her breath is bubblegum sweet, and this is the greatest thing that ever happened in my entire life.

"Hello!" comes the sound over the water, breaking through the pounding of the surf and the euphoria of that kiss. Maggie breaks away, and then she's standing, waving to her uncle coming in on his boat. I get up, too, smoothing out my t-shirt, my jeans, pressing my hands against my face because I'm blushing redder than a crab.

Uncle Harry makes landfall, and Maggie helps him drag in his dinghy. He waves at me, grinning, and then he's hauling his bait and tackle and a bucket of catch from the boat.

"I came to look at that weird thing you found," I tell him, hands in my jean pockets.

"Oh? Oh!" He says, dropping his buckets at his

feet. He pokes through the various pockets in his vest until he finds the right one, a smile coming across his craggly, wrinkled face. I don't think the guy has ever frowned in his life. "Here. I don't know what it is. Do you?" He pulls the shiny thing from his vest pocket and hands it over to me.

It's small and curved and iridescent beyond belief. I stare down at it, turning it this way and that. It's not part of a shell—that was my first thought.

"Thought it could be a mermaid scale," says Harry, leaning back on his heels. "But thought we'd ask the mermaid for confirmation."

I glance up at Maggie who's watching me closely.

"I'm sorry," I tell him, shaking my head and reluctantly handing the pretty thing back. "I don't know what it is."

"Could it be a mermaid scale, though?" he asks, and I shrug, biting my lip.

"I don't know," I repeat. He shrugs, too, pocketing it again.

"Well," he says, winking. "Stranger things have happened, I suppose." Maggie laughs a little and when we leave Uncle Harry, he's swearing about some fish making off with his best hook.

"What's it like?" asks Maggie as we walk up the dunes. The sun sets behind us, so beautiful it makes me catch my breath. We watch it slipping away into the folds of water. "Being a mermaid?"

I watch the last bits of sun for a long moment. "I love it, sometimes," I tell her. "But it's all weird. I don't want to be a mermaid forever. I want to go to school. I want to be a chef," I say, all in a rush. "I really love to cook. I've thought a lot about it. But the family business, you know? It's hard. I don't know what to do."

She stays quiet for a moment, and we both watch the water. "I know it's superstitious," she finally says, "but you know the day I saw the mermaid? Uncle Harry got married to Aunt Ann. He was never happier than when he was with her. He still misses her." She sniffs, sighs. "I think mermaids are luck. You're a mermaid." She grins sidelong at me. "A 'real, live' mermaid, even. So you must have a lot of luck. It'll work out. I really believe it."

This time, I lean in. I don't even care. I lean in, and I kiss her, but just a little peck, because I'm not really *that* brave. "Thank you," I whisper to her, smiling. "That means a lot to me."

She just grins and turns, and we both start walking back.

But…it's kind of weird. I thought I saw, out against the sunset, something rush and leap out of the water. It wasn't a dolphin, but I couldn't really see it—just a glimpse, out of the corner of my eye. When I really looked, it was gone.

"Coming?" says Maggie at the top of the dune. The wind moves through her hair, and her grin is all jaunty and gorgeous.

"Yeah," I whisper, and—digging my hands deep into my pockets—I follow after.

BLUEBOTTLES

by Jennifer Diemer

Barefoot, I tiptoe over the wet sand. There are man-of-wars—bluebottles, my dad calls them—glowing cobalt all along the shoreline. Before I moved in with my mom, Carolina and I used to walk this beach every day, and we imagined the brilliant blue creatures were fallen stars, or gleaming beads carved from the moon.

I'm not ready for this. Why am I here?

Even the waves are bioluminescent, alight with bluebottles rising, cresting, and then washing ashore. I kneel down, peer at one of the beached man-of-wars and feel a pang: the sorrow, the loss. "I'm sorry," I whisper, but my voice is stolen by the sea.

When I glance back up, trail my gaze over the water, my eyes shift out of focus for a moment, and I make out a pattern, a necklace of bright blue flickering beneath the sunlit surface.

I stand and stare into the ocean. It's unmistakable: there's a line of bluebottles winding through the waves— not moving toward the beach but away, spiraling deep and away.

Without a thought, I strip down to my swimsuit and dash into the water, running until I'm in up to my neck, shivering, floating. I lick my lips and taste the salt and think of Carolina again…

No.

My feet tread water, and I blink, scanning the surface for the bluebottle trail. Its tail end hovers just below me—hovers, like it's waiting—and then begins to slowly whirl and glide further out from shore.

I follow it.

There's a pool at Mom's apartment complex in Pittsburgh, but swimming in placid chlorine is nothing like swimming in a living sea. I've missed it. I was so preoccupied with missing *her* that I failed to notice the ocean-shaped fissure inside of me. My muscles move instinctively, slicing through the blue, and I'm only half-aware of the string of man-of-wars gliding below, guiding me. I swim farther than I ever have before, until my heart hurts and my arms ache.

Until I see the boat.

"Ramie?"

I freeze and sink, swallow salt.

"Ramie, is it really you?"

She's wearing the rainbow headscarf I tie-dyed for her. Her blue hair is drawn into a side ponytail, brushing against her bikini strap, her bare shoulder.

"Oh, my God, Ramie, it's you!" Her little boat tilts as she hangs over the side, motoring toward me.

I take a deep breath and inhale water, start to cough, sink lower, cough harder, but then she's there, sitting in her boat beside me, and she hooks her hands under my shoulders and drags me out of the sea, onto the white-painted planks. Freshly painted.

"You fixed it," I say, because I don't know what else to say, and she stares at me for a long moment before answering.

"My uncle rebuilt the bottom, yeah, and I just refinished it. It's still not totally seaworthy, but…" Her mouth twists into a lopsided smile. "You know me. I live for danger."

I bow my head, sit up, pull my knees to my chest. I'm afraid to look at her again, afraid I'll find she's disappeared, because I thought I'd never see her again, and I had nurtured the pain of that knowledge like a sharp, wild reef inside of me, scraping away, hour by hour, minute by minute, at my soft parts. Until I was numb.

Until I could look into a mirror, into darkened windows and glittering car doors, into the fake blue water of the pool at Mom's complex without seeing the ghost of Carolina's face there.

I thought I'd never see you again.

I hoped—prayed to every deity I could beg by name—that I would.

"What are you doing so far out?" Carolina asks, leaning down, trying to catch my eye. "Did you swim the whole way?"

It's my turn to smirk, but my mouth feels stuck in a sort of disbelieving frown. "I followed the bluebottles. I guess…" *I guess they led me here, to you.* "I just felt like swimming."

"Hey. Ramie. Will you look at me?"

I bite my lip, and there are tears in my eyes, but I look at her, anyway. She's seen me cry before. "I like it," I whisper, gesturing toward her hair. "The blue."

"Thanks." She shoves off the seat, kneels down beside me. "Ramie. I—I've missed you. A lot."

I've missed you, too. More than a lot.

I swipe a fist over my face, catching tears.

She breathes out hard. "Why didn't you reply to any of my emails?"

Because I printed them out, smeared them with sobs, and hid them, folded into origami hearts, in my pillow. Because writing to you, knowing we were so far apart, would have hurt too much. I hurt too much.

"Ramie. Talk to me."

I lift my gaze. Something inside of me dissolves when my eyes connect with hers—so blue, bluer than the ocean, than the sky, and shining. "I should have never left you," I whisper, covering my face with my hands.

Carolina's cool palms—her skin is always cool, even in the sticky heat of Florida summer—encircle my wrists. "Don't," she says, moving close, gathering me into her arms. The comfort of her nearness, the sea-claimed scent of her, the pulse of her heart beneath my ear… I can't control myself; I cry against her shoulder, and the salt of my tears stings my face.

"Ramie, you had no choice," she whispers, her voice gruff with emotion. "The judge gave your mom custody—"

"But I should've fought harder. I should've convinced her to stay here." I nearly choke on my tears, so I tilt my head back and, through a watery haze, stare into Carolina's sad, lovely eyes. "I shouldn't have left without saying good-bye. I just couldn't…"

She bows her head, and tendrils of blue glance my forehead. "You were devastated when your parents split. And your mom—" Her mouth smirks. "Well, I was never her favorite person. I think 'that lesbo girl' was one of her…kinder nicknames for me."

"I'm sorry about that. I'm so—"

"I know." She smiles softly, but her eyes remain downcast. "I've been saving up, you know. Working double shifts at the restaurant, and helping my uncle out on his hauls. I almost had enough to hop on a plane to Pittsburgh. One way." Her hand grazes my hot cheek, smoothing away the tears there. "But then you showed up. Splashing like a mermaid." Her smile stills, then ebbs. "Why are you here, Ramie?"

"Why are you? I thought you were going to go to that theater internship in Atlanta over the summer, and then on to L.A.—"

"No." She shakes her head, tousling her azure hair, and she looks so *right*, perfectly placed, her outline synthesized with the backdrop of the ocean. *She's* the mermaid. My siren. Her eyes glisten. "I was waiting for you."

I touch her—her hand, poised on her knee. I trace the lines of her fingers one by one, and she inhales but keeps her eyes trained on me. "I lied," I say. "I told Mom that I got accepted at Florida State—which I did, though I don't know if I even *want* to go to college—and I told my dad that Mom wants alone time with her boyfriend, without a teenage daughter moping around in the background." I sigh and trace a heart on the back of Carolina's hand. "Not entirely untrue."

Her eyes roam my length; I flush. "So you're here." She swallows, watching me hopefully. "To stay?"

I bite my lip, because I don't want to cry again, but she's a vision: it's like a dream to be here with her now, close enough to see, to touch, kiss. "They'd need a steamer to drag me away from you, Care." My blush deepens. "I mean…if you still want me. I'd understand if you didn't, after the way I treated you, after I *left* you—"

"Ramie."

"Yeah?"

"Shut up and kiss me."

"Okay." I breathe in, trembling, and lean toward her.

Kissing Carolina is like kissing the ocean. All of my bottled-up emotions from the past few months fill my chest until I'm certain it will burst, *I* will burst, and the longing for her rises within me like a never-cresting wave, higher and higher, still higher, until there are no clouds, no sky. Only water. Only her.

Our connection is salted and sweet and long, and when we separate—with room for only a breath between us—Carolina gasps and startles me by leaning over the edge of the boat, rocking it treacherously to the side.

"Oh, Ramie. It's so beautiful," she whispers, grasping my hands, looking to me with wonder shining in her eyes.

All around us, the bluebottles spiral, glowing like submerged beacons beneath the broad, soft, rippling sea.

PEARLS ENOUGH

by Jennifer Diemer

I wait for her at the dock.

There's no one about. It's a warm and still summer night, heavy with longing. Before me, the full moon hangs low, its reflection a half-circle of white on the sea. I stare unseeing at the ripples of light, and, despite the heat, an otherworldly shiver rakes my spine.

Breathe, breathe.

I dab a handkerchief at my forehead, but the lacy square slips from my trembling fingers; I watch with detached eyes as it flutters like a flag of surrender, lost to the opaque waves below. At night, the ocean is as black as the sky.

How does she see, I wonder, when her world goes dark? How can she tell up from down? How does she find her way to the shore, to me?

These are questions I've never thought to ask her.

Somewhere a ship's horn blares, and I start, leaning hard against the wooden railing.

Lottie will have noticed my absence by now; I failed to appear for dinner. I can't imagine what she'll think, finding me gone from the house at such an hour, but I know what she'll *feel* after the shock has worn away: relief. She will no longer be burdened by a disagreeable younger sister, will never again be forced to contrive excuses to explain away my "strangeness."

Oh, the poor thing had such a fright when our father passed on. I'm afraid she's not quite recovered from the upset, and allowances must be made for odd manners in circumstances such as these.

No, I'm certain it wasn't Portia you saw wading in the sea—how absurd, the mere thought!—because she was here with me all day, embroidering daisies on a shawl for Lawrence's mother.

As if I would ever engage in such frippery as embroidery. When Lottie caught me returning from the shore that day, she ordered me to strip out of my wet things and burn them in the hearth-fire, because they were *mucky* and *ruined*—was I determined to bring scandal to the family name?

I'll not miss her a bit. Perhaps that makes me an ungrateful person. But I am not naïve, despite my years; I know when I'm unwanted, and I prefer not to linger. I'm certainly old enough to make up my own mind. Before Father died, I was the one managing his accounts, and I nursed him during his illness. Lottie claimed to be too busy with her duties as wife and Lady of the House to visit or offer any assistance to her ailing parent and fifteen-year-old sister.

Now—after residing for a full year under her smothering roof—I know precisely what those so-called duties of hers entail: bobbing her head along with every word to escape her idiot husband's lips; making faces at her mirror and pinching her cheeks until they bruise rotten-fruit purple; spying on the servants and reprimanding them for trivial crimes; and, of course, napping. Lottie sleeps more often than a cat, and snores just like our father did: evenly, moistly, openmouthed.

Father told me on several occasions that I take after Mother, the mother I've never known, with my black eyes and unruly black hair. But I suspect our resemblance runs deeper than that. Mother ran away from her life, just as I'm running away from mine now. I wonder if she had an extraordinary secret, too? I wonder if she tired of this place, as I have, and sought out another world? I wonder if she slipped away, slipped *through*...

A splash.

I gasp behind my hand and turn toward the sound, but nothing is distinct in the undulating expanse before me.

Still…I know she's here. Near.

"Mea?" My whisper sounds rough and dry in the humid night.

"Below you," she says softly, and I tilt my chin down over the edge of the dock to spy a pair of white hands on the wooden ladder sunk into the sea, and then a dark head heavy with coiled, dripping hair.

She's climbing up, and as I watch her, I press against the railing, and the realization washes over me that soon—how soon? Minutes, perhaps?—there will be no more railings for me. There will be no space between myself and the sea.

Between myself and Mea.

I cough nervously, though my heart beats like rain within my chest as she crests the top of the ladder, as she places her bare feet—toes webbed, too long; they separate and shorten before my eyes—between the rails and stands nose to nose with me, with only wooden slats and the salted air separating us.

"You came." She looks flushed, exuberant—her skin shining like scales, iridescent, beneath the moon. "You're certain, then?"

"I'm certain of this." I pull her against me and claim her mouth in a kiss; she's cold and warm all at once, and she tastes of colors I've never seen. The wet length of her imprints my dress with a Mea silhouette.

"I'm certain of you," I whisper, leaning my forehead against hers. A droplet of ocean glides from her cheek to mine, and its salt startles my tongue.

"And I, you." She smiles against my lips, kisses me again. "But you know what I'm speaking of."

"I know."

Together, hands twined, we gaze outward, over the surface of the sea, but my eyes fall—sink, as if by an anchor's weight—down into the black waters. For a moment, my breath catches as I imagine *not* breathing, never breathing for the rest of my days. I watch Mea's still, airless chest, and she moves her eyes back to me, stares, then nods.

"You will be frightened, Portia. Your body—by instinct—will revolt. As mine did." Her hand traces a cold line down my hot cheek. Tenderly, she lifts my chin, and I drown in the green of her gaze. "But then, after the change, you will feel more alive than you ever have before."

"I only feel alive when I'm with you," I tell her, the truth. "Everything that *isn't* you is dull, gray as graves. My sister has no dreams in her, no hopes, and she seeks to mold me in her image, but I cannot—*will* not melt myself down. Mea…" I wrap my arms around her once more, and she settles her mouth against my neck, lips cool. "The day you came to me was the first day I felt my own soul."

Her laugh is a rivulet, wending deep. "Well, you were drowning. Mortal thoughts are common when death is near."

I bite her ear, and laugh, too. "Don't tease—"

"Shh, someone approaches."

I still, throat too dry to swallow, and slowly turn. A man in uniform stands outlined in moonlight at the far end of the dock, peering in our direction. When he notices my glance, he nods and begins marching toward us.

I gasp and cling to Mea. "Now! We must hurry! If he sees you—"

She stills my tongue with her steady, patient gaze. "Carefully, Portia, lift one leg over the rails. And then the other. I'll hold onto you. You won't fall until…"

I do swallow now, and cough. "Until we jump," I finish her sentence. She nods her head, tapping the railing with a hand.

I'm wearing my thin muslin gown, the one Lottie hates—*You look like a washerwoman, Portia. Have you no pride?*—because it is unencumbered by decoration and has a wide skirt, so I'm able to swing my legs over the railing easily, expertly, as if I've made a living of making escapes. My heart rattles around in my chest like a tooth come loose.

The officer is only a few strides away now, and he's shouting. I can't hear his words over the rushing in my ears—of my blood, of the sea.

Mea embraces me and whispers, "Dive."

I take my last breath: it's warm and thick and briny, and as I exhale, little thoughts like waves ebb and flow… Will Lottie shed a tear for me? Will I miss her, after all? Did my mother miss me? Did she lose her dreams, too, like Lottie, or is she dreaming still, like me?

Will it hurt when the sea claims me, when my blood turns to salt?

I sling an arm around Mea's waist, and we kiss, and we leap—

Ice.

I shatter.

Pain.

I thrash. I wail and drown…

There is only cold and black and—

Portia, I'm here.

"Mea," I say, and sink, choke, but I reach for her, and our curves come together, and our mouths are one, *one*…and everything within me lets go, reforms, and I can see again, white—no, blue. No… So many colors. Colors I can't name, don't know. And I'm warm, so warm, and Mea's in my arms, and I laugh without breathing, sigh without air.

My nets—real and imagined—drift away along with my gown, the pearl necklace Lottie clasped on my neck like a collar…

Mea and I will have pearls enough here.

Together we swim, twin-tailed, through a thousand secret hues.

BREAKING THE ICE

by Jennifer Diemer

I grew up wild and motherless in a frozen land. My father taught me how to survive. He insisted upon it: self-sufficiency, independence. Before I had all of my teeth, before my baby-fine hair thickened and darkened and fell in slow waves against the back of my neck, I knew the secrets of Earth and Water, Fire and Air. I mapped the stars. I studied the animals, learned their languages, burned into memory the shape of their tracks in the snow. Each feathered wingbeat slicing the cold, sharp air was distinct, as clear as voices, to my ears. Birdcalls and plaintive, bestial howls sprang forth from my throat more often than human words. But I was not lonely.

During the tenth month of my tenth year, my father took his final steps out of doors and remained bedridden, confined to the modest pile of timber we called home, from that moment onward. He was not old, or ill, not of body. He was lazy, I thought. Weak. I resented his stubbornness, his seeming determination to die and leave me, a small child, in this wasteland alone. But dutifully, every day (until the last day), I fed him, cooked for him my killings: bony hares, bland fish with scales warmed to crisps over the fire, the rare fowl felled by my primitive, hand-sharpened darts. I bathed him in our wooden tub, shaved his face with the silver blade I kept strapped inside my boot, and I sang to him songs of my own invention,

173

blue-white melodies about winters without end.

I feel no bitterness toward him; he was not a brave, spirited man, but as a man, he did the best he could with my upbringing. He made certain I understood the natural laws, the basics of survival. Because, I know now, all throughout my childhood, he was planning and awaiting his exodus from this world, and he did not want the guilt of my abandonment weighing upon his conscience. My father's heart had failed him more than a decade before, when my mother died with the birth of me, but his chest did not cease its rise and fall until I was eleven and had learned all he felt capable of teaching. I could not read, and I could hardly love, but I could live, and so his soul departed.

With a strength borrowed, perhaps, from the beasts watching—for they were always watching from the snowfields nearby—I hoisted the corpse that was my father onto my splintered sled and dragged it over the ice. In preparation, and at his request, I had widened one of my fishing holes with an ax days earlier, and as I tilted the sled, his body lurched toward its watery grave, but slowly, reluctantly. Skin caught on the jagged wood fragments; then came the blood—so red against the snow that my color-starved eyes fixated upon it and missed the moment that the cold waters swallowed my lost and last relative.

"I am alone."

And so I remained…for months upon months, years upon years. Time and seasons mattered little in such a place, to such a person as me. I woke, I ate, I slept…and at night, I dreamed. Dreams of warm things, soft things. But dreams are quickly forgotten in subzero solitude. Snow, ice, white, stillness. Cold water slushed through my veins, and I was numb.

On the morning that I first glimpsed her eyes

beneath the ice, the sun was shining heroically, its pure light gleaming upon glaciers. I sat cross-legged on the frozen sea, stitching hides together for leggings and gloves, and allowed myself, for just a moment, to imagine that large yellow star puffing up its cheeks, squinting its eyes and pushing, radiating with all its might, determined to melt this summerless island into a tropical paradise. An arctic smile warped my chapped lips. "Old fool." I inhaled deeply, laying my handiwork aside to tilt my head upward and bask in the rays. "But I appreciate the gesture."

I was 17 and had not seen, heard or spoken with a fellow human being in six years. In an effort to prevent myself from forgetting my tongue (and losing my mind), I had taken to talking aloud to trees and rocks, stars, fish. A water-stained photo of my mother. Granted, these conversations were brief and, excepting the occasional remark from a sociable bird, entirely one-sided, but they kept my sanity more or less intact—or so I liked to believe.

Funny, I suppose, that the thought of leaving that barren place had never with any seriousness occurred to me. What use would it have been, though, to go elsewhere, to learn a foreign landscape, when I had all I needed here? I did not know longing or desire. Want was not yet part of my emotional vocabulary. The aches of hunger, of physical pain, of biting winds and stark beauty...these alone moved me.

And then I saw her face.

It wasn't uncommon to spy movement under thin expanses of ice. A lifetime without the security of solid ground had taught me to avoid such tracts. But there were fish visible below, of course. And then, less often and still too often, the seals—unfortunate creatures that had swum too far, too long, desperate for air, encased and drowning. In rare, wonderful moments, my father told me stories about the seals and their undersea kingdoms of seal people, seal gods. He loved them, I think, because they reminded him of my mother. "Those eyes," he said, "could make a desert sky weep."

But these eyes...staring back at me through the frost, looking at me as one person looks at another person, and blue... No, they did not belong to a seal. Perhaps, the last remnants of the little girl in me wondered, there are seal people, after all? Or perhaps, the cynic nurtured in me these last years decided, there is a dead body floating beneath me—a drowning, a murder victim...a suicide.

Death did not frighten me. Was I not, myself, Death's maidservant, daily killing the animals of land, air and sea so that I might eat and cover naked skin? There were wolves, bears, but only I played predator to them all, with my pink flesh and thin wrists and tangled, night-black hair. I did not belong with these beasts, and yet with whom did I belong?

Something odd stirred inside of me; my chest tightened. With whom...? I lay a hand upon the ice, over the cheek of the unfortunate someone floating beneath me. She was a woman.

"And what is your story?" I whispered, half-frightened, though I could not guess at why. "What brought you to this end, here, where there is nothing and no one...but me?"

As if in response to my question, the pale lids over her eyes—eyes blue as sky on snow—closed and opened.

They blinked.

I started back and slid a full foot before gaining my bearings and skidding to a stop upon my knees. My palms, ungloved for ease of stitching, were now raw and bleeding. Red... Too red. My father...

Shaking fingers grazed my temple. A drop of blood fell to my thigh.

But I couldn't have seen... It defied reason. The cold water alone would, within moments, stop any human heart from beating. And there were insufficient holes in the ice for swimming meaningful distances without dying from a basic lack of air. That's why the seals died. That's why I couldn't have seen...

"Mad." An idea took hold, winning favor over the incomprehensible alternative. "I've gone mad at last. I'm imagining things that aren't possible, that aren't even there." I risked a glance. Her hand—it was pressed flat against the ice now, as if attempting to push through…

"No!"

On my feet, gripped by an unfamiliar emotion—fury, disbelief, fear…what?—I seized my hides and glowered down at the bleary visage. "My world," came the whisper, from lips that seemed possessed. "This is my world, mine. Alone. That's how… That's how…"

She was wincing. She was…pleading.

All feeling drained from my body, puddled at my feet. "That's how it's meant to be. This is no place…for someone like you. Go. Go away. Go now!"

And I turned my back on her. And I trudged back to my shack, with its leaky roof and empty heart, and I sobbed for a shamefully long time; finally, the tears crystallized upon my face, and sleep gathered me into her deadening arms.

The night passed, dreamless.

Lonely, loneliness—such words never had meaning for me before. Alone, yes, for I was always alone, even before my father's passing. But lonely, no. Yet in the morning, a revelation, a certainty: I was lonely. It was something internal, like a sickness. My father had taught me many cures—for fever, for frostbite, for pain in the head and joints and lungs—but none for this. And I realized, with a tremor, that loneliness had proved fatal for him. It stole away his will, his dignity. His last breath.

"I am nothing like that man," I said calmly, evenly, in a tone so detached that I doubted its origins. "This will pass. All things pass, in time."

A shiver coursed through my body; I felt chilled to

the bone. With a charred branch, I stoked the weak flames of my little fire, fighting against the determination of my teeth to chatter from the cold. It was not so cold, truly. Only as cold as it ever was, always was—freezing, scarcely bearable, mind numbing. But I was used to this climate. I knew nothing else. I was born on the ice.

Still, another shiver.

With stubborn resolution, I slung the fishing sack over my shoulder, grabbed my pole and went outside, inhaling deeply the harsh wintered air into my dry throat. Activity would warm my blood and occupy my thoughts. In retrospect, I probably looked quite frightening, stomping like a great wild bear across the frozen landscape. My lips were set in a tight, sinister line, and my eyes had the pinpoint focus of one who refuses to see anything beyond the real and the obvious, blindly ignoring all else.

But somehow, of their own accord, my feet found the place again, the shallow ice over sea which had, only hours ago, covered her face like a veil. No, I will not think of her. I will not. I will not look –

I looked.

She was not there.

"Oh…" And I threw down my fishing pole, and I stooped to peer closer, and closer still; my nose touched the cold surface, and my breath frosted the ice.

Fathomless depths. Vacant, black. No one. No one gazed back at me, needing me, begging me. Wanting…me.

"Oh…" I sighed again, rising to my elbows, pressing my gloved hands together, as if in prayer.

But the small part of my brain still capable of reasoning suddenly gained control. Perhaps— No, no. Certainly. Certainly there had never been anyone there, under the ice, at all. The madness… It truly was madness.

Unless she drowned. My cheeks paled at the possibility. Unless she died because I refused to help her when I had the chance. And of course she would have died. Any person would have died. She should have been dead…already.

A fish, small, with scales that glinted silver, swam through the waters below, jolting me out of my reverie.

I sat back. I stared at the snow-capped mountains straight ahead, far away, neutral geography for my weary eyes. And I made a decision.

From my boot, I pulled the knife that had once shaved my father's face, and I began stabbing at the ice with a careful violence. An ax would make quicker work of it, but I had no desire to ease these labors. I wanted to hurt; I wanted to strain. I wanted to feel something recognizable, besides the cold.

How much time passed, I could not say. The repetitive motions grew painful; my arm and back ached. But my mind remained blessedly free from thought, and for that, I was more than grateful.

At last, the first breakthrough. Water which had never hoped to flow beneath the sun trickled out over shocked ice—warming it, cracking it, softening it to slush beneath my knife. The newborn hole widened, like a mouth gasping for air. I dipped my own mouth down to drink from the fresh, invigorating flow.

Then, I began to sing.

They were sharp songs at first, like icicles. Simple melodies, simple lyrics. I did not know as many words then as I know now, and so I found myself returning to the same ones, over and over again: silence, broken, lonely, heart. Another gulp of the water, and my voice became stronger, louder, and I remembered other words: *aching, longing, hungry, love.* My lips cracked, and my throat grew hoarse, but still I sang. The water on the ice under my legs seeped through my clothing, stung my skin. My empty stomach growled.

Minutes became hours. The sun faded from gold to slivers of red. My eyes drooped wearily, and my body sunk down to rest.

But still I sang.

Eventually, I suppose I slept, yet I think…my songs continued, carried on by the tireless wind.

I awoke—dry, comfortable—and she was bending over me, smiling, brushing the hair back from my forehead, petting me so gently that I felt only a faint tickle against the raw, sunburned flesh there. In a rush, I realized that we were indoors now, under the roof of my house, lying together beneath the coverings of my bed. Skin to skin. One of her arms rested beneath me, cradling my neck and shoulders.

I hesitated…and then I lay my head upon her breast.

"Are you real?" I tried to say, before comprehending that I had no voice left. Are you real? Are you here? Will you stay?

And then: Who are you? How are you? Why are you…with me?

A tear slid from the corner of one sky-on-snow blue eye. She lowered her face toward mine. I felt her silken lashes brush my cheeks, and her lips, softer still, parting at my ear.

"Please," she breathed, "let me into your world."

Warm. I had never grasped the concept of warm until that moment. It was a flood: two dams burst from my head and my toes, converging at the center of me, the now-hot—aching, hot—center of my being. And, oh, I pulled her close, and I wept into her yellow-gold hair, and I understood, finally, what it meant, what it all meant: my mother, my father. Companionship, trust, devotion…

Desire.

And I understood, too, that I would never understand how this impossible creature had chosen me, found me, filled me with more doting heat than any summer. She was all the summer I needed. My soft, warm Dream come true.

She rose from my side, then, and I cried out from the cold that assaulted me in dearth of her nearness. "No," I whispered, reaching for her desperately, half-crazed. But she only smiled again, shushing my fears with a gentle flutter of her fingers. There was a rope tied round her narrow waist with something white, like bones, jangling against her thigh. She unknotted the rope and removed the white strands—not bones, after all, nor teeth—and I saw that she held two necklaces in each of her two hands.

"What…?" I whispered, confused but curious.

She lay down once more, melding herself against my welcoming curves, and pressed a finger to my lips. And, then, slowly, with a shine in her eyes that signified reverence, she took one of the necklaces and looped it over my head, settled it against my throat. A thin white stone— later, she would tell me it was a seashell—dangled from the center of the pearl-beaded strand.

The other necklace she poured into my hand, bowing her own neck meaningfully as she did so.

I stared down at the gleaming white sea jewels in my palm. I gazed into the pure blue sincerity of her eyes.

At once, my father's voice called out to me, a faint but persistent echo: "Independence," it argued. "Self-sufficiency. Autonomy."

"Love," I countered, and encircled her throat with my promise.

We sealed the covenant naturally, with a kiss warm enough to melt a heart of snow.

UNCHARTED SKY

FALLING HOME

by S.E. Diemer

"It's not working!"

Det flicks the needle, trying to shove it into his arm, the Glow pulsing in the syringe like a hundred thousand suns. His hands are shaking too hard, though, and I have to take it from him, patting the white skin around his crow tattoo, trying to find a vein.

"Hurry, hurry..." he glances over his shoulder, shaking his head. "They're coming..."

"There..." I mutter, inserting it. He hisses in pain, but then I'm pushing down on the syringe, the Glow shooting under his skin.

He becomes luminous as something bangs against the metal door, like a body was hurled against it.

"Do you, c'mon, c'mon," he mutters, becoming almost too bright to look at as the Glow takes hold.

"Fuck..." I whisper, trying to draw more Glow into the syringe. The fear's making me shake too much and I'm clumsy. Push it down, don't listen to them pounding against the door...there, got just enough.

The door shatters inward, metal flying, red-hot pins everywhere while I inject enough Glow into myself to ascend.

And we do, while they scream in frustration, claws just missing us. Too late.

"Oh, for the love of…" I mutter, spitting sand out of my mouth. I'm blinded by the grit in my eyes, try to drum up a few tears to wash it out. Fail.

"Fifth level," says Det, resting his head next to mine on the gritty red ground.

"How do you know?" I can just see how red everything is now, the undulating, blood-colored hills bending off in all directions.

"The fifth level of hell is all about discomfort," says Det, grinning widely as he sits up, offers me a hand. "Aren't you itchy, Silver?"

I am. I've been trying to ignore it, but I scrub at my upper arms now, hissing out.

Det's wings are crawling with lice.

"That's disgusting," I frown at him, but then glance back at mine. Yup. Lice-covered. How lovely. I arch them back, try to shake them, but I'm still too clumsy from the ascension, and they sort of flop down like a drunk seagull's.

"I can't believe we haven't found her yet…" Det mutters, scrubbing at his face with one too-white hand. "Actually, you know what? I can. What I can't *believe* is that you had us start in the *seventh* level. Watch, she'll be in the first just *waiting* for us, and I'll proceed to kill you for all of this torture."

"You never used to call spending time with me that," I pout as a pack of demon dogs crest the nearest hill. Their eyes are on fire, a blaze licking upward from each sunken hollow in their rotting faces.

"Well, it is," says Det huffily as he takes out his angelic blade. It *shings*, shining in the dull, half-light of hell. "We used to do *lovely* things together. Remember that time we went to the party the seraphim were throwing, and you made out with that girl from the angelic host…what was her name?"

"Mariah," I tell him, drawing my own blade as the

dogs leap closer, maggot-covered tongues lolling out of their mouths. "And she wasn't even *nice*."

Det slices two of the dogs in half as our blades meet, and I get the last three. Pieces of flesh litter the sand and are sucked down and in, as if the earth is hungry. I grimace at my dirty blade and try to scrub it off on my pant leg before sheathing it again.

"Silver," says Det, breathing out. I wince, preparing myself for his "I'm out" speech, but he says nothing, only steps forward and places his hands on my shoulders. "I'd do anything for you," he says then, mouth turning up at the corners. "But next time, can you fall in love with a girl who *isn't* mortal?"

"I'll work on that," I promise him, fighting my tears. He can be such a *dork*, but he's my brother, and for fuck's sake, I don't know what I'd do without him.

"Okay," he says, nodding, taking the pocket watch out of his vest. "We have fifteen minutes before they catch up with us."

I nod, too, kneeling down so that the sand prickles me through the jeans. I close my eyes, still my breathing, my wings spread over me.

I *listen*.

All around us, the souls drift, in various stages of agony and annoyance. It's like a river at night—they're all the same shade of spirit, all stuck together, all moving with the rotation of hell and all its levels.

But…wait. No.

They're not all the same.

My eyes spring open, and I'm running across the packed sand, wings arching over me before I pump them, and then I'm flying, Det right behind me.

"She's here?" he asks, panting, and I nod, veer off from the bone creatures that give a strangled cry—the flock of which I almost fly through.

She's *here*.

"Ten minutes before they show, Silver…" my brother mutters, flying into formation beside me.

I gulp, breathe out.

Ten minutes.

My blood thunders through fear-filled veins.

Will it be enough?

I'd always hated Earth duty. *Everyone* hated Earth duty, but you had to have it every hundred years. It's what made things fair, said the angelic host. And, really, it wasn't *so* bad, said the angelic host.

They'd never *had* Earth duty. They *didn't know*.

Transitioning humans' souls fucking *sucks*. Humans are mortal. They don't know what comes after, though a great deal of their mythologies is all about, no, *totally* there's pearly gates and harps and haloes or no, *totally*, there's devils and brimstone and a lot of fire. They have so many pieces wrong and right, and it's this whole jumble of fear that makes human death so messy that no angel wants to touch it.

But we have to help them transition. That's the system: angels help mortals transition off of Earth. There's no way around it. So we take turns and are miserable for a handful of mortal years while we deal with death and dying and really terrible shit.

And we have ways of coping. Like donning mortal forms to make the time pass in an as-close-to-enjoyable-fashion as possible.

"You know what's *really* terrible is being a teenager," my brother Det had told me. "You have to try it. They have to go to school, and it's a little like a gladiator arena there. You remember those?" I told him that I did, thank-you-very-much, and I had no intention of reliving that. "Oh, they don't hack each other apart anymore," he'd told me, eyes alight. "They're just assholes to each other."

"That makes it so much better," I'd grimaced. But

because Det was on duty with me (lucky him), and he'd decided to take a mortal teenager form (he always makes stupid decisions without consulting me), I really had no choice. So I did, too.

And the very next day, I'd met Sophie.

"*Five* minutes," Det mutters when our feet touch hell sand again.

When I gather her soul into my arms.

She flutters her translucent eyes open, looks up at me, *stares*.

"Silver..." she whispers, ghost mouth moving into a soft, tired smile. I almost cry as I press her see-through head to my shoulder, holding her as close as I can, her fragility pulsing beneath my fingers.

She murmurs: "you came to get me."

"What's the number one rule?" asked Det, the night that I'd taken her to the prom, wearing a mortal tux because it's what I felt most comfortable in, slicking back my spiked short hair into what he'd dubbed an "unholy Mohawk."

"Don't get involved with mortals," I'd told him, adjusting my tie in the mirror.

"And what the hell are you *wearing*?" he'd bemoaned.

"I like boy clothes," I'd tossed over my shoulder, grinning. "Screw you."

"This is very, very bad," he'd managed. "If they find out, the balance will have to be restored. You know that there are consequences."

"No one's gonna 'find out,'" I told him, hissing at him as I lowered my voice. "Shut *up*, Det. Don't jinx me."

But it was already begun.
Prom night was when the accident happened.
When Sophie died.

"Hurry," Det hisses as I crouch down on the red sand, digging through the knapsack for the vial of Darkness and the syringes.

"I'm hurrying, and you're not helping…" I mutter in a sing-song voice as I hear the clicking and clacking, the tell-tale sign that they're getting closer.

"We just *assume* that if we inject Darkness in the lower levels we'll fall below the last level of Hell and start all over again at Heaven. We don't *know* that."

"Shush, Det, we discussed this. It's got to work."

"We're out of time…" says Det, crouching next to me, hands shaking. "Where is it, you're not fast enough…"

We both glance up at the veritable *wall* of demons crawling toward us across the sand. I grit my teeth, draw up enough Darkness in the syringe for Sophie. I inject her translucent skin, and she goes dark and disappears. Okay—okay…Det next. I inject him through his tattoo's crow eye, and then me next.

I close my eyes as the closest demon reaches for me, pressing down on the syringe top.

I feel claws across my skin.
And then nothingness.

"Was it enough Darkness to get us there?"
A flare of light.
"Yeah. Just enough."
I open my eyes.

Det sprawls beside me on the glowing sand. He's spread-eagled, looks *exhausted*, but is glowing and beautiful again, as any angel is when they're Home.

And Sophie is here. I begin to cry as she opens her beautiful green eyes, sits up, hand to her head. But she glances at me, brows up in a quizzical frown, but then I gather her face in my hands, pepper it with kisses.

"You so owe me," Det sighs as Sophie puts her arms around me, squeezes me tightly.

"I don't understand..." she whispers, glancing past me. I know she'll see the Ocean of Stars, and beyond that...space. It probably looks like a dream, she probably doesn't understand it...but waking up to this is definitely better than hell, right?

She stares up and up and up at my wings, eyes wide.

"I always knew you were weird," is what she finally says, then, grinning at me, drawing me into her arms, kissing me.

I'm so relieved, I laugh.

"Are you ready to go back?" asks Det, brow up, eyeing my knapsack. Sophie looks beyond me, out to the ocean, out to space.

"Is that...is that a galaxy up there?" she whispers, as a shooting star roars by so close, its thrum is deafening. "Oh my God, it's beautiful..."

"Soon," I tell him, patting the bottle of Light.

Regenerating a dead girl.

I've had to explain worse.

I kiss her hand, so relieved I feel light as feathers. When she wakes up on Earth again...things will have to change.

But that's not right now. And if there's anything I've learned, it's this:

Take each moment as it ticks.

NIKE

by S.E. Diemer

My knuckles are bleeding.

I punched the bathroom wall until they were red red red, white and battered and red and white and they taste like metal and they bring me back here, now, God dammit I want to die.

I sniff hard, bring the snot back up my nose, lick my lips, stare at the stupid shit written on the bathroom stall door, Tim's a dick, Sammie's a whore, call this number for a stupid slut. Every day they try and fix the doors, but the janitor's not a miracle man, can only scrub off so much shit before it gets all fucked up again tomorrow.

Like me.

I hear the door swing open, heels clicking across the soap-gray floor. "Beth?" she whispers, pausing outside of my shut stall door. "Beth, are you in there?"

"No," I mutter, grab some toilet paper, try to clean up my face, my hands.

"Beth, Miss Gramone said…"

"*Screw* Miss Gramone," I mutter, pushing the door open. Allison stares at me, face paper white, eyes round and big and shocked, she looks *shocked*, because she should. I don't cry, you know? Yeah fucking right. Totally got it together. That's me.

"Beth, are you…"

"No, I'm not *okay*." She winces at that, and I hate myself so much in that moment I can't breathe, my insides squeezing me. "I'm sorry, I'm sorry…Jesus, I'm sorry." I step forward, bring my arms around her and crush her to me. She lets me. She holds me, too, thin arms around my middle, and then I'm sobbing like the mess I am, my snot running down onto her perfect blonde hair.

"I hate her," I whisper.

"I know," Allison says, holding me up. "She's stupid. I'm sorry. She's *stupid*, you know that—don't let her get to you."

"Like she hasn't already." The words are so small, so voiceless, from my mouth, I wonder if I even said them. But then Allison is making little concentric patterns on my back with her small hands, pressing her palms to me.

"Beth, I promise, it's going to be okay…"

I back away from her, stare down at her. Her mouth is so small, pressed into that tiny line. She's so pretty, my best friend is *beautiful*, and as straight as a streetlamp.

She tries. But she has no *clue*.

"You tell Miss Gramone to go fuck herself," I mutter, grabbing my backpack from the stall. And then I'm past Beth, out into the hall, sprinting down it as fast as my sneakers can take me.

If I get expelled, it won't matter.

I can't take this anymore.

I'm a ball of nerves, jangled, tight, spiky. I'm all spikes, all sharp things, all broken bits of glass, of knives. Everything I am is sharp, sharp, sharp. I'm shaking. I'm gonna throw up.

I kick my backpack as hard as I can so that it bounces off the wall, settles limp on the living room carpet.

I can still hear them laughing.

God dammit. I tear at my hair, and then I curl up on the couch, sobbing again, trying to breathe in and out around the wails of despair that I jam my fist into my mouth to try and stop up. I don't manage it, but almost.

I stay shaking on the couch until I feel nothing but a great weight of emptiness that presses down on me, limitless and never-ending.

I want things to stop. Please, fucking let them stop.

Sleep takes me into dark, distended jaws, biting down.

I'm four, kicking my legs against the stairs, staring up at my grandmother who holds my hairbrush in one flawless hand. She's beautiful, radiant. Everything's whites and blues. We're in the backyard in our first house, before the divorce. Bella is rolling around in the dirt, shaggy coat sopping wet and muddy. Gramma's laughing.

"You know," she says, inclining her head toward Bella, "things change. What once was beautiful grows ugly. What's ugly becomes beautiful again."

It's one of her favorite phrases. She's a little woo-woo, even then, even when I didn't know what woo-woo meant. Metaphors. I just keep smiling up at her as she runs the brush through my hair. It feels good, her hands against my head, her smiling down at me like I'm something pretty and nice and worth something.

"Be a good girl, Beth," she whispers, and kisses my forehead.

"What the hell." My mother's voice, hard and cold, as the door shuts. "Beth?"

I burrow further into the couch, rubbing the sleep

from my eyes with scabbed knuckles. "What, Ma?" I bellow. It's getting dark outside. I don't know how long I slept.

"I got a call from your teacher. Again." She's standing over me, hands on her hips. "You're facing expulsion."

"Good." I'm standing, sharp again, everything's sharp. "I want to be. I'm never going back. What are they gonna do? Nothing. Just like always." My hands are in fists. I keep breathing, in and out, but it doesn't seem to give me any air. I'm so hot, burning.

"What's the matter with you?" she asks, mouth in a thin line. "What's wrong? What happened?"

"Every fucking day is a nightmare. You don't fucking *get* it. What didn't happen would be a shorter list." I'm brushing past her, already crying, of course I'm crying again. The weight presses down on me, choking me.

Pitifully, I wish Gramma was here. She knew. She helped.

My phone in my pocket is vibrating. I take it out when I shut myself in my room—I expected it to be Allison, to tell her I was sorry, but it's not Allison calling me, it's a Facebook notification. I was tagged in something. I'm so sick, suddenly, I'm going to throw up. No one ever tags me in anything. I have fifteen friends on there. I don't want to click through, but I don't have a choice because I'm going to throw up, I am.

It loads.

Ann McKenzie tagged a photo of me. The photo from gym today.

I hit "untag" immediately, but there are already "likes" and comments.

I drop the phone on the floor. I'm shaking, everything's shaking. I stomp down so hard on the phone that I crack the screen, pathetic little plastic pieces ricochet across the room.

I pace in tiny circles, around and around and

around, everything a blur of color, the posters and postcards on the wall, the green bedspread, the rainbow rug on the floor. Tighter and tighter I spin until I sink down onto the ground, put my head in my hands, breathe in and out, stare down at my shaking fingers.

I crawl toward my bed, everything spinning. Under my pillow is the post-it note. I put it there a few weeks ago. Sharp, tiny numbers are scribbled on it in sharpie. I stare at the pile of phone in the middle of the floor, and then I pick up the landline beside my bed, the ancient thing actually giving me a dial tone.

I stare at the phone and then at the number and then at the phone again. I punch in the number and it rings.

"Hello, my name is Elle, can I please have your name?"

I can't believe I did this. I can't believe I called. I reach under my pillow again, feel the slick curve of the knife that's rested next to the post-it for weeks.

"Give me one reason," I manage, teeth clacking together.

"I'm sorry," she says, voice soft, "I can hardly hear you. Did you say your name?"

"Maxine," I whisper into the receiver. My middle name. "Give me one reason to live."

"Maxine, I'm sure you have people who care very, very much about you…"

"No, they don't. They don't give a shit." I squeeze my eyes tight. "They don't understand."

I hear a breath on the other end of the line. Elle. She said her name was Elle.

"Are you gay?" I mutter.

"Yes," says Elle. I can hear a little smile in her voice. "I am."

"Were you bullied?" God, I hate that fucking word. Tortured. Tortured is a better word.

"I was very much. Maxine…"

"I want to do it." A tear leaks out of my eye, runs

down beside my nose. "I really want to fucking do it. I've got nothing anymore. No reason."

"Please listen to me," says Elle softly. "I don't know what happened to put you here. I'm so sorry you're there. I want you to take a couple of really deep breaths with me, okay? I want you to relax a little, if you can. Are you in a safe place?"

"Yes," I whisper, staring at the bright poster of squares and circles across from me.

"Have you self harmed today?"

I suck at my knuckles, close my eyes. "Yes."

"Do you have a plan in place for how you would commit suicide?"

I stare at my pillow, breathe in and out. "Yes."

"Okay, Maxine, thank you for telling me this. I want to tell you that though things are very dark right now, I promise they won't look so grim in the morning. Do you live with someone who cares about you?"

"Yeah, my mom," I tell Elle, closing my eyes. My shoulders lower from around my ears. Her voice is soothing. Kind.

"Your mom is okay with your being gay?"

"Yeah, she is actually."

"That's really great. I'm happy for you. That's wonderful. Was there something specific that prompted your thoughts today?"

I can't think about that. I keep breathing in and out, and I manage: "Yes. I don't want to talk about it."

"That's okay—you don't have to. Tell me about your friends?"

"I have this one. Allison. She's straight, though."

Elle laughs a little. "That's okay. We'll let it slide."

For whatever weird reason, I smile a little at that. I wipe at my tears, sigh. "Yeah, I guess we will."

We talk for a half hour. I'm surprised when I hang up the phone, look at the clock. Elle's kind, gentle, talks me through everything. I don't know why I'm surprised, but I am—I didn't expect kindness.

I stare up at the ceiling. Things aren't sharp anymore. Heavy. Empty. But the sharpness has mellowed. My stomach growls. I open my desk drawer, grab out a candy bar and tear open the wrapping, letting the soothing scent of chocolate wash over me.

My shoulder blades itch, and I reach around behind my neck, scratching under my shirt. Odd. My fingertips scratch against something soft and thin, and I grasp it, pulling it out.

A feather.

I dream about Gramma again. This time, I know it's a dream, can see myself from overhead, like the camera's angled all weird. She's braiding my hair and singing to me in Russian, and I'm holding Annie, my old teddy bear.

"Things change," she tells me in a sing-song voice. "What once was beautiful grows ugly. What's ugly becomes beautiful again."

"Geez, Gramma, I know, I know," I mutter to her, making the teddy bear dance in my lap.

She's tying blue ribbons at the bottom of my braid, blue as the sky, blue as her eyes, blue as the icing on the cookie I take a bite out of, the crumbs falling into my lap.

It's sweet.

I wake up to an email from Allison. I don't want to read it, but I do anyway.

"I got Facebook to take it down. Do you want me to talk to Gremlin? I will. Love you, bb."

Gremlin. I don't want to bring him in, our

principal wouldn't know what to do with this, he'd get all stiff and awkward and wave his arms a lot. And be completely useless. I email her back, tapping on my phone: "no, it's ok. Love you, too."

"Are you coming to school?" is sent a second later.

I stare at my phone, panic beginning to eat the edges of my stomach. I close my eyes. I remember Allison coming to find me in the bathroom. I remember Elle's voice from last night.

I don't know where it comes from, but this coolness begins to settle over me. It makes the sharpness soften. I think about the gym. I think about *her*, and her stupid friends laughing. And I think about Allison and Elle and my mom.

And Gramma. Yes. I think about my grandmother because her picture is beside the bed, in her awesome glasses and super-awesome bouffant. She was hot. And she was amazing. And she loved me no matter what, and she still does, I guess, if ghosts come back in dreams.

"Yeah," I reply. "Whatever. Fuck them." But my phone autocorrects "fuck" to "duck" and I don't fix it. I actually grin at it a little.

Yeah. Duck them, too.

When I get up, I wonder if my pillow is molting. There's another feather on my bed, white as a marshmallow.

"Tell me a story," I beg my grandmother for the eight millionth time. *She rolls her eyes and sighs and draws me up onto her lap and presses my head under her chin.*

"You know all of them," she says, *but I tug on her hands, wrap them around me. I've never taken "no" for*

an answer yet.

"All right, all right," she groans, laughing and squeezing me. "I shall tell you the shortest one."

I squeak with joy, leaning back against her. She smells of lemons, all bright and warm.

"There was once a beautiful Goddess," says Gramma, her tongue rolling out the words. "But she was smart, too. The smartest in the world. Her name was Athena, and she was smart and beautiful and had a pet owl..."

"Gramma, you're telling it wrong," I huff. "Slow down!"

"Well," says Gramma, squeezing me tighter. "She had many friends, but her closest was a beautiful creature named Nike. Nike was one of the last angels, and she had magnificent white wings. Athena loved Nike because Nike was always victorious...especially in the gods' battle with the Titans..."

"You're not telling it right!" I whine. "You didn't say anything about Nike's chariot!"

"If you know it so well, you tell it," she laughs, poking my stomach with her finger. I sit up straight, puffing myself up.

"Nike had the best chariot, and the Titans didn't stand a chance! That's why she was victorious!"

"Now you're telling it wrong," says Gramma, poking me again. "Nike was victorious because she never gave up."

"What does 'victorious' mean?" I ask her, placing my little hand against her big one. My fingers are so small, and I want them to be like hers someday—long and curving and beautiful.

"Overcoming," she says, curling her fingers around mine.

My shoulders ache. It takes all of my attention in Calc., making me scratch at them with my pencil.

Blessedly, the asshole leaves me alone.

Allison comes up to me between periods, gives me the tightest hug in the world. "Are you doing okay? I got your favorite." She presses my favorite energy drink into my hand, leans close with a smile. "And I have another in my locker."

"Thanks," I manage, smiling at her. She returns the grin, squeezes me again.

I drink it walking to my next class, can feel it vibrate through me. My shoulders keep itching and I duck into the bathroom to pee, leaving the can on the sink.

When I reach up to touch my shoulder blade, I feel something…wrong. Something small and pointed beneath my hand, like my bone's broken. It doesn't hurt anymore. It just…aches.

I feel weird, but I pee, wash my hands and get to my class. It's stupid—when isn't it stupid?—but when the period is over and I get up to leave, I stare down at the feather beneath my seat.

It's getting…strange.

Gym.

I hate gym.

And she's there. With her stupid groupies. And they're talking behind their hands and *looking* at me.

"Ignore them," Allison mutters, brushing past me, her hair high in a ponytail. I breathe in and out, stare down at my sneakers.

"Mrs. Anderson," *she* says, raising her perfectly manicured hand. Mrs. Anderson turns and looks at her, and suddenly I'm so sick again. She's going to say something, I know it.

"Mrs. Anderson, Beth was *looking* at me in the

shower yesterday. I feel really unsafe around her." Her smile is so pretty and lip-glossy, you'd never know it's hiding a snake underneath.

Mrs. Anderson sighs, turns and glances at me, shaking her head. "If you have a problem, Ann…"

"I shouldn't have to shower with a dyke," she says, clipping the words so that they fall between us, around all of us, sharp and jagged and infinitely stupid.

"Class…" says Mrs. Anderson, raising her hands as people begin to laugh. I feel myself redden, redden, and then I just…stop.

"I mean, what if she tries to touch me? I mean, that would be the most disgusting…"

"Why," I say, the word soft and loud in the stillness that descends, "would I ever want to touch *you*, you asshole?"

The silence is so absolute I can hear my heart hammering against my ribs. Ann stares at me, the girl who has tormented me my entire fucking life *stares* at me as if she's seeing me for the first time.

I'm turning, following Mrs. Anderson's finger pointing toward the door which will lead to the principal's office, surely.

It's going to get worse. They'll step up their game now. I know they will.

But I'm not going to sit there, silent and defeated.

One more year. That's all there is. And then freedom. And Ann McKenzie-less days. And the rest of my life, stretching out with possibilities, rampant and wonderful and *possible*.

I close the gym door behind me, a single white feather falling to my feet.

I pick it up and keep walking.

THE GARGOYLE MAKER

by S.E. Diemer

Her hands are always dirty, clay-dusted. Gray as death. The bread-seller's daughter, Rose, notices this, every day, watching.

The gargoyle maker's hands are dirty.

But she's still beautiful.

Beautiful like a bird-song or a cold winter's dawn, walking through the streets with that thin, small basket at her elbow crook, looking at the market's stalls without really seeing. Rose watches her, waits for her, everyday, knows that she'll come close to sunset. Rose's heart pounds when the gargoyle maker enters the square, her thick, black hair neatly braided down her back in a lustrous coil. Rose swallows, watches her move through the stalls, among the vendors and barterers and buyers and sellers, moving like a whisper. No one notices the gargoyle maker.

No one but Rose.

Rose thinks she's the most beautiful woman she's ever seen...not that Rose is much of a judge. "You will marry a good girl," says her mother, the bread-seller, every morning when they bake the loaves. "You don't want to set your eyes on a strange one...not like the gargoyle maker. Get yourself a *good* girl, Rose."

But Rose never listens.

The gargoyle maker set up shop in the abbey's tower, one long winter's night, a year ago. Rose knows this because the pennant flies from the dilapidated window, high overhead, red and rampant in the dying sun. On it is a ghoulish face, a gargoyle's face, cleverly painted so that it looks like it's laughing.

The gargoyle maker's prices are reasonable, the butcher told her mother. For all her strangeness, they're reasonable.

And doesn't everyone need a gargoyle?

Like every afternoon, this one is no different. The gargoyle maker enters the square, her beautiful black hair in a thick braid, her young face expressionless, her eyes unseeing. And her hands dirty. She holds the red shawl tight about her, nose up, proud, as she moves among the stalls, her small basket empty at her elbow.

There is nothing different about this afternoon—it is the same as all the ones before it. But as the gargoyle maker comes closer to the bread-seller's tent, Rose finds herself moving, as if in a dream. And it must be a dream. Because Rose steps out from behind the stall as the gargoyle maker comes closer, and then they're standing nose to nose. Just like that.

The gargoyle maker's eyes are a deep brown, like rich earth, and her lashes are long and lovely. Rose blinks, swallows, as the gargoyle maker cocks her head, staring at the girl.

"Hello," Rose whispers, and then—dying inside, slowly and with great pain—she says: "would you like to buy some bread?"

"Oh no, thank you." And the gargoyle maker moves around her, continuing on through the square.

Her voice was soft and warm. Like honey.

Rose finds herself turning.

"I mean…" The gargoyle maker pauses, snared by Rose's words, and she turns, too. Back. Toward Rose.

"Yes?" she asks, brown eyes flashing, mouth twitching at the corners. But she does not smile.

"I've always wanted to see the abbey," says Rose, all in a rush, feeling her cheeks burn like day-old biscuits. "I almost wandered through it when I was very small. But I never got up the courage…"

Not like now.

The gargoyle maker watches her, head still to the side. "It's an abandoned building. Like any other," she says, voice quiet. "But my gargoyles seem to like it."

"Oh…" whispers Rose, the ache in the word almost physical. "I would love to see *that*."

The gargoyle maker is smiling now, mouth truly curling up at the edge. She looks even younger when she smiles. Rose wondered if maybe she was eighteen. Maybe. A grown woman. But she might be Rose's age, with that smile.

The gargoyle maker steps closer.

"You could come see them," she whispers, breathing out. "If you'd like."

"Are they very frightening?" asks Rose, turning back to see her mother scowling over the loaves of bread and the pies. Rose unfastens her apron, pressing it back into her mother's hands. And then she's walking through the square with the gargoyle maker, feeling naked without the apron.

Her mother doesn't say a word. There will be hell to pay later. But not. Right. Now.

"The gargoyles?" The girl tilts her head back and laughs a little. It's clear, that laughter. Like bells. "No, they're not frightening. They're good creatures."

"I'm Rose," says Rose, breathless, disbelieving in her own good luck. "What's your name?"

"Annabella," says Annabella, the gargoyle maker. "Here…this way." The front door that faces the village square to the abbey was boarded up long ago, but there is a grouping of bushes, and through that, the cook's entrance. The door is gone, and when Rose and Annabella move through it and into the echoing, empty kitchens, a flock of disturbed pigeons take off in a rush of feathers. Rose starts, but Annabella puts her hand against the girl's shoulder. Her fingers are so warm. Rose stills.

They climb a narrow, rotting set of stairs, and then a great, open room sprawls before them. The windows are boarded up, but some candles burn, flickering in the dark. And there are the gargoyles.

They turn, swiveling heads and clicking claws against the stone walls. Rose's heart hammers against the cage of her ribs as, in the guttering light, they come into view. They are hideous creatures with lolling, stone tongues and sparking eyes and horns and wings and fangs and scales and tails and they are all messy imaginings of animals, really. This one has a horse's head but a ram's horns and a dragon's body with cruel, clawing wings, and this one has a winged monkey's body but a dragon's head and goat horns. Like a jumbled mass of chaos, they move forward across the floor, dragging themselves or pacing on too-large stone claws.

"We have company," says the gargoyle maker cheerfully, squatting down on the floor as the smallest gargoyle waddles over toward her, depositing itself in her lap. It has the body of a small dog, but the head of an eagle and a unicorn's horn. "This is Rose, my lovelies," says Annabella to the stone monsters. "Rose, these are my creations…the gargoyles."

"How do you do…" Rose manages to get out, not because she thought it the best thing to say, but because pure instinct has taken over. The guttering lights and hideous creatures fill her with fear, but Annabella doesn't seem to be frightened. In fact, she laughs a little as the small stone dog-eagle-unicorn rolls over onto its back in her lap, as if it's a puppy begging for a scratch.

"You…you make these?" Rose asks, then, as Annabella stands, patting another of the great beasts. Annabella nods.

"All of them," she smiles, scratching the tallest gargoyle behind the ears. "My father was a gargoyle maker. And his father before him. I am the last in a very long line," she says, voice wistful. She shakes herself from her reverie, grinning sadly. "And, as you know, everyone needs a gargoyle."

Rose shudders, thinking of nightfall. "I'd...I'd better be getting back," she says, mouth dry.

Annabella is watching her, eyes round and full and sad. "It was lovely meeting you, Rose," she whispers, stepping forward. She kisses the girl on one cheek, and then the other. And then Rose is stumbling backward, back down the stairs, hand against her cheek, heart pounding.

Annabella places her own hand along the smooth, stone flank of her newest gargoyle, closes her eyes.

Night falls.

The nightmares squirm along the ground on misty, clickety-clawed hands. Perched over the doorway, the bread-seller's gargoyle watches it closely.

The nightmare comes no closer, wailing its defeat as it turns an eyeless face away from the door.

There was not always a gargoyle to protect them.

The nightmares did not always leave.

Rose lets the curtain fall, shudders.

But not before she sees the light in the abbey tower, burning.

There is peace in that.

The gargoyle maker comes to the market, empty basket in hand. Rose is out of the stall in a heartbeat, apron off, smile wide.

But Annabella is not smiling today.

"What's the matter?" asks Rose, taking a step back. Annabella will not look her in the eyes.

"I'm needed elsewhere," she says, tiredly. "I have to go on to Shroud City. Everyone here has a gargoyle, now. It's time for me to go."

Rose's heart is in her throat. She remembers her mother's lectures. She remembers being told this would happen.

She remembers hoping it wouldn't.

"I'll...I'll come visit you, in Shroud City," says Rose impulsively. Annabella smiles, but only for a heartbeat, shaking her head.

Rose is a village girl with a village heart and she'll marry a nice village girl, and they'll live in the village until they die.

For the gargoyle maker, life will be very different.

Annabella has always known this. But still, as she packs her great trunks that night, she cries, tears falling against the stained wood.

The gargoyles are no comfort, then.

She wishes that Rose had never noticed her. She wishes she had never noticed Rose.

Annabella moves to the window, the high and lonely window. Down below, the nightmares move across the cobblestones, crawling and quivering. And the gargoyles with their beautiful, baleful eyes keep them in the streets, out of the houses.

Safe. The gargoyles keep the village safe.

Annabella knows Rose's window. Every night, Rose goes to the window and watches Annabella's tower. She's seen Rose do this. But tonight, as the nightmares move past the bread-seller's house, the window *moves*. And Rose climbs out of the window, feet hitting the cobblestones.

As one, the eyeless nightmares move in their worming across the ground. As one, they turn toward Rose.

Annabella watches for a single moment before turning from the window, heart in her throat. She runs down the steps and down the stairs and out the open door hidden behind the bushes, the open door her oldest gargoyle guards.

And Annabella, too, is out and in the square.

Rose is running toward her, pack banging against her slight back, eyes wide with terror. The nightmares move slow, but there are so very many of them. Rose runs into Annabella, crashing against her as they tumble, and they're standing, holding hands, turning as one toward the wall of moaning creatures that squirm across the cobblestones toward them.

Annabella closes her eyes. She stills her heart.

And that great, burning spark that exists just *there*, above the pulsing heart, ignites. It is the spark that begins a gargoyle in her hands. It is the spark of strange, stone life she carries. As her father before her. And his father before him.

And when she opens her eyes again, they are not good, brown eyes, but the roaring spark of a gargoyle. And the nightmares pause in their pursuit, mewling beneath her gaze. And, as one, they turn away.

Annabella breathes out, sagging, and Rose embraces her tightly.

"What were you *thinking?*" Annabella hisses, shaking Rose, but just a little. And then she crushes the girl in her embrace.

And then she's kissing her. But just a little kiss. There are still nightmares about.

"I'm coming with you," says Rose, voice all resolute and quavering. Annabella shakes her head quickly, but is pulling her through the bushes and through the door and up the stairs.

"And what of your mother?" she asks in a rush, her heart beating wild. Rose watches her, mouth quirked to the side.

"She knows," whispers Rose then, quietly. "And she doesn't like it. But a girl's got to make something of herself. And Shroud City is so large...surely I can bake bread there, can sell it...maybe open a bakery..."

"This is really what you want…" asks Annabella, voice soft. Shaking.

"Yes," says Rose. "I want to try, anyway. This. Us." And then, shyly: "you."

Beneath the sparking eyes of the gargoyles, Annabella kisses Rose.

But then they turn away with stone smiles behind stone eyes, giving their maker privacy.

BONE SHIP

by S.E. Diemer

"I don't believe in ghosts."

Her words sound bratty, but she's pale when she says them, mouth in a tiny, firm line, like she's holding her fear behind her teeth. I shrug, press the elevator's "down" button.

"What does that *mean*?" she asks, watching me closely. I shrug again, fold my arms carefully, biting down on my lip.

"I don't either," I tell her slowly, carefully.

And then, like the ultimate joke, I think: *but they believe in us*.

The elevator door *whooshes* open, letting in the stale air from floor seventeen—the basement. There are only seventeen levels on the ship…I know that sounds like a lot, but I haven't seen planet-side in ten months.

Seventeen levels grows as close as a coffin when you spend ten months with the dead.

She wrinkles her nose, grimacing when the door opens. I know she can smell it. We recycle the air, put it through countless filters, but that's the thing about death…it touches you whether you want it to or not. It clings to my clothes, my hair, that wretched scent, the formaldehyde sickly sweet and cloying. I run a finger through my hair now, cast a tight, sidelong glance at her. But she sees me do it, raises an eyebrow.

"This way," I clear my throat, gesture down the right angle of the hall. She moves out and I follow, keeping my eyes carefully attached to her boots and not any higher.

Well. Maybe just a little.

"I can't imagine…" is what she's saying, voice trailing off into silence when we round the bend. I turn my direction, glance over what she's staring at, mouth open.

I remember feeling that awe, once. It's crazy, isn't it? Bring up enough earth for an eight-foot deep graveyard. In a ship. Between planetary systems. It sounds like something from a book, but then that stupid Starchild religion makes otherwise smart people do stupid things, and…well. Here we are.

On the Bone Ship.

With the dead.

The dirt goes on for a good, long while. The opposite wall—made entirely of five foot thick glass—seems to be a towering, distant skyscraper. And there, in the dirt, are the grave markers, smooth stone carved with names and dates, like an idyllic, spooky New England cemetery. But we're not in New England. We're not even on Earth.

"So much trouble…" she sighs, crosses her arms. She glances at me when she shakes her head. "*So* much trouble. And for what? So bodies aren't cremated into ash, shipped out into space…it's just a bunch of carbon, anyway…" She sighs for a long moment, glances at the nearest gravestone. I dug that grave this morning with the press of a button, depositing the little metal casket into it as the machine creaked around me.

"It's creepy," is what she says, her words clipped short. I shrug again, laugh a little.

"Yeah," I agree, crossing my arms, too. "But it's what they want."

She's watching me. A shiver runs through me—I can't help it. I glance up and into her eyes, and they're an icy green. Green. Like a planet.

"Don't you get lonely?" she asks then, voice soft, sweet. It cuts me deeper than metal. My palms are slick, suddenly. I rub them against my thighs, the chemical fabric warm beneath my fingers.

"I mean, I've got Dad," I say, snorting, tossing my nose up like it's not *true*.

Of course I get lonely.

"I've just…Stars…" Her voice quavers as she looks away, rubbing at her eyes. Her fingers glisten…was she *crying*? "I've just *missed* you, Ellie."

I promised myself I wouldn't do this, but I am. I'm beside her in a heartbeat, my fingers at her waist, pulling her toward me, and then we're kissing.

*This is stupid, this is stupid…*I keep thinking.

But I'm feeling something else entirely.

A puff of air against my cheek. I back away, breathe out. Her eyes have gone wide and she's staring across the graveyard, hand to her cheek, too.

She felt it.

"What…what was that…" she whispers, staring at the graves. The artificialness of the fluorescents overhead casts everything in a sickly white glow. There's nothing frightening about the angular lines of the gravestones, but I've never liked being down here alone, just the same. Dad calls it superstition.

But he never feels the hands on his shoulder, the breath against his face.

He never hears someone calling his name. Never sees the blur along the corner of his eyes.

Never feels someone watching him.

"It's nothing," I tell her smoothly, easily, but she's watching me with wide eyes, stepping away from the dirt, shoes clicking against the metal walkway.

"It's fucking *creepy*," she says, a shiver passing through her. "Can we go, now? I'd like to see your room…" She threads her fingers through mine, single brow raised. I swallow. When Dad took this position, I knew I'd have to leave the school…leave her.

But yes. I've missed her, too.

Fiercely.

"Sure…" I murmur, and we move toward the elevator.

As the door shuts, I swear I see a shape against the glass.

But then she's kissing me.

And I forget it.

I don't remember anything.

I don't know why I'm here. I'm tied to this thing, this slab of stone on dirt. It bears a name and a date. AnnaMaria Chovin. Born, 8210. Died 8227.

Outside the glass: a hundred thousand stars.

Inside the glass, she moves.

She's beautiful. Ellie. A girl named Ellie. I try to speak to her, try to get her to notice me, but she never does. I don't know why. I've tried so long and so hard.

I love her. Ellie.

Please hear me, Ellie.

Please.

POPPY AND SALT

by S.E. Diemer

"Do we have enough?"

Celia dips her hand into the bag, letting the tiny black seeds run through her fingers. The sound they make, a sweet *shushing* as they fall back into the bag on their brothers and sisters, is like a sigh.

"I think so…" She looks up at me, dark eyes flashing in the half-light of a setting moon. "I think we're ready, Alice."

"Says you," I retort, turning up my nose to stare at the dancing constellations. It's a bitter night, so cold the wind steals your breath. Celia lays a warm hand against my fingers, squeezes.

"It'll be *fine*," she says, grinning widely. "After all, it's not like this is our *first* vampire."

"Small comforts," I mutter, as we begin to ascend the hill.

We left the shaggy ponies in a small valley outside of town. The vampire would smell them easier, and we needed silence. As always, though, I missed their comforting bulk, the way Rosie would nuzzle my hand for bits of carrot, her nostrils warm as blood.

"Alice, come *on*," Celia hisses over her shoulder, already outpacing me. Her hands on her hips beneath the cloak, her red hair sticking out at odd angles, she looks like a slight demoness, rising above me in the dark. Surely not a creature to trifle with. I sigh, double my steps and reach her, putting my arms about her waist.

"Patience," I whisper into her ear. She laughs against me, breath coming fast against my neck, and then she puts her hands on my cheeks and draws me down for a kiss.

As always, she tastes of blood and mint. The mint to hide the taste of blood. The blood because only a vampire is good at hunting other vampires.

She backs away, pushing her hair from her face, gazing up the hill again. "Let's hurry and be done with this," she whispers, elfin features puckered into a sudden frown, as if she's heard something.

"You always enjoy this," I mutter, following her. "Why hurry?"

"Alice, come *on*," she repeats, for what seems the millionth time that day. I sigh, roll my eyes, and hitch my skirts a little higher, staggering over the rocks after her. Like all her kind, she moves like shadows over the terrain. And I, the token mortal girl, struggle after her like I'm a graceless dog. I think she almost likes it that way, that my clumsiness amuses her. But she's not paying attention to me tonight. She's standing, nose to the wind, sniffing, hand at the bag on her belt, running her fingers through the poppy seeds again.

"She's coming," Celia breathes, glancing down the hill, her dark eyes wide in the moon glow.

The skin on the back of my neck pricks, and I glance down the hill, too.

She's there.

She crawls over the rocks like a spectacular spider, blonde hair streaming milkily over her shoulders and dragging over the ground along with her gigantic bat wings. She's still a ways down, but I can see that she has no whites to her eyes, can see the mound of fangs dripping out of her mouth. I shudder, breathe out, feel everything else fall away.

If she flies after us, we're done.

"Come along, darling," Celia breathes, untying the bag from her belt, holding it out before her. "Come along home."

A handful of blackness is in Celia's hand as she begins to walk backward, letting the seeds fall upon the ground. I follow her quickly as Celia takes out more seeds, and more still, stalking up the hill toward the vampire's resting place—a small cave on the western edge of the hill's summit.

The poppy seeds fall quickly, scattering on the ground, but it doesn't matter exactly where they lay, as long as they lead back to the vampire's grave. I'd always thought it an old wives' tale, really...a vampire is controlled by poppy seeds? It was said that if a trail of them led back to the vampire's resting place, the vampire must obey them and return to its den, never to come out of it again. But the story was only half true. Poppy seeds will lure a vampire, surely.

But it's the salt that does the final trick.

I gulp down air, hearing the vampire's claws scrabbling on the rocks not-so-far behind us, its wings thumping in the dead air, but never truly taking flight. Celia keeps her eyes on the creature, never daring to look at me as she glances over her shoulder, trailing the poppy seeds out of her hand. I feel the bag on my own belt, tear it off as we near the great standing stones that mark the entrance to the cave. Celia enters the dark maw of it, spilling the last of the poppy seeds at the entrance, and the vampire moves past me, ignoring me as my heart thunders, dragging its body through the cavern entrance, its wings glistening and mangled, tearing over the rocks.

Blood drips on the stones behind it. I shudder, gritting my teeth. It fed in the village, then. One more victim, gone.

I breathe out, watching the entrance. I can't seal the cave until Celia's out. But sometimes, she cuts it far too close...

Like tonight. Celia dances out of the cave, face alight, wiping at her mouth as she laughs. "Seal it, seal it! I made her angry," she says in a sing-song voice as the piercing scream curls out of the cavern entrance. I take a great handful of salt, breathe over it and lay it across the entrance as the vampire barrels out of the cave, the wound on its neck silver in the moonlight.

It crawls toward us and stops at the edge of the salt as it must. It hisses, more animal than human now, the blood driving it past the articulate stage into something monstrous. Celia simply laughs, throwing back her own head, throwing an arm around me.

"We did it, she whispers," and she's kissing me. I swallow my disgust at the taste and gingerly peck her back as the vampire roars in front of us, and then I'm backing away, dragging her by the wrist.

"Don't be so cocky," I whisper over my shoulder, but she's not watching me now. She's looking back. Back at the vampire.

"What you do comes back to you," the vampire growls around a mouthful of teeth. And then she's laughing, too, dripping blood on the ground.

Celia closes her mouth, grips my hand tighter.

A cloud blocks out the moon.

On her back on the bed, red hair fanned out around her shoulders, Celia looks more like a doll than a girl. She stares up at the ceiling, unseeing, and stirs only when I kiss her too-pale cheek. She smiles at me, then, putting her arms around my neck, and I kiss her deeper…but her heart isn't in it.

"What's the matter?" I whisper to her, my own heart pounding against my ribs. Celia is always the reckless one, the one who never worries. That's *my* job. But she seems to be taking it.

"I'm just thinking…" she sighs, sits up, draws her arms around her legs. "Do you think what we do is wrong, Alice?" she whispers then, looking up at me with wide eyes. I sit on the edge of the bed, watch her. She's never talked like this before.

"What do you mean?"

"I mean, I'm betraying my own kind," she grits out, picks at the blanket beneath her with a long-fingered hand.

"You're betraying the ones who kill people," I remind her gently. "Who go on rampages. Who destroy entire villages..."

"I mean, we've gotta eat," she sighs, leaning back on her hands. I roll my eyes, shake my head.

"There's a difference between a willing victim..." I pat my own chest, "and a non-consensual victim. And I know you know this..." I mutter, holding up my hand to still her protests, "but it needs reminding sometimes. You're not like them, Celia."

She looks so young, her hair spilling about her shoulders, her wide, green eyes searching mine.

"I was, once."

Celia runs her fingers listlessly through the poppy seeds, listening to the sound of them in the bag. *Shush, shush.* She bites her lip and stares out the window, watching the rainfall, the downpour as rhythmic as the seeds beneath her hands.

I kiss her forehead, but she doesn't acknowledge me.

I had a dream last night. A nightmare, really. I sit down beside her, press my thigh against hers, my arm against hers. Feel the solidity, there. Her soft coldness.

Celia closes her eyes, tilts her head, listening.

I dreamed about the vampire I was partnered with before her. I was sixteen, then. She lasted me an entire year. Her name was Tallie, and she had short, brown hair and quiet eyes. I'd loved her so much…fiercely. I'd believed we'd be together such a long time that I'd fallen in love with her.

It was my first mistake. I'd been told by the elders not to. That a vampire in our…profession…cannot last.

She had died twelve months into our partnership. Two months into our relationship.

And then I'd been partnered with Celia.

"This one should last longer," said one of the faceless elders. Almost as if he was sympathetic.

That was eleven months ago. We restrain one vampire, sometimes two, in an evening.

How much longer can this last?

I've already fallen in love with her.

I rub my eyes, breathe out. Celia rests her fingers along my arm, humming something tuneless, softly.

She runs her other hand through the poppy seeds, fingers parting them like shadows.

Shush, shush.

In this moment, we're together.

I close my eyes, lean against her and listen.

MERCY BROWN

by S.E. Diemer

"Andy, I'm serious…" My voice is thin and whiny, even to me, the wind snatching it up and away as I shove my hands deeper into my pockets, peering into the dying light of the cemetery. "I'm *not* going with you…this is *so* stupid…"

"I can't go *alone*," she says, voice hushed, grinning hugely. She comes running back, grabbing my arm, spinning me. "*C'mon*, Layne, what are you…afraid?"

I toss my hair over my shoulder, straighten my knees in my skinny jeans so that I hope she can't see them shaking. "No," I manage, but it's weak, and I grit my teeth together.

"Then come *on*," she says, plucking at my parka with fingers ending in sea-green nails.

I can't refuse her. And she *knows* it.

"I hate this," I say, gulping, dragged after her as she steps over the threshold, onto the cemetery grounds. "*Right this minute*, we're breaking the law." My voice squeaks as I glance over my shoulder, staring up and down the road, looking for cops. And I'm not being a goodie-goodie, either, I mean cops are seen on this road *all the time*.

"Oh, whatever," she says, rolling her eyes, picking up the pace. Her sneakered feet practically race over the frozen grass. "Cooper says he saw her, and I want to prove he's wrong. And you're going to be my witness that we were here and that she does not, in fact, exist."

"I'm your girlfriend," I point out huffily. "He's going to say it's nepotism or something…he's not going to believe you if you say that *I'm* your witness. See? This plan is terrible." I try to turn, disentangle myself from her grasp, but the sun is long gone, and the last of the light is drying up, and I trip over a gravestone for my troubles, sprawling on the cold ground.

"Well, shit," I mutter, scrabbling up. I cut my fingers on the edge of the stone. I wince down at it, gingerly shoving my hand into my pocket.

"Did you hear that?" Andy whispers.

I stare at her, her wide eyes, feel my heart pounding too. "It's a cop, isn't it? I told you," I whisper shrilly, but she's shaking her head, finger to her lips, glancing past my shoulder, behind me, and up.

I turn slowly, my entire body a thundering pulse.

But there's nothing there. Nothing but pine trees and some more manicured graveyard and an unending litany of stupidly old headstones.

"I hate you," I manage, but she's still shaking her head, her eyes are still wide. "Andy, *what*?" I ask her, and she jerks her finger up, above the pine trees, up and up at the first star edging out of the blue-almost-black sky.

A bat wheels through the air in slow, lazy circles.

"What?" I ask, crossing my arms, shivering under my parka. "It's just a stupid bat…"

She shakes her head, stares at me. "Are you *crazy*?" she practically squeaks. "Bats don't come out in the cold. Not like this."

"Oh, thank you, miss Zoologist, for that charming introduction to Bats 101…"

"No, seriously, Layne…" Her eyes are wide, hunted. "I think it's Mercy Brown."

"This isn't a cartoon," I point out. "Bats don't automatically equal vampires."

"But it's what all the legends say…" she whispers, watching the bat turn and arc. "Mercy Brown could turn into a bat. And a black cat. And a mist."

"I'm fairly certain that those are pretty recent twists to her story…" I reply, staring up at the bat, too.

"I've never seen a bat so big…" Andy whispers, and I know without a single bit of doubt, that I've lost her rationality somewhere behind a gravestone.

"This is *stupid*," I tell her then, the millionth time today, really. "Mercy Brown is a stupid old story that stupid kids make up and use to frighten each other with. There was *never* a Mercy Brown, and she was *never* a vampire, and…"

"Tell that to Wikipedia," Andy breathes. "There *was* a Mercy Brown. Her gravestone is here. She was dug up because people thought she was a vampire, and they burned her heart and made her poor brother eat it in a soup. And people still believe she's a vampire. And that she still haunts this town."

"I'm not one of those people," I point out, watching the bat descend in lazier and larger arcs. "And I think that thing is rabid. Would you *come on*? Let's go get some pizza or something like *normal* teenagers…"

"I want to see where it's going…" she breathes, and then my girlfriend is actually *following* the deranged bat as it begins to fly through the pine trees, toward the other end of the graveyard.

And I'm just stupid enough to follow them *both*.

"I hate this…I *really* hate this," I whisper to no one in particular when I trip on yet another gravestone. I manage to save myself from sprawling, not that Andy notices. She keeps staring up at the bat, who's flying lower and lower. Funny that, as I watch it, it doesn't *seem* like the normal size of a bat. You know, small and rodent like.

This actually seems pretty big…I know the dark can play tricks on your eyes and stuff, but it looks…I mean, I thought it looked hawk-sized.

It looks bigger than that now as we draw closer.

Andy pauses at the edge of the trees as the bat

spreads its wings and stops flapping. It dives down, long and low, and then it's landing on the ground. I've never seen a bat land, but I never imagined it would look like that, and then it's…

"Oh my God…" Andy whispers. I grip her arm, nails probably drawing blood I'm gripping so hard, because the bat turns, and then…somehow.

It's changing.

A girl stands there with nut-brown hair. She's wearing very strange, old clothes like someone out of Williamsburg, and even though it's pretty dark out, I can see her skin is pale as snow. She watches us for a long moment, unmoving, and then she turns. In an instant, she's gone from view. Andy is ripping away from me, running across the grass and falling to her knees before the gravestone the girl had been standing before.

"Oh my God," I can hear her mutter. "Layne? *Layne!*"

I already know what the gravestone will read. I walk toward it in dread, heart pounding so fast, it's going to plunge out of my chest.

Sure enough:

Mercy Brown, carved deep into the stone.

"Let's get out of here…" I whisper, tugging on Andy's arm. Her hand is pressed against the cool stone of the grave marker, and she remains like that for a long moment, breathing steadily.

"She's real, Layne," she whispers, standing, turning to face me, eyes burning. "She's *real*."

"I'm not so sure…" I have my hands at the small of her back, practically shoving her down the path toward the entrance to the graveyard. "I'm pretty sure that we just had a mass hallucination, brought on by all of the hi-fructose corn syrup in the ten Cokes we had today for that Biology final…"

"She's *real*," Andy repeats.

I refuse to believe it. I *refuse*. But as we stumble out of the cemetery, back into the street-lights and safe sidewalks, I dare to glance over my shoulder and look into the graveyard just one more time.

And Mercy Brown is there, watching us.

And, in the darkness, she smiles at me.

A BIT OF SPACE

by Jennifer Diemer

The owl shows me the way.

I wait for it every night. On the back porch, I bite my nails and tap my foot. I pace back and forth or sit with my arms wrapped tight around my knees, scanning the sky for wings until my neck aches.

Sometimes the owl comes—brilliant white against the middle-of-nowhere, black-as-soot sky. More often, I linger alone, anxious and shivering, until sunrise.

But tonight feathers brush against the crescent moon, and the owl swoops low, circles the yard three times. And then I'm chasing it across the snow-dusted lawn, plunging headfirst into the evergreen forest.

The woods are a thousand acres deep. I might never find her, if not for the owl; she's unable to arrive in the same place twice. It's hard to be precise, I imagine, from such a height.

And she can't come to me, because someone might see her. And if they saw her, they'd know. They'd be afraid. And they'd talk: call the newspapers, the *Enquirer.* The FBI.

So the forest is our rendezvous. No one around here takes walks in the woods. They're too busy watching giant televisions, fingers tapping on phones, to remember there's a whole world—a whole universe—evolving just beyond their double-bolted doors.

My heart beats hard as I run, breathing in the cold,

white air, boot heels crunching over thin patches of ice. I slip and grapple for a nearby branch, but I'm careful to keep my eyes on the owl, because it doesn't wait for me, doesn't care whether I'm following or not. It isn't really an owl, of course, or even alive. She made it for me—out of stars or machines or something more mysterious. Whatever it is, or isn't, the owl is my compass, pointing always to her.

My nose and ears smart in the chill air, and I tug down on my hat, press a hand to my frozen face.

There.

I stop, panting, and gaze into her endless eyes. "Cel. Oh, Cel, I missed you."

She's leaning against a spindly birch and smiling at me as if I'm a wonder. Her silver gaze is misty, gleaming. The owl alights upon her shoulder, folds its wings neatly and goes as still as the trees, as silent.

"It's been so long," I whisper, holding back tears. "Nearly a month. I was afraid—"

She's beside me. She didn't walk, didn't *move*, but she's crossed the space between us to wrap her arms around my waist and press her lips to my cheek. In my ear, she breathes, "I promised I'd always return for you."

"But anything could happen. What if—"

"Molly." I feel her mouth arc into a smile against my neck. "Would you like to know where I've been, what I've done?"

I swallow and turn toward her. Our eyes lock. A thrill races through me at the strange loveliness of her—familiar and alien, known and unknown. "Yes," I say, voice gruff with emotion. "Please tell me."

She rests one long-fingered hand against my cheek. "I made something for you. The parts were difficult to acquire. But..." Her eyes flash with mischief, and she casts a glance over her shoulder, toward the large boulder beyond. "I think you'll be pleased."

I wrap my arms around her neck and land a kiss on her nose. "You're in a playful mood tonight."

"I'm excited. And I hope you will be, too." She takes my hands and pulls me along. "Come."

We run together—a brown-haired girl in a red hand-me-down winter coat and a black-haired girl in a bodysuit that shimmers and pools like mercury. Cel's hand is cool in mine. She tosses bright, eager smiles at me as we race past the trees, and I catch her excitement, grinning up at the leaf-laced night sky.

"How much further?" I ask, when we pass the marsh. "Where is it?"

"In the clearing," Cel smiles, ruffling my hair and laughing when I blow her a kiss.

But we reach the clearing, and I whirl around, making circles in the snow. There's nothing here. Nothing but paw prints in the slush and sharp, white stars dangling above us.

I tilt my head questioningly and raise a brow. "I don't understand. Where are we—"

"Look," Cel says, and she draws something from the pouch on her belt. Upon her palm rests a perfect circle of silver: dainty, plain, and thin. It looks like…

"A ring?" I blink, confused. "It's pretty, Cel. You made it?"

"Mm. I modeled it after the rings around my world, Molly. But it's more than that." She takes the ring between her thumb and forefinger and holds it up to her eye, stares at me through the hole. "It's a ring of space. *Space,* Molly. A pocket. A hole." With each word, her voice grows louder, more excited, but I bite my lip and shake my head.

"What do you mean, a hole? Like a black hole?"

"No, no. A hole like…" She glances about, her gaze resting upon the pine trees surrounding us. "A hole like a hiding place. Like a nook. Here." Hand in hand, we walk over to a thick tree trunk pitted with woodpecker cavities, and Cel nods. "A hole like a carved-out space. A safe area." Her eyes fall closed, and when she opens them, they reflect my own eyes, wide and pale.

"I mean a haven, Molly. A place for *us.*"

A hundred questions take shape within me, but before I can speak, Cel takes my hand—so gently, as if she's grasping something fragile and precious—and slides the smooth ring onto my second finger. It fits as if it were made just for me. I hold my hand up to the stars to marvel at the cool, shining circle, silver as Cel's extraordinary eyes.

"All you have to do now is stand in an open area and think of me," she whispers, kissing the back of my palm before raising her gaze to meet mine. "Think of me, Molly, whenever you need me, and we'll be together. In a space of our own."

"You mean, the ring—"

"Yes," she smiles, tilting her head to capture my mouth lightly. "Try it."

Perplexed, and dazed by the warmth of Cel's nearness, I breathe deeply and close my eyes, imagining the lovely, lithe shape of her, the electricity of her presence, and my stomach falls, as if I've ridden over the peak of a mountain, and I hear Cel's voice, as if from far away, call out for me.

Slowly, I raise my eyelids, and I see only stars. And Cel. She looks like a star, gleaming just as brightly, undimmed by the heavy weight of my Earth. Because we aren't *on* Earth. We're in the sky, or space, or nowhere, but there's solidity beneath my feet, and I can move, walk, breathe…

"What—" I begin, but I can't finish, because I don't know what I meant to ask.

Cel's smiling at me, reaching for me, and I fall into her arms and laugh and cry a little, but then I lift my head from her chest and look up at her, and I know what to say. "Our own world," I whisper, truly crying now. "You've made us our own world. Haven't you?"

"A bit of space," she says quietly, kissing my tears away. "Safe space. A bridge between your world and mine. We can meet here whenever you'd like. And stay for as long as you'd like. And maybe someday…" Her gaze softens as she brushes my hair back from my face. "Maybe someday I'll show you *my* world. When you're ready."

I kiss her, tasting the stars within her, and cradle the ring against my heart. "Thank you. I don't understand how you did this, or what it cost you to do it, but—"

"I'd do anything for you." Cel pulls me close, so that there is no space between us. I feel her chest rise and fall in a laugh before she kisses my hair. "There's little need for this now," she says, leaning back to remove the motionless owl from her shoulder. She thrusts her arms up toward the stars, and the bird takes off, flying around the two of us in bright spirals of white before ascending up, up and up to claim a place amongst the stars.

FINDING MARS

by Jennifer Diemer

So, I'm in love with a UFO nut. A saucer chaser. An X-phile.

Don't get me wrong—I love a good conspiracy theory, and when Diana suggested this alien-hunting summer road trip, I thought it sounded like a blast (pun totally intended). But we've been roaming around Mars for, like, an hour now, and there's no sign of the flying saucer anywhere, and I can't find a Starbucks, either, so I'm ready to throw in the proverbial towel and take a nap—or, you know, "a nap," wink, wink—in the giant '70s van we borrowed from my wannabe rock star dad... But Diana's still in UFO adventurer mode and wants to keep searching for the stupid fake saucer.

"It's not even a real saucer, Di. It's just a joke. A roadside attraction. Because we're in *Mars*, Pennsylvania. Ha. Ha. C'mon. Let's go."

"No, wait. Let's ask this guy if he knows where it is."

This guy turns out to be a gas station attendant hunched over the greasy innards of a beat-up Ford. He stares us up and down with crazy suspicious eyes before spitting something on the ground and grunting, "Nope, dunno where that thing is. They like to move it around, y'know, for parades and that. Festivals. Brings out the tourists." He smirks and slams down the hood of the truck with a *bang* that makes me jump. "And the weirdos."

I open my mouth to tell him a thing or two about

"weirdos," but Diana stills me with a glance—and unintentionally turns my knees to jelly. (Wow, her eyes are gorgeous.) So I repress my simultaneous longings to kick the guy in the shin *and* sweep Diana up in an uber-romantic kiss—despite the decidedly unromantic locale and the noxious aroma of spilled gasoline—and continue walking to the end of the block. Diana catches up and falls in step beside me.

"Hey, if you really want to head back to the van, we can call it a day." Her hand brushes against mine, and little electric sparks zip and zap along my arm. "You've been amazing, Tab. I know this alien stuff isn't your thing—"

"You're my thing," I smile, tracing a finger over the inside of her forearm before hooking my hand around her elbow. "And it's been fun." I laugh. "The acorn spaceship in Kecksburg. Chasing you around those crop circles in Idaho—"

"Which were totally a sham."

"*Totally*. But worth the drive just to see you so excited, so...alive." I stop walking and wrap my arms around Diana's neck. "I love having adventures with you."

"Oh, Tab. It's been awesome, hasn't it?"

"Yeah. I can't wait to upload that photo of us to Facebook—wearing tin foil hats in Roswell."

She shakes her head, grinning. "We're such dorks."

"We're such *awesome* dorks." And I don't even care that Gas Station Guy is still watching us with his beady, distrustful, we-don't-take-kindly-to-strangers-here (especially-strangers-with-piercings-and-weird-blue-hair) eyes. I take Diana in my arms, tilt her back like Frank Sinatra or something in one of those old movies, and kiss her right there on the sidewalk in middle-of-nowhere Pennsylvania. Thoroughly kiss her. And I'm not sure what I believe about visitors from outer space, but right now I *know* I believe in UFOs, because *I'm* a flying object, floating above the ground with sappy, galaxy-spanning love for the alien-crazy girl in my arms.

"Listen," I say, even as Gas Station Guy gapes and grossly salivates behind Diana's back, "let's circle the town one more time to look for the saucer."

"Are you sure?"

I kiss her again, grab her hand and tug her along. "First one to find the UFO calls dibs on the last cupcake in the van."

"Well, then…" Diana grins, and we race through the streets, chasing each other and laughing and winning lots of stares from the townspeople—Martians, ha!—as we descend into silliness, peering beneath the lids of garbage cans and under parked cars in our search for the elusive saucer.

At sunset, still UFO-less, we choose a bench in the park and sit with our arms slung around each other, gazing up at the orange-purple sky.

"I can't believe our trip's almost over," I sigh, tilting my head to rest it against Diana's shoulder.

"I know." She laughs lightly and pulls me closer. "So, Ms. Skeptical, have you changed your mind about life on other planets yet?"

"Oh, I don't know. But I'm pretty content with the life forms on *this* planet." I smile up at her, and she leans down to kiss me. "Your life form, in particular."

"Ah, so smooth."

"What can I say?" I waggle my eyebrows at her. "It's a gift."

We snuggle together in silence as the sky grows darker and darker and the first stars fade in, faintly twinkling.

"Excuse me, girls."

In the yellow glare of the streetlamp, I see a middle-aged woman in a grey flannel shirt and blue jeans approaching from our left. As one, Diana and I sit up straighter, untangling our very tangled limbs. My temple begins to throb as I brace myself for the inevitable homophobic comment or some ranting religious diatribe, but the woman only nods in a friendly way and gestures toward Diana's t-shirt.

I got the t-shirt for her last May, for her birthday: a black babydoll screenprinted with a neon-green UFO that glows in the dark.

"I assume you girls were looking for our flying saucer? I saw you walking around town earlier."

"Yeah," Diana says, standing up. "Do you know where it is?"

"I'm so sorry to disappoint you. It's in repair. Some kids vandalized it on the Fourth of July, and we're working on cleaning up the spray paint and popping out the dents. If you come back in a few weeks, it'll be back here in the park."

"Oh, well, thanks for letting us know."

Diana slumps back beside me as the woman moves on with a little wave.

"We could come back if you wanted, Di." I weave my fingers through her wavy black hair. "It's only a couple of hours from home. I know you really wanted to see it."

She shrugs her shoulders and turns to smile at me. "It's not a big deal. Bad timing. But maybe we could do another tour next summer, to celebrate senior year—Alien Adventure Part II: Return to Mars."

I laugh and gather her into my arms. "Totally. I'd fly to the moon for you, you know."

"I'd fly to *Pluto* for you."

"Hmm." I brush her hair back from her eyes and plant a kiss on her forehead. "A secret lesbian colony on the non-planet Pluto. I like the sound of this... It would make for a great, *terrible* movie."

We kiss and stand up, stretch, and kiss again. Then Diana pulls back, her gaze latched onto the stars above our heads. I look up, too, and gasp.

"Hey, Tab—"

"Yeah. I see it. Oh, Di—I *see* it! What *is* it? Is it—"

"I think so. I think it's—"

"A UFO!"

Hovering many miles above our heads, a gathering of bright white lights in a triangular formation glows amidst the blackness and the stars. I can't speak, can't move, can't even close my mouth in a dignified manner, because *this*... This is *amazing*. The longer I stare, the more details become clear, and my eyes trace the vague outline of a ship around the lights.

"Is this really happening?" Diana breathes.

I nod my head, willing away the sudden urge to faint.

There's no sound and no movement, not until, heart-stoppingly fast, the UFO streaks across the whole sky with a whir that makes my body buzz. The trail of light it created lingers for a handful of seconds, and then, with a shocking finality, the light is gone, and the sky is empty again, black. Save for the sprinkling of far-off stars.

"Um," Diana says.

"Yeah," I say.

And then we look at each other, and I take Diana's hands, and we look back at the sky for a long while, as if we're waiting for an encore.

"Well," I whisper finally, when the dizziness passes, "that was… That was a flying saucer." My voice sounds alarmingly matter-of-fact.

"Flying triangle," Diana corrects me, making a triangle shape with her fingers in front of her face.

I kiss her through the triangle, and she laughs and flings her arms around my shoulders, whispers, "Let's go back to the van and share that cupcake."

I grin. "And other earthy delights."

Hand in hand, silent, in awe, we stroll the now-deserted streets of Mars, the flying saucer glowing on Diana's t-shirt lighting our way.

THE GIRL ON THE MOUNTAIN

by Jennifer Diemer

They call her Goddess, the Deliverer, She Who Moves the Sky.

I am the one who must bring the gifts to her every summer because I'm the one who found her, the only person from my village who has ever seen her or spoken with her. The only person who does not fear her.

My heart stills within me now at the thought of seeing her again after so many months away. Will she think me changed? Will she see the confession in my eyes? What will she say when I tell her that Lem proposed to me three months ago, and that I refused him, that I told him I was in love with someone else?

Will I summon the courage at last, or will I leave her mountain with the burden of my heartache once again?

Nine years ago, I was eight, and I was lost.

While my father's hunting party stalked a herd of elk across the cliffs, I lingered behind in a patch of laurel, singing to myself and weaving a flower chain to take home to my mother.

Mother was sick then, and she died a few weeks later, but I believed, as children are wont to do, that my

241

wishes and flowers could make her well, could reignite the spark in her pain-dulled eyes. I imagined presenting her with my white-petaled necklace, looping it over her head... She would be so pleased by my gift that she'd whirl me around until both of our dresses flared, and then she'd bake blackberry muffins and tell me a story at the fireside. Just like she used to do, before the fever came.

So many of the villagers had fallen ill over the winter, adults and children both. Rumors spread that Sun Valley was cursed, that we had angered a god by dancing on Rest Days or by overindulging in wine and song. Soon enough, dancing and drinking and singing were forbidden, and we prayed together from noon until dusk. But the fever raged on, and by summer, it had claimed a dozen lives and threatened several dozen more.

I begged my father to take me to the cliffs with him because I knew the laurels grew there, and they were my mother's favorite flower, for she had grown up in the mountain range to the south of Sun Valley. Father agreed but made me promise to hold silent and stay out of the hunters' way. He had neither the time nor the desire to child-watch a small, curious girl rambling over tricky crags and slick, mud-stained knolls.

But I fell to daydreaming there in the laurels, and I never noticed that the party had moved on until a cool breath of wind gusted my brown hair over my face, and I looked up, toward the cliffs, and saw no one there. My father and the others were gone. Possibly long gone. I stood, forgetting my flowers, heart beating like a hoofed stampede inside my chest. I had never been alone before, and here I was, lost in an unknown wilderness, too many miles from the village to walk back on foot.

I thought about crying, but it seemed a misuse of energy, so I fell back onto the ground, crushing my laurel chain beneath my knees, and simply stared. I stared at the space the party had occupied when last I'd noticed them. The scrub was still mashed down from their stamping horses, and I spied muddy boot prints upon the speckled granite. Perhaps, if I ran, I might catch up with them... But what if I followed the wrong path? What if I couldn't find my way back here, where they surely must pass in order to return home to Sun Valley?

It seemed best to remain where I was, no matter how long I must wait, and no matter how frightened I felt—so lonesome in such a wide, sprawling place.

With a shaky sigh, I spread out on my back amongst the fragrant laurels and unfocused my eyes to find shapes in the clouds. The game calmed me. I lifted my arm and traced a finger along the fluffy white back of a newborn lamb, curled on its side with spindly legs tucked beneath its chin. I found a tall, narrow church with a towering spire; a hunchbacked woman carrying a small child in her arms; a sleek cat floating on fat, feathered wings.

My eyes were just beginning to slide closed with weariness when I saw something amongst the clouds that was not a cloud and not a bird, either. I widened my gaze and raised up onto my elbows, head tilted back so that my hair grazed the laurel bed and caught on the leaves.

I blinked and rubbed my eyes, but the vision remained.

A child.

There was a child—a girl—hovering above me in the sky.

She had no wings and appeared to be suspended, bare toes pointing down, as if she were held up by invisible strings. But then, in a heart-stopping instant, she curled toward me, headfirst, and drifted down the sky like a leaf caught in the wind: erratically, arms and legs sweeping wide. Her close-fitting, blue-grey gown billowed a little at her ankles.

I bit my lip and straightened my back, watching

her descent with slitted eyes, a skeptic's gaze. Surely I was dreaming, though the hard ground made my young bones ache, and I felt the air shift around me with her unpredictable movements.

Pinching myself, I wished with all my might that I would waken to find my father and his party gathered around me, scolding me for lagging behind. I wouldn't mind the punishment, any punishment. I just wanted home and Mother and a soft, warm bed to lie upon.

But I didn't wake up, couldn't, because I wasn't asleep, no matter how dreamlike the world now seemed as the floating girl alighted upon the granite beside me and knelt down to meet my stare eye to eye.

"Are you a cloud?" she asked me in a strange wispy voice, delicate as a wishing flower or a spider's web.

I almost laughed at her question, it was so silly, but her earnest expression made me tilt my head and frown. "I'm a girl," I told her simply. "A girl like you."

Her small mouth tightened. She took my hand and placed her own hand flat against my palm. Our fingers were the same length, though her skin was paler than mine, nearly as white as the laurels beneath our feet. "No." She caught me in her steady gaze, watery blue and bottomless. "Not like me," she whispered, letting my hand fall. She sat back on her knees, calm and still.

I crossed my legs and leaned toward her. "How did you do it? How can you fly? I thought only birds could fly. I never saw a girl do that before. Can you teach me how—"

"No," she said, and the word contained such profound sadness that I regretted my hasty questioning. But then she shook her head and tried to smile. "I wish I could teach you. But you're too heavy for flying. That's the difference between us." She plucked at the laurels and cradled a small bloom in her hand, then placed it in my hair, just behind my ear. "And that you're lovelier than me."

I bowed my head, suddenly shy. When I looked

back up at her, she was smiling softly, and I smiled, too. "My name is Kivrin. What's your name?"

"I've never had need for a name. I don't have one."

Puzzled at this, I wondered if her lack of a name had something to do with her ability to fly. I was reluctant to broach that subject again, so I licked my lips and picked up my chain of flowers. "Would you like to be called Laurel?" I asked her. "You live here amongst them, or above them, and you look a little like them—soft and white."

The girl laughed, though her laughter sounded more like sighing. "You may call me Laurel, yes, if you wish to."

Happy all of the sudden, and humming an old lullaby to myself, I began to work at my chain again, bending and slitting the flower stems. I noticed Laurel watching me and preened at the attention, showing off for her by making wide, sweeping gestures and putting on a serious, grown-up face. "If you don't slit the stem just right," I told her importantly, "the flower chain will break. And then Mother will never get better, and Father will get angrier and angrier and stay away from home all night long, and I will…" I ducked my head to hide my childish tears, but Laurel patted my cheek and gazed at me gently.

"Is your mother sick, Kivrin?"

"Yes." I nodded, wiping at my leaky nose. "Many people in Sun Valley are sick. Father says Mother will die, but I don't believe it. I think she'll be well soon, and she and I will take walks like we used to do, gathering mushrooms and berries. And she'll teach me how to dance, like she promised she would, before it was forbidden, before…"

Laurel rose to her feet. "Perhaps I can help you—you and your village. I have seen the sickness you're speaking of. And I know its cause: a disease in the air."

I swallowed, blinking up at her. Her strange silver hair was haloed with golden light. At once, the full weight of my situation struck me, and I slumped, overwhelmed. Had Laurel truly…flown? How had she done that? She had said we weren't the same, that she wasn't a girl like me. What, then, was she? Now, gazing up at her, I was reminded of the statues in the village chapel, the smooth-faced goddesses with crowns of light encircling their heads.

I stumbled to my feet to stand beside her, surprised to realize that I was a little taller than her, though I naturally stooped beneath her piercing gaze. "How do you know," I began, voice shaky, "about the sickness? How…how can you help?"

Laurel smiled broadly at me and pointed to her feet. I looked down at them, confused, and then watched in awe as, with a gentle scraping of skin on stone, her toes—her whole body—lifted from the ground, and she was floating beside me, bobbing a little, like a paper boat in a stream.

"How—" I began again, but she tapped my mouth with her finger, mischief in her eyes, and then swept up so quickly that my heart fell away, and I gasped, gaping toward the sky, toward her, because she was far above my head now, out of reach.

"I can't tell you how I fly any more than you can tell me how you walk," Laurel said lightly, still smiling. "It's simply what I do, who I am."

"Who…are you?" I took a few steps backward, keeping her in my sights.

"That depends on who you ask, Kivrin. People have given me—my people—so many names. None as lovely as Laurel, though." She swooped down suddenly and suspended herself beside me, face to face—but upside-down. I laughed at the funny way her face looked from the odd angle; her long hair dangled down to tickle my neck. "Would you like me to help you?" she asked, slowing turning in the air, tucking in her arms and legs as she whirled. When she was right-side up, she lowered to the ground again—silently, effortlessly—and looked up at me, awaiting my answer.

"Yes," I breathed, unable to hide my tears now, because I believed her; I believed she truly could help my village, could save my neighbors, my mother. "Please help us," I choked, sobbing.

Laurel took me in her arms, and I gasped quietly, startled by the softness of her skin and the *light* feeling of her, as if she truly were made of air or clouds. I wondered again what she was, who she was, to be able to do such extraordinary things, but her scent surrounded me, soothed me, and I grew relaxed in her embrace.

Everything would be fine now, I knew. Laurel would save us, all of us, and it didn't matter how she did it, or who she was, only that she was kind and my friend.

"Kivrin," she whispered against my hair, "there are men approaching. I hear their voices in the wind."

"My father!" I let her go and peered over her shoulder, craning my neck to catch sight of the hunting party.

"They're many paces off but will be here soon." Laurel rested her hands on my shoulders and stared into my eyes. "They mustn't see me. I have to go. But..." She lowered her gaze and smiled softly to herself. "I'm glad we met today. I knew you wouldn't be afraid of me, that you were brave and good."

"Brave and good?" I repeated, mystified, because I had never been called either of those words, nor anything like them. My father favored "lazy and wild," and my mother called me her little goat, because I was always rambling out of doors, upon the hills, and striking up mischief.

Brave and good. The words circled in my mind, again and again, until they made a sort of groove and became a part of me, until they began to feel *almost* true. Perhaps I wasn't truly brave and good, but I could aspire to be, for Laurel. I would try to be brave and good for her.

"I'll do what I can for your village," she said then, exhaling a little sigh. "But, Kivrin, your mother... I can't promise—"

"I know," I said, and I did know, deep down. I knew that my mother was dying, that nothing and no one could save her, not a laurel chain, not even a girl made of clouds. And I couldn't think about it, not too long or too hard, because then I'd shatter, and I wasn't prepared to shatter, not yet.

I took a trembling breath and smiled. "I'm glad to have met you, too."

Something sparked between us, something I could never explain, or try to, because it was at the borders of my vision, and I felt it more than saw it. But it happened: a lightning moment, a bolt zapping from me to her, or her to me, and when our eyes met afterward, Laurel looked older, somehow. Softer... Beautiful.

I took a step nearer to her, but then the voices were upon us, and Laurel swept upward, so high so quickly that I lost track of her as she arced across the sun.

My father found me blinking up at the sky and knocked the laurel from my hair with his big, fisted hand. "Last time you're coming here, you wild, lazy—"

Frightened by the finality of his words, by the prospect of never returning to the mountain, of never seeing Laurel again, I told him everything, though the words tasted profane as they fell from my lips, too ordinary to explain what had just happened and all I had felt, all I now knew.

Still, Father—and his hunting party gathered around me—listened to all I had to say and, in the end, chose to believe me, because what else did they have to hold onto? Maybe Reiner's flighty daughter had fallen asleep in the laurels and had a fantastical dream...or maybe she truly had seen a mountain goddess who had promised to heal Sun Valley and make its people well.

They clung to the latter possibility, to hope, and sent me back to the mountain every summer with the village's offerings, because Laurel did chase the diseased air away, as she'd said she would. My mother was the last fatality of the sickness, and her death nearly broke me, but only nearly.

I still had Laurel. She Who Moves the Sky.

The basket is heavy this year with my stepmother's canning and the pastor's wife's knit goods, "to keep the poor thing warm up there. Gods forbid she catches a chill!" I smile a little to myself now, imagining Laurel festooned in the bulky wool sweater, her hands weighted down by giant mittens the color of apricots. She'll laugh when she sees them, and she'll admire the canned tomatoes and pickles, but she won't take any of it, and she'll tell me again that the offerings make her feel uncomfortable, and I'll tell her again that Sun Valley is grateful for all she has done, and this is the only way they know to express their thanks. And she'll say—

I drop the basket to the ground and run, stumbling over stones. I press a shaking hand to my temple, to the place that always throbs whenever I imagine telling Laurel how I feel, how I've *always* felt, and how that feeling torments me every hour of every day... When I'm milking the goats, I think only of Laurel, of her soft, white skin and graceful limbs. When I'm hanging up the washing, I think of the way Laurel's dress shimmers as she moves, as she floats beside me, a pale silhouette against the sky. And when I'm lying in bed, I think of Laurel up there on the lonely mountain, and I wonder if she ever thinks of me, if she ever wishes—

"Kivrin?"

I startle and trip, falling to my knees.

"Oh, are you hurt?" Her hands glide over the backs of my arms, lifting me up, holding me suspended—for just a heartbeat—above the ground.

I find my footing and shake my head, dusting off my skirt and inspecting a little gash on my wrist. "Elegant as usual," I smirk, and Laurel smiles down at me from her lofty height, bowing at the waist to tap my nose.

"I never meant to surprise you. I just knew you were coming—I heard your footfalls ages ago—and so I hurried to meet you and to lighten your load, but..." Her blue eyes flicker to my hands, narrowing. "You haven't got a load this time."

"No," I murmur, ashamed at my brash abuse of the village's offerings, but I take a deep breath and shake my head again, frowning to myself. "I thought—Well, you have no use for those things, anyway, so I left them behind, but of course Sun Valley send its gratitude and prayers, as always, and wants you to know—"

Laurel waves her hand and drifts down until she's seated on the flowers, legs folded beneath her. I sit beside her, brushing my fingers over the laurels and biting my lip.

"I wish they wouldn't send their prayers," she sighs, raising her eyes to the sky. "You know I'm no goddess, no deity. I'm only..." She sighs again.

A wonder, I think. A treasure, a dream.

"A girl on a mountain," she says, turning her gaze to me. I fall into the blue of her, and when my own eyes flutter and water, I look away.

"A girl on a mountain," I repeat, swallowing hard. "Well, so am I, here and now. But you're more than that."

"Am I, Kivrin?"

I glance at her, and she snares me with her softness. "Laurel..."

"Yes?"

"I've been meaning to talk to you about—I mean, I've been coming up here for nine years. We've grown up together, and the moments I spend with you are...They've been..." I swallow again and shift my gaze to the flowers carpeting the mountain beneath us.

Just say it, Kivrin. Say it, and then you'll know. One way or the other, you'll know. Just say it.

Laurel covers my fidgeting hands with her own and ducks her head to catch my eyes. "They've been what?" she prompts me gently, and my gaze is drawn to her mouth, pink as the wild roses that grow in the forest at home.

I groan and cradle my head. *Just say it. Say it!* "I love you." My throat starts to close, to stop the words up, but I cough and fill my chest with air and look right into Laurel's eyes and say it again: "I love you. I think I've always loved you, from the moment you fell out of the sky, but I couldn't tell you, because you're *you*, and I'm just—"

"*Just?*" Laurel whispers, smiling faintly and leaning near. "Kivrin, you aren't *just* anything. You're grand and lovely and good and brave and..." Her voice falters. She glances away, at the flowers, at our entwined hands.

"And?" I squeak, trembling beside her.

"And..." Her eyes flit over my face, restless. "And you have been so loyal to your village, so—"

"My village?" I mutter miserably, finally catching her gaze. "Is that what this has all been about, Laurel? My village? You have protected us from sickness and storms, and we have prospered and worshiped you, and laurels bloom in every garden, and is that all it's about? Is that all I am to you?" I swipe a tear from my eyes, even as she moves nearer, reaching out to lay a hand upon my cheek. "Am I a messenger, nothing more?"

"No," she says, and there is power in the word— water and wind and lightning. My skin prickles as her palm brushes hair back from my face. "No, Kivrin. It was never about the village. I'm a selfish thing, if you must know the truth."

"Selfish?" I blink, red-faced and confused.

"I didn't blow away the disease and the floods for *them*, Kivrin. Never for *them*."

"I don't—"

"It was all for you."

A blast of air sweeps through me, chilling me and warming me at the same time, as her words claim a place inside of my heart and upon my history. *It was all for you.*

"Do you mean..." I whisper, hardly daring to hope.

But she takes my chin in both of her hands now, and the lightness of her fills me, lifts me up...*truly* lifts me up, because we're floating together. Her arms are wrapped around my waist, and we're so far above the ground that the flowers below are barely freckles upon the vast grey stone. "It means," she whispers, as the air gusts around us, "that I love you, too, and that I always have. And that *you,* Kivrin, are much braver and more good than I, such as I am, could ever hope to be."

There's mischief in her eyes and her smile as she kisses me upon a bed of clouds.

"I'll build a little house at the top of the mountain," I tell her, as she kisses me again. "And sometimes you'll come down to me, and sometimes you'll carry me up...here, with you, and we'll live—"

"Forever," Laurel says, and I feel the lightning between us again, and we float together so high that I lose sight of the ground.

All around me, there's only blue. A beautiful, bottomless blue.

I cradle my wonder in my arms and move with the breeze, lighter than air.

KYRIE

by Jennifer Diemer

I'm staring sleepily at the periwinkle bubbles in my mug of Blue Fizzy, trying to summon the energy to leave the café and slog through the rain back to my dorm, when Lulu slides into the empty seat beside me with a riotous crash, dinging her alumi-bag against the side of my chair.

"Did you *hear*?" she squeaks, bouncing up and down and going all blurry—and double—before my sleep-starved eyes.

I point at the Fizzy and wince. "Headache, Lu," I whisper. "Maybe you could tone it down a little?"

"Oh, right. Sorry." She stills for a moment, but then she starts bouncing again, and I notice that her face is aglow. And kind of...purple.

"I thought you said your Test's tomorrow, same time as mine?"

She shrugs. "Yeah, so?"

"*So*—you got a Facelight instead of studying?"

"Well, the salon was having a special, 'cause of Test Week." She models her luminous lavender face for me with a flourish of her hand. "Audacious Amethyst, the newest shade. I think it brings out the green in my eyes."

"Mmm." I frown blearily into Lulu's Enchanting Emerald contacts and sigh. "You wanted to tell me something?" I chug down some more of the Blue Fizzy, hoping it'll take the razor edge off of my migraine, but the bubbly drink tickles my throat as it goes down and makes me cough. I groan; my head throbs with pain.

"Yes, yes! Oh, you'll never guess!" Lu's hopping around in her seat, and she claps her hands together cutely. I give her a half-smile as I massage my left temple.

Really, I love Lu. We've got zero in common and *should* have nothing to talk about, but somehow there's never a dull moment between us. Two years ago, she and I met on a blind date set up by my old roommate. We shared a few giggly kisses in the back of the Holoplex before mutually deciding that we'd make better friends than lovers. Now Lu's going out with some spike-haired girl from the flyball club, and I'm in a serious relationship with my history textbooks.

I take another Fizzy swig but pause mid-swallow, because Lu's eyes have gone all huge—eerie in that violet face—and she leans forward over the table, her long yellow hair brushing against my arm, to whisper, "They found another Kyrie."

I choke, spitting up bubbles. "They *what?*"

She eases back into her chair wearing an adorable—but unmistakably smug—grin. "You heard me. I got the news firsthand from the witness."

"Who?"

"Landon Milbaugh."

"That gamer guy who works at the library?"

Head bobbing, Lu leans toward me again. "Yeah! He told me the whole story. He was locking up when he heard—"

"Wait." I shake my head, stunned. "You mean… The Kyrie was *here*? At school?" Wild thoughts stumble through my pain-addled brain. My stomach lurches a little, and I push my mug away.

"Outside the library," Lu announces dramatically, tossing sidelong glances at the tables around us. "Maybe we shouldn't talk in public. This is all top-secret information and—"

"Well, Landon had no qualms about blabbing to you, apparently."

She chews on one blue-painted fingernail. "I can't help it if I have a trustworthy face."

I burst out laughing. Because she's right. Even with the Facelight, Lulu looks like an angel, the kind of girl you can trust with your deepest, darkest secrets. And you can—for the most part. But there hasn't been a Kyrie sighting in more than three years. (Three years, seven months, sixteen days.) This is big, exciting news, especially since it happened on campus.

"Well, Landon's my Test partner—Prof Rinkle paired us together—and so we met up at Pizza Ship last night and…" She spreads her hands wide. "He spilled. It happened just before we met up. He was super late, actually, 'cause the authorities had to question him. And that's why there were all those black trucks in the student parking lot. Did you see them?"

I bite my lip, smile fading quickly. "No. I was studying in my room."

Lu tilts her head at me. "All night?"

"Yeah."

"You know, you've got to be careful, Mille. Too much studying and you'll fry your brain."

I clutch at my forehead. "Maybe I already have."

A waitress stops at our table, and Lu orders an Orange Fizzy, her usual, "with a rainbow straw, please!" It's a superdose of solar energy, and I used to think the drink was the reason Lu couldn't seem to sit still for more than three seconds straight, but now I know the truth: Lu's just innately…bouncy.

She orders Orange Fizzies because they taste like summer and make her tongue turn gold. And I order Blue because my head is a constant muddle of dates and names and theories and questions and memories I'd be better off forgetting. And because it tastes like a kiss in a snowstorm. And kind of…I think…like flying through the clouds.

I swallow some of my drink down and close my eyes. It's weird, because I can almost feel the wind on my face as I reel and arc across the sky—

Then I realize that Lulu is blowing on me.

"Wake up, dozer! C'mon! I've just told you the story of the century, and you're, like, falling asleep?"

"Sorry." I take a deep breath and muster up a smile. "You're right. I'm just...overwhelmed. Shocked. A Kyrie *here*? That's unheard of, you know. They've all been sighted to the west, or south. Never up here. Never so close to—" I stop myself. I was going to say, "so close to me," but that might make Lu curious, and it's never a good idea to make Lu curious—not when you're trying to keep something from her. And from everyone else.

"So," I say in a way-too-cheerful, not-like-me-at-all voice, "how far away was it when he spotted it? Could he make out any details? Which direction it was flying?"

Lu's mouth forms a perfect O of surprise. "Oh, no! I forgot to tell you the most important part!" She raps a fist against her forehead and rolls her eyes. "Landon didn't see the Kyrie *flying* at all. It was on the ground. Maybe its wings were broken or something. So the authorities came and took it away."

The world stops. I can't hear, can't breathe, can't speak until I force down another gulp of Blue Fizzy to wet my dry throat. "They *caught* it?" I finally whisper-croak.

"Well, yeah." Lu tilts her head at me again. I catch her eye for a moment before glancing away and fidgeting with my mug. "Landon said they didn't put her in one of those black trucks, though. They took a bunch of photos and measurements and things, and then they carried her into the Syence Hall." She sips at her drink. "Maybe she's still there."

"She." I feel my eyes glazing over, and my shoulder blades itch—no, burn. I have to go. I have to *think*. I have to...

I have to go to the Syence Hall.

"Mille? Are you all right?"

I leap to my feet, knocking over my mug, and toss a couple of tokens onto the table. "Yeah, sure. I've just got to get back to studying. Test's tomorrow and—Yeah." Stumbling, I wave a feeble good-bye over my shoulder. "See you later, Lu."

"I'll be at the Pizza Ship with Landon again, if you want to meet up! All day. Buy you a slice."

"Okay, if I'm not too fried, I'll stop by," I hear myself say, but my brain is operating on automatic now, and I trip again as I cross the café threshold and dash out into the puddled street. Without another thought, I cut across campus toward the boxy brown building at the base of Scholar Hill.

I remember the day that it happened vividly, though I remember so little that happened before. Nothing, really. My childhood is a void. No matter how much I pry at the locks and kick at the door, I can't break in. Someone stole the key from me.

The same someone, I think, who stole my wings.

It's for your own good, they said. A man or woman, I couldn't tell. I couldn't see. I was strapped, stomach-down, to a hard table, and everything was dark and cold, and I tried to scream but couldn't make a sound. Muted, blind but not deaf, I listened as they talked about me, as they clacked metal instruments together, as they walked around me, pressing their gloved hands against my back. I arched beneath their touch, against the restraints, but then they injected something into my neck, and I couldn't feel anything at all.

Except for a sinking. A dissolving. A feeling I came to recognize as loss.

When I woke, I was in a strange bed in a room full of empty beds, and there were bandages wrapped around my chest and shoulders, beneath my t-shirt. I sat up, and my body was lanced through with a pain so hot and ferocious that I fainted.

Days passed. I think.

Finally, I could sit up without passing out, and the ladies who fed me and bathed me were kind if distant, avoiding my questions, and I understood, in time, that I was in an orphanage, that I was an orphan, parentless, without family. Entirely alone.

It felt...wrong. It felt like a lie, like someone else's story. But I believed it because they told me it was so again and again, and soon enough, the pain in my shoulders faded to a dull ache, though the scars never healed properly. I wouldn't let the wounds heal. I picked at the scabs until blood soaked my bed sheets, and the ladies scolded me and trimmed my nails to the quick.

They said I was in an accident. A terrible crash. They said my parents were killed, that only I survived.

They said nothing about the hard table or the restraints or the gloved hands. Nothing to explain the phantom limbs I felt opening and closing on my back.

Every night until I was sent away from that place, sent to school, I cried into my pillow—not for my parents and not even for myself. I cried for my wings. They had been so beautiful, black feathers tipped with grey. I remember the way they pulled at the muscles in my back and shoulders, the way they fit against my shape like a child nestles, instinctively, against its mother's body.

I don't think I'm supposed to remember them. I mentioned them to one of the women at the orphanage, and she ran from the room and returned with a man in a white coat who asked me questions for hours and pricked me with foul-smelling needles.

I pretended after that. Lied. Recounted the accident story and faked tears for parents I couldn't remember.

But I remember my wings, if nothing else.

Now, in quiet moments, I summon up the thrill of ascension, that moment when the earth gave way beneath my feet and became something mysterious, foreign, unknowable.

I was a Kyrie. And now I'm just Mille.

As a history major, I've never had cause to enter the Syence Hall before, but my student passcard still unlocks the glass double doors.

I step through them and start to run but then stop, a hand against my pounding heart as I stoop over a little, breathing hard. I don't know where to go. I don't know what I'm doing.

I don't know what I'm hoping to find.

I've followed the Kyrie sightings fanatically, even tracked them on an old map that I keep folded up in my desk drawer. They're rare—or at least rarely reported— and no one claims to have ever seen one up close, only from a distance as they swoop and soar through the sky.

Some people don't even believe they exist. They equate them with alicorns and fire-breathing cats. But they're hot news, no matter what you believe. And there have been at least a dozen holofilms made about them— sappy star-crossed weepfests.

I never knew Lu believed in the Kyrie, honestly. Not until today. I tend to avoid the topic with my friends, if I can help it. I'm a terrible, clumsy liar. I'm surprised I haven't ever given myself away. But it's been ten years since the "accident," and I've lived a life of careful normalcy, motivated by some self-preservation compulsion built into my atoms. But now that I know there may be a Kyrie nearby, occupying the same space, breathing the same air as me…

Seeing her, even for an eye-blink moment, would be worth any risk, any price. For proof that there's someone else in the world like me, I'd pay anything.

I need this.

I'm walking. Fast. Too fast. I slow my pace a little, but my muscles move of their own accord, and my eyes dart from door to door, scanning for...I don't know what. I hope I'll recognize a sign when I see it. Or maybe I'll sense her. Maybe I'll just *know*—

A man dressed in black—there's an official-looking badge clipped to his lapel—emerges from a grey-painted door at the end of the hall and pauses, giving me a hard stare. I gulp audibly before bending over to relace my shoe tubes, wobbling a little on my shaky legs. Despite my ridiculous performance, the man trots past me without a word, hands jammed deep into his pants pockets.

I catch my breath and walk slowly until he's out of sight. Then I throw my weight against the door he exited, fully expecting it to be locked. It's not.

It's *not*?

Maybe I distracted him enough to forget to relock it.

Maybe no one thinks a lock is necessary, since the Kyrie is a secret, known only to Landon and the people who arrived last night in the black trucks. (And Lulu. And me.)

Maybe it's a trick, a trap, and when I step through the door, an alarm will sound, or an officer will slap Permalinx cuffs around my wrists, or—

I'm in.

The door shushes and clicks closed behind me, and I panic, worried that someone will hear the noise and come to see who's here, but minutes pass—excruciating minutes, infinitely more painful than any study-induced migraine—and I'm still alone. I exhale silently, moving forward on tiptoes. There's nothing to look at. I'm in a small, unfurnished room—a little smaller than my bedroom in the dorm—but it appears to be an entryway of sorts, because it opens up to a hallway winding off to the left.

Swallowing hard, I step softly over the tiles, grateful for my Whisper-soled shoes. I work part-time in the library—morning shifts, so I never see Landon there—and all of the staff is required to wear Whispers to set a quiet example for other students. It's a nice thought, but the library's the hottest spot on campus with its Stellar Coffee franchise and the three-story bookstore—which sells far more techno gadgets and gag gifts than it ever does paper or electronic books.

There aren't any decorations or doors in this branch of the hallway, but then the corridor turns again, off to the right this time, and just ahead, a few paces away, is another grey-painted door.

It's halfway open.

I stare.

I take a step forward. A deep breath.

Then, trembling, I take a step back.

What if...

Dry-mouthed, I take another step back. Two.

I mean, no one's ever seen a Kyrie up close—or admitted that they have—until Landon. From far away, making circles in the sky, they look lovely: winged people with streaming hair and graceful limbs. They look like angels.

But what if they're...something else?

What if they're horrible? What if they're monsters? What if the gloved hands took my wings away to save me, to help me? *It's for your own good.*

I back up to the wall—pain blossoms where the paneling connects with my old, old wounds—and lean against it, sliding down to my knees. I swear, balling my fists on my lap.

I need to know. I *want* to know.

I'm so afraid.

But I'm *not* afraid of the man in black or anyone else who might be guarding the Kyrie in that room.

The truth is that I've been searching for another Kyrie for ten years without ever expecting to *actually* find one. Because finding one would mean finding myself. Not the girl with her head bowed behind a book, wearing the mask of a student, a scholar, a historian.

I don't even *like* history.

I just can't seem to come to peace with my own.

My hands rake through my hair, and I make up my mind, stand, march toward the door with its sliver of yellow light. I tilt my ear toward the opening, but there are no sounds within: no machines, no voices, no footsteps. Maybe the room is empty. Maybe the Kyrie isn't even here.

I know she's here. It's not a feeling so much as a scent: cool, bottomless air.

I watch my hand rise and push at the door, watch the door glide open slowly, unhurried, watch the scene unfold before me with the silent awe of a child gazing out at the world for the very first time.

"I came for you," she says, and her voice moves through me like wind, gusting away my acquired humanity to reveal the sleeping Kyrie beneath.

I gasp from shock and relief and panic and joy.

She's strapped to a table, strapped stomach-down, but her wings are intact, folding, unfolding, effortlessly graceful and startlingly misplaced in the dull, square room.

We're alone.

"You're…" I stammer.

"Yes." She regards me coolly with her midnight eyes, pale cheek pressed against her midnight hair. "And so are you."

"Yes," I whisper, staring. I have to stare: she's so lovely, too lovely. I forget to breathe and gasp again. My eyes trail her body, wrapped in cloud-white gauze, and linger over her back, her wings—comprised of small white feathers with fine black striations. Different from my wings, the wings I remember. "You're beautiful."

She smiles, pink mouth closed but upturned coyly at the corners. "I hoped you would come. I've been searching for so long. I tracked your scent to the library, but you weren't there."

"No. I'm there often enough… But not last night." I shake my head. "I don't understand. You were looking for me? How did you—"

"I was with you when they caught you. Took you. I guess you don't remember."

I shake my head again.

"I didn't know you well. We were so young, and there were so few of us…" She bites her lip. "But I failed you. I couldn't save you. I escaped and vowed to find you, no matter how long it took."

"All this time…" I'm bewildered and can scarcely form words to match my thoughts. "I guess I was looking for you, too."

Her dark eyes delve deep within me, deeper than I've ever allowed anyone to see, and I feel warm and safe and somehow…home.

"There's a knife at my hip, tucked beneath the wrappings."

"What?" I blink, leaning against the table, confused.

"To cut the restraints," she says calmly, but I notice now that her breath is shallow, and her nails are scraping at the metal beneath her.

"Sorry, I was just… One second." I step nearer and move my hands awkwardly over the fabric against her hip. She's wrapped so tightly that I almost fail to notice the slight bump in the gauze, but then I peel back a bit of the wrappings and slip my hand beneath them, startled to connect with the warmth of her bare skin. I blush horrifically but somehow manage to tug out a knife by its wooden handle.

Its blade gleams strangely in the yellow light from the ceiling fixture. I can't tell what sort of metal it is, or even what color.

"Hurry."

"Right. Sorry."

The restraints are made of Permalinx, and it takes several minutes of frantic sawing to cut through them. I free her hands first, and then she sits up on her knees while I set to work on the ankle restraints. Her velvet eyes watch me, glancing back; my own eyes flit from her face to the knife in a dizzying rhythm. I feel woozy, drunk. I'm probably going to cut myself, but her gaze rests upon me with perfect trust, with a bone-deep surety that makes my heart stumble inside of my chest.

Her wings burgeon out from her back, brushing against my elbows, my neck, my face. I shiver every time a feather grazes my skin. It's intimate and familiar, the feel of feather on flesh.

"Almost there," I whisper through gritted teeth. My hands and fingers are sore, but time presses on me and makes me saw twice as fast. It's been at least half an hour since I arrived, and who knows how long that man intended to be gone. Maybe he left for the day, or just to grab a late lunch, or to fetch a jagged tool strong enough to hack through a pair of glorious Kyrie wings.

Why? *Why* would anyone mutilate such a magnificent creature, take away such remarkable limbs?

Why did the person with gloved hands steal my wings from me?

Maybe this girl knows, but there's no time to ask her now, because the second ankle restraint comes loose with a metallic thud, and then she's swinging her legs over the table and standing beside me—looming over me, really, because she's tall, though we appear to be around the same age.

My legs turn to Jelliblobs as I look up into her eyes and sense the heady smile within their dark, blustery depths.

"Thank you," she breathes—her voice more like a breeze than a whisper.

"You're…you're welcome." I don't know what to do with my hands, with the knife in my hand, with my face, with my heart… I bow my head and then shift my gaze to the door. "We should go."

"Yes. But don't run. Not until we have to."

"Okay," I squeak, and follow closely behind her, stepping upon the broad shadow of her wings.

It's Test Week, so there aren't a lot of people milling about, and the sun's beginning to lower, daubing the horizon with glimmers of pink, but we're so conspicuous—the Kyrie's made no effort to conceal her wings, and I can't think of any suggestions for covering them up, anyway—that I can't envision a scenario in which we *don't* get caught. It's only a matter of time before someone glances up from the virtual Test on their PalmPad and notices that there's a walking, breathing—not to mention gorgeous—Kyrie in their midst.

Two Kyries, really, but the white-faced one gripping her head in her hands while tripping over her own stupid feet looks more like a frazzled history student stressing about tomorrow's Test than a creature who inspires awe and crazy-romantic holofilms.

Still, I think I'm going to skip tomorrow's Test. Somehow it doesn't seem so important anymore.

The launch pad-shaped parking lot at Pizza Ship is empty of people but packed full with autocycles. I lead the Kyrie behind the restaurant and gesture toward a stand of pine trees. "Wait there. I need to talk to my friend. I think she'll help us get out of here."

"Your…friend?" Her eyebrows arch.

I blush again. I *never* blush. Seriously, I feel like I just downed three Red Fizzies. I'm hot-faced, stupid, reckless. "Just…a friend," I stammer, turning away, toward the Pizza Ship entrance. "But we can trust her. I promise."

"I believe you," she says, and the words whoosh through me; I'm weak, practically swooning, when I fall—literally—into the restaurant. The motion-activated doors whiz closed behind me, scanning my perso-tracker, and a bright electronic voice declares, "Welcome aboard, Passenger Mille. Step up to the command module to place your order. We promise you service that's *out of this world*! And intergalactically delicious!"

I whirl around in circles until I spot Lu's head bouncing up and down in a corner booth. Landon's sitting across from her, his forehead furrowed with concentration. I'm surprised to note he's got a Facelight, too. Green. It makes him look like he's really sick. And maybe he is. He looks nervous enough to throw up.

I dash across the floor and skid to a stop beside Lu, pressing my hands flat on the table, narrowly avoiding mashing my palms into the Asteroid P'za she and Landon are splitting. It's covered with Spicy Space Peppers and splotches of cheese shaped like stars.

"Whoa, nice catch, Mille!" Lulu grins, dropping her PalmPad to the table and patting the empty space beside her. "Saved you a seat. Do you want to order a Blue Fizzy?"

"No, no," I mutter, sliding into the booth and cradling my head. It feels so good to sit down, but I refuse to get comfortable. I've been far too comfortable for far too long. And it's cost me too much.

"I need to talk to you, Lu." I cast a glance at Landon and smile weakly. He nods in my direction, eyes glued to his Pad as he jams pizza into his mouth. "Um…outside?"

"Oh! A secret?"

"Yeah, kinda. No offense, Landon. It'll only take a sec." My voice sounds hollow to my ears, but Landon pays me no further mind, and Lu's already bumping me out of the booth.

"Let's go, then! Landon, I'll catch up when I get back, 'kay?"

"Mmm," he grunts, and I wonder how he can be so engrossed in his studying when he witnessed something incredible last night, something few people will ever have the opportunity to experience. I guess the Kyrie was only a blip in his storyline.

I feel like my whole life's been nothing *but* a blip. Until today.

Lu's three steps ahead of me, bounding outside like a puppy excited about a walk. I jog a little to catch up, but then she whirls around and sticks out her tongue: it gleams with a metallic sheen beneath the twilight sky. "Is it gold yet?" she says with her tongue between her teeth. Her eyes cross as she tries to get a look at it herself.

"Yeah, it's totally gold." I loop my arm through hers and pull her back toward the pines. Luckily, the parking lot's still deserted. "Listen, remember what you told me earlier today, about…" I swallow. Am I really going to do this? After years of hiding, am I really going to—

"About the Kyrie?" She tilts her head toward me, face glowing. "Of course I remember. I was just talking to Landon about it. I think he mixed up the story a little the first time he told it to me." Her mouth twists into an uncommon frown.

"What do you mean?" "Well…" We pause before the stand of pines, and Lulu reaches up to pet one of the soft-needled branches. "I *thought* he told me that the Kyrie's wings were injured, and that's why she was lying on the ground, but now he's saying that he used an Icer on her."

The butterflies in my stomach flutter off, replaced by something sharp-edged and infinitely hotter. There's fire in my gut and in my voice when I growl, "He *shot* her?"

Lu stares at me, alarm dulling her Enchanting Emerald contacts. "Yeah. I thought he might be trying to impress me, bragging or something. But then he showed me the Icer. He has a license for it, but only for gaming, you know. I guess he plays this game where you hunt Kyries, and he got confused…"

"*What?*"

She shrugs. "I don't know. It's so messed up. And the authorities didn't even care that he used the Icer on the Kyrie, just told him not to tell anyone what happened. Which he obviously *did.*" She shakes her head.

"At least icing never causes permanent damage. They'll probably look her over and then release her back to the sky."

Oh, Lu. If only.

"So! Thanks for stopping by. I was pretty upset by it all and didn't really feel like studying with him anymore. I mean, I treated him to a Facelight and everything, and—"

"Lu." I want to stomp into Pizza Ship and punch Landon's sickly green face. But there's no time for that. The man in black may already know that the Kyrie's missing. He may be searching for her, may have a team of people searching for her—covering the campus, scanning the sky. She nearly lost her wings because of Landon's stupidity. I can't *bear* the thought of her losing her beautiful wings.

I take a deep breath. "She's here. The Kyrie." I gesture toward the trees.

"What? How... Where—"

"I need to get her somewhere safe. Without getting caught. Can you help? I didn't know who else to turn to. You're the only one I..." My voice trails off, because I'm not using the right words, not saying what I *need* to say, what Lu needs to know.

She places a hand on my shoulder and squeezes gently, her eyes glossed with worry.

"Okay, I'm just going to say it," I breathe, peering into the trees. I feel the Kyrie there, though she's hidden herself well. Just knowing she's nearby—with her cool surety and core of calm—gives me the strength to speak. "I'm a Kyrie, too, Lu."

Lu blinks. Blinks. Tilts her head and blinks again.

I sigh. "I used to have wings. Someone...took them. And the Kyrie—the one from the library... She knew me *before*. I don't remember anything from my Kyrie life. All I've known is *this*—hallways and books, a perpetual string of boarding schools, because I've never had a *home*, Lu. But now, with her…"

We both stare into the deep green gathering of trees.

I can't say anything else, don't know what to say. I'm shaking, and my head hurts, and suddenly I wish none of this had ever happened. I wish I were in my room, bent over a book, losing myself, losing my sense of time, as everything that is *me* becomes absorbed by other people's stories.

It's so much easier to study history than to make history yourself.

I exhale heavily, rake my hands through my tangled hair.

No.

No.

I'm done with what's easy. Easy brought me nothing but dull days and restless nights. And a longing I could never ease, a pain I could never soothe.

I'm never going back.

I'm a Kyrie.

I gaze into Lu's eyes and square my shoulders. She looks back at me with the strangest, softest, most *serene* expression I've ever seen upon her face. Then she throws her arms around my shoulders and squeals into my ear, "I'm so proud to be your friend!"

Tears spring to my eyes. I hug Lu back tightly, and I realize in that moment that I'm going to miss her—every day I'm going to miss her—so much. "You're the best friend I've ever had."

She gives me a squeeze, hiccups a little, and then lets me go. "Okay, turn around."

"What?"

"Your perso-link. I've got to deactivate it. Otherwise they'll be able to track you down no matter how well you hide."

Brow furrowed, I turn so that my back's facing Lu, and I lift up my shirt to reveal the perso-link tattoo at the base of my spine. "You can *do* that?" I ask her, bewildered. "Deactivate a perso-link?"

Lu giggles. "Of course, silly. What do you think I've been studying all year long? Biosy is simple, really, once you get the hang of it. Aaaand once you get your hands on some super-fancy gadgets!"

I stare over my shoulder as Lu produces a tiny ball-tipped wand from inside of her bra. "Never know when you might need to go incognito," she winks.

I feel her hand press against my back, and then there's a small flare of light.

"All done!"

"Just like that?"

Lu tucks the wand back into her cleavage and grabs both of my hands. "You're basically invisible. Now! Grab your girl, and let's hop on my autocycle. I'll drive you as far as the city, and then you two can take off from there. I'd suggest heading north. Less population, more places to hide."

"You're amazing, Lu."

"I know," she grins, sticking out her golden tongue at me.

Her name is Pathne, and mine, she tells me, was Corin, before I forgot who I was. (I'll never forget again.) Wingless, with her I fly, and someday we'll find others like us, and someday we'll end the mutilation of our kind, spearheaded by techno-worshippers who fear everything they can't replicate with bits and bytes.

In passing moods, I feel crushed by the weight of all of the years I wasted: gravity-bound, indoors, hiding, alone. Studying for a Test that doesn't matter, memorizing names that are only names—not beating hearts.

Now my textbooks contain chapters of clouds and odes to the sweet breath of the sky. I study Pathne's mouth, learn the contours of her shoulders and hips, and rest in the discovery of a winged heart within me.

I am Mille. I am Corin. I am a Kyrie.

I'm not afraid.

And my head—and my wounds—never ache anymore.

FIN

EXTRAS

S.E.'S
AUTHOR NOTES

"Witch Girls"

I spent all of my growing up years running wild in the woods—as a wild little hooligan, really--and that made me into the person I am today. Independence and freedom can be found beneath the dark trees, and that secret is what I spun into "Witch Girls," a story I've been wanting to write for over a decade.

"Surfacing"

I love everything about mermaid mythology—I'm a little obsessed with it, actually. The idea and concept of mermaids is actually a lot darker than the sparkly, seashell-bra-wearing ideal we've drummed up in recent times. Pair that with wanting to cheat from "The Dark Woods" theme with an ocean-based story, and I got "Surfacing."

"Curse Cabin Confession"

Contrary to the dark stories I write, I have a really weird and constant sense of humor (I promise!). Normally, I take a very serious approach to shapeshifters, but for once, I let that fly out the proverbial cabin window: simply put, I wanted to write a ridiculous, but believable, story about shapeshifters. And "Curse Cabin Confession" was born.

"Wolves of Leaving"

I was out walking at twilight, watching the beautiful colors spill across the sky, and I began to imagine a conversation between two girls...one afraid and one desperate. I was walking our Collie, Link, and he looks a little wolfish in the growing dark, so I turned the girls in my head into werewolves, and came home quickly and wrote their story. Link was not amused that his walk was cut short, but I hope he understands. The treats helped.

"Devil May Care"

The aforementioned Link was staying over at my parents' house while we were traveling in the spring. Link was adopted as a puppy from a shelter—he'd been terribly abused by his previous owners, and was afraid of *everything*. We worked gently with him until he was happy and healthy, but he definitely still has specific triggers—including bad storms. There was a *terrible* storm, and my parents put him out in their very-tall-fenced-in backyard. And somehow, impossibly, he leapt the fence and ran away in the middle of the night during a monstrous thunderstorm. Jenn and I had just returned and rushed over and then spent the next twenty-four solid hours traveling the hundreds and hundreds and hundreds of acres of woods around my parents' farm, trying to find him. I'd assumed that since he was terrified of most people, and terrified in general now, that he'd get run over and I would never see him alive again. These were some of the most painful hours of my life—I love Link with all of my heart. He's my baby. Finally, through a set of magical miracles, we found him and were reunited (so very many tears, so very much relief and joy). I turn experiences into stories, and this was the seed of "Devil May Care." (No, I did not actually summon any demons to help us find Link. *Fairies* on the other hand...)

"A History of Drowning"

This is an amalgamation of many memories and dreams I've had over the years: I drowned as a twelve year old in the town pool (and was saved after not breathing for a touch too long), I had the worst crush in the world on a girl who was a dear friend (and, unfortunately, straight and didn't have a clue how I felt) when I was a teenager, and I've had a reoccurring dream my entire life (after the drowning) that I drown in a car that falls off a bridge. I often take memories and dreams and turn them into stories with new characters to help process them. This is where "A History of Drowning" came from.

"Melusine"
The story of Melusine is one of my favorite myth fragments. I had a vision of a novel, but was working on another novel at the time, so wrote the short story. I may revisit this as a novel someday.

"No Bigger Than the Moon"
I'm fascinated by the idea of kelpies...their need for satiation, their unabashed hunger. The fact that they're usually, awesomely, in horse form. I also love writing twisted endings. I wrote this story right before one of our trips to New England, and I was turning over the idea of the hungry sea, and the story was born.

"In the Garden I Did Not Sin"
I wrote this note that accompanied the story when it was first published:

...The story you are about to read is very strange. It has an even stranger history.

And there is much more to it than what you see here.

"In the Garden I Did Not Sin" is part of the larger world of the novel I've been working on and off again for many years, tentatively titled The Apple Queen. *I am heavily influenced by the bones of myth in my writing, and* The Apple Queen *is no different. However, when working with "living" myth, it is not so easy as retelling a story no one has believed for thousands of years.*

The Apple Queen *recounts the love story between Eve, the first woman, and Lilith...the* first *first woman. And the story of their daughters. It has gone through many* incarnations...what you see below is the beginning of the saga that would be serialized in novella format.

Here's the thing. I'm working on many more projects than I have space to list. I'm swamped. I now have two amazing agents. This project has always had the softest spot in my heart, but let's be honest: it's weird, it's blasphemous to a large portion of the population, and lots of people are interested in retellings of myths. But retelling a Christian and Judaic myth? Maybe not so much.

But maybe I'm wrong.

If you want to see "In the Garden I Did Not Sin" become something more than this short story, tell me. You guys know that I listen. If something about this project tugs at your heartstrings, let me know. If you want this in its whole form, spread the word about it. I'm listening. You guys are amazing, and reading and sharing the Project Unicorn stories, but this one is a little different from the others. There is a great and expansive story behind what you see here.

I'm leaving it in your hands. If the world wants a lesbian retelling of the myth of Eve, I would be overjoyed. If you want this, tell me.

Either way, enjoy. <3

A Word About Blasphemy: My intention with this story has nothing to do with blasphemy. If you are Christian and believe the word of the Bible, that's awesome. I don't—I believe the Bible to be myth, and as a myth reconstructionist, I have long worked with the myths of the Bible as I have with many other myths. I respect your religion, and am not making any Blanket Statements with my reinterpretations—I am merely retelling the story as I would any myth.

Many, many people went on to share the story and ask for more...*The Apple Queen* is now tentatively in the works!

"Two Salt Feet"

I'm a vegan, though not anything like Sam in my

story (she's pretty "in your face!" about it). I was thinking about how having a voice is crucial for having rights (when S.E. enjoys metaphors!), and began thinking about gay rights and voicelessness, and "Two Salt Feet" evolved from a lot of thinking about such things. And having wandered through an open-air market in New England recently, where I probably would not have been completely shocked to see a mermaid for sale. In a tasty way.

"Daughter of Blue"

I'm a lifelong Pagan who finds it utterly tragic that there are not more Pagan stories. "Daughter of Blue" was a story that I'd written very differently about five years ago. I wanted to rewrite it for a YA audience and add the Pagan element (it was more fantasy based back then), but I kept the very first line that had always haunted me, asking for the story to be retold.

"The Mermaid Circus"

There's a little town in Florida called Weeki Wachee. For over fifty years, young ladies have donned mermaid tails and performed underwater acts of amazing grace to crowds of tourists. Lately, the amazing mermaid theater has become quieter...a beautiful relic of times gone by that people still journey to. From the tiniest of kids, I wanted to go to Weeki Wachee (hello, mermaid obsessed girl), and when I finally got to go, it was everything I'd dreamed of...but it was also bittersweet, seeing how far the place had gone. While there, I got so much inspiration for so many different stories, and "The Mermaid Circus" is one of them. No, Weeki Wachee is nothing like the Mermaid Circus in the story—if you ever get a chance to go, you should. It's beautiful and worth the journey to see the old magic that remains there.

"Falling Home"

This is part of a novel that I have not yet written

(but can't wait to—I love this story so, so much). I got the idea from talking about the deadly sins and the levels of hell with my wife. Because, you know, that's polite and romantic dinner talk fodder. And this, ladies and gentlemen, is always how we roll.

"Nike"

I wrote this note that accompanied the story when it was first published:

This story, though incredibly fantastical in the end, is based on real life events.

As I have my main character, Beth, call a suicide prevention hotline in the story, I had been doing research on hotline prevention scripts and what they can do.

And one night, I called the Trevor Project hotline myself.

(The Trevor Project Lifeline is a crisis intervention and and suicide prevention service for LGBTQ youth. It can be reached at 1-866-488-7386.)

"Hello, this is Paul, how can I help you?" answered a kind man's voice after two rings. I was surprised. I didn't think it would be answered so quickly, and without any sort of menu.

"Hi, Paul, this is S.E. Diemer—I'm a lesbian young adult author, and I'm working on a short story about a teen lesbian with suicidal thoughts. Can I ask you two or three questions? I promise it won't take more than a minute or two. I totally understand if you're busy taking calls and can't answer."

"Absolutely I can answer!" said Paul. He went through the scripts they use, how they respond to specific questions, like "I'm thinking of killing myself right now, please help me." Throughout it all he was wonderful and engaging and kind. I was so impressed that at the end, I thanked him profusely and told him he'd be mentioned at the end of the short story.

"I know you said this was for a short story, but this is a question I have to ask every caller," said Paul.

"Are you thinking of contemplating suicide?"

"No," I told him.

"Have you in the past?"

"Yes," I said truthfully. "When I was a teen, I came out when I was fifteen, and it was very, very difficult for me. That's why I'm writing the story."

"We're here twenty-four/seven, and we will talk with anyone, anytime," said Paul. "Please know that, okay?"

"I do," I promised him. "And I'm going to tell others, too."

Regardless of what you think of the Trevor Project, the grace and kindness of those who answer their Lifeline is top notch and nothing short of amazing. The lengths they go to to help a teen on the phone are astronomical.

If you are a queer kid who is contemplating suicide, please call the Trevor Project. There is a kind person waiting to listen to you and to help you.

1-866-488-7386

I am very grateful to Paul who took a few minutes out of his day to help this author with her story—and who spends time in his day to help people who need it.

"The Gargoyle Maker"

This is one of my favorite stories I've written to date. I have a small collection of gargoyles, and a lifelong obsession with their mythology. This story has been living in my head for many years, waiting to come out--I wanted to write it as a novel, and I still might, some day. This story is dedicated to my friend, Bree, who has the heart of a gargoyle: loyal, fierce, protective and innately awesome.

"Bone Ship"

I was giving a small tour of a local graveyard to some friends, and was talking about how the Victorians needed to make absolutely certain that people were buried in the earth, their toes pointing to the rising sun, so that they would be able to *bodily* rise when Christ came back to the world (yes, totally like zombies)…and I began to wonder what would have happened if we fast forwarded time a little, and people still held that belief as absolute and true.

"Poppy and Salt"

I was flipping through one of my weird books, in my collection of weird books, and came across a paragraph on how it was once believed, in old Europe, that vampires must follow poppy seeds back to their final resting place. I thought that was a very ill-thought out plan, because once the vampire gets home, he might be quite put out at whoever had made the trail of poppy seeds. And I began to think that, really, blessed salt might be the only thing to *seal* him there…and then I began to write this story. Vampires are one of my first literary loves…when I was a teenager, I wrote bad vampire book after bad vampire book. I still love them, even though they've been "done to death" (I don't believe it!), so feel that I have to be even more creative and weird when I write about vampires so it's original and compelling. Out of all of this came "Poppy and Salt."

"Mercy Brown"

Poor Mercy Brown. This short story of mine is actually based on a *true* story. In the nineteenth century, an entire family was plagued by consumption in Rhode Island…when Mercy died, they dug up her other family members, then took her out of the crypt where they'd been keeping her until the spring thaw to bury her. She looked fresher (she hadn't been dead that long), and because her family was hysterical at this point, they tossed reason to the wind and cut out her heart, because they assumed she was a vampire. They *then* thought it'd be a fantastic idea to burn her heart on a rock until it was ash, and feed it to her brother. Mercy has been called the "Last American Vampire," and because I love her and feel pitifully sorry for her, I wanted to write her into a story. I've still not visited the grave of Mercy Brown, though I will someday. If you're ever in Rhode Island, look her up. I'm sure she'd love a visitor.

JENNIFER'S AUTHOR NOTES

"A Craving"

The fairy tale Snow White has always occupied a place in my heart, and, as a writer, I find endless inspiration in its strangeness and its symbolism. My novella *Seven* is a Snow White retelling, and I also have a full-length speculative fiction novel in the works based upon Snow White. It's a story with mythic qualities for me, and I love experimenting with its motifs.

"Natural"

I have gone with S.E. into the woods several times to visit her beloved childhood tree, which she shared secrets with when she was a little girl. This story was sparked by her old, majestic, towering Magnata.

"Haunt"

I was in the mood to write a ghost story set in a graveyard. Problem was…the Project Unicorn theme was *The Dark Woods*. So, I cheated and just put the graveyard in the woods!

"Dreaming Green"

I sat down with my laptop, determined to write a spaceship story. Again, though, the month's theme—*The Dark Woods*—presented a pretty serious obstacle. But with careful plotting, I mashed the spaceship and forest together and came up with a story that would likely have never occurred to me otherwise. In this case, I think the confines of the theme made for a more original tale.

"Mirrors"

I love the concept of turning ordinary objects into containers for magic and mystery—like the book in *The Neverending Story*. Maybe that's just the treasure hunter in me. When S.E. and I go thrifting, I'm always on the lookout for strange and special things. The antique store compact in "Mirrors" may be seen as an embodiment of the idea on which S.E. and I centered our Etsy store slogan: Within small things waits great magic.

"Blue Bottles"

On one of our visits to Florida, S.E. and I strolled the beach to find the sand speckled with brilliant cobalt blue—hundreds of man-of-wars washed ashore by the sea. That experience provided my inspiration, and the setting, for "Blue Bottles."

"Pearls Enough"

The Victorian era was a particularly confining time for women, so I thought the symbolism of Portia eschewing society in favor of a wild existence under the sea was powerful. And…I just loved the idea of Victorian mermaids!

"Breaking the Ice"

In the early days of our relationship, S.E. and I often wrote poems and stories for each other, and "Breaking the Ice" was one of my gifts for her. It is deeply symbolic and meaningful to both of us. For those reasons, I was a little reluctant to share this story with the world, but my intuition told me that it was the appropriate time.

"A Bit of Space"

This story was completely spontaneous, based solely upon the image in my head of a girl following an owl into the woods.

"Finding Mars"

S.E. and I love to visit weird roadside attractions, and, because some of my family lives in Pennsylvania, we often find ourselves driving past signs for Mars. Sadly, we've never had the opportunity to visit the town—or its infamous spaceship statue—ourselves, but it is on our must-see list. We have, however, driven to Kecksburg, Pennsylvania, to see the acorn-shaped spaceship replica there!

"The Girl on the Mountain"

Originally, I had envisioned Laurel as an alien being, primarily because I love writing about alien beings... But when I immersed myself fully in the story, it became clear to me that she was nearer to the earth than that—a sky spirit, like the cloud nymphs—*nephelae*—of Greek mythology.

"Kyrie"

I had a lot of fun with this story. I loved the way that its setting—a technology-obsessed society—contrasted with its central conflict: the appearance of beings who defy known science with their natural-growing wings. Mille's bubbly friend Lu was a big surprise to me, honestly, and turned out to be my favorite character of the story. Because I loved Lu and the Kyrie and this world so much, I am considering returning to it in some form or another in the future.

AUTHORS' INTERVIEW

Authors Jennifer Diemer and S.E. Diemer interviewed each other in late December 2012 about Project Unicorn, writing lesbian teen heroines and about the stories themselves, using the magical technology that is known as Google Drive and while drinking copious amounts of tea and coffee. The interview went as follows...

Jenn: So...do you like purple?

S: Seeing as I married a purple-haired lady, the answer is YES.

J: Good answer.

S: We asked, and you guys answered: You said you wanted an interview by and of the two of us as an extra feature in this volume. And yet just look at that very first question! Everyone is immediately sorry they asked for this. ;D All right, let's get dangerous...I mean serious (sparkling, virtual vegan cupcakes to whoever gets that reference). Honey, do you believe we've already done one *quarter* of Project Unicorn? It feels surreal.

J: It does. We have this habit of setting crazy, insurmountable goals for ourselves--and then achieving them, but I have to say, this has been a challenge! But an endlessly rewarding one.

S: I just remember being all like "ha, two stories a week! Piece of *cake!*" And then quoting that line with extreme sarcasm whenever we were past deadline and staying up until four in the morning to finish a story...

J: Yeah, "piece of extremely complicated, fancy, five-story tall wedding cake" might be more applicable...

S: Wasn't it somewhere in our wedding vows that we would love each other and cherish each other with or without extreme writing deadlines? I'm sure it was in there.

J: I think it must have been.

S: It was right next to the part of "will help each other come up with eight million story ideas on two hours of sleep." WRITERS: when they get MARRIED. Okay, serious time again! (Ha!) What was your favorite story out of all of these to work on?

J: Well, as far as themes, I was definitely most excited to work on *Uncharted Sky*, because I'm all about alien stories. But I'd say my favorite stories overall were "A Craving" and "Kyrie."

S: I know you loved "A Craving" because "Snow White" is your favoritest thing of ever (scientifically proven fact), but what about "Kyrie" made you love it? (I, personally, loved how you stitched together the otherworldly and very mundane. And how you wrote it. But then I'm your biggest fan so this is NO SURPRISE! <3)

J: With "Kyrie," the characters and the whole world, really, just came alive so effortlessly, and I found it was a place I enjoyed spending time in. I also loved writing about angel-like beings who weren't technically angels but still evoked that feeling of awe and mystery. So, how about you? What were your favorite stories to write?

S: I was physically sick the entire time I was writing "Nike," and it's not really a story one could ever call a "favorite," considering the subject matter, but it was incredibly cathartic and cleansing to write that one. It dealt with so much that I went through, that I know a lot of lesbian teens go through, and it was powerful to put it out into the world, though incredibly draining, if I'm being honest. My *favorite* story is probably a cross between "The Gargoyle Maker," "Falling Home" and "Two Salt Feet." I love writing supremely weird things because I think surreality can unlock a lot of magic, and that makes me so happy to bring into the world. I also loved the main characters deeply in all of them. I know that I have my own ways of differentiating characters (especially since all we write are lesbian stories, and we write so many of them!), but how do you keep your characters fresh, alive and different in your head?

J: Honestly, I'm very intuitive about the whole writing process and just write words as they come to me, and present characters as they present themselves to me. I do try to make my characters different enough to be distinct from one another, though.

S: I love that all of your stories are different enough that they always shock me (in the best of ways), and yet they always have that seed of "this is a Jenn story." There's that shock of wonder-full awe in almost everything you write. That there's strange, surreal magic in the world if you look for it, and even in yourself if you seek to find it.

J: Really, those are the same qualities I most love about your stories. I might think I know which direction you're heading in, but then you always surprise me in the most unexpected, sometimes-weird, sometimes-delightful sort of ways. <3

S: Thank you, darlin'. <3 And that's the "awwww heard 'round the world," ladies and gentlemen! <3 Before we get SUPREMELY mushy (as we tend to do), I think this is a great segue into addressing the lesbian teens who might be reading this. Look at the above mush. Just look at it. I remember when I was fifteen and I thought that I would never fall in love because there was no one in the world for me. And then I fell in love with a purple-haired writer who loves me not *despite* of the fact that I'm obsessed with monsters, graveyards, fairies and tea and sparkles, but *because* of that.

J: It really was magic, the way that we found each other, fell in love and came to spend our lives together. But I think it's magic that's available to everyone, and that's, I guess, kind of what I--and I think, you--try to communicate with these Project Unicorn stories. All of our stories have a bit of magic to them, and that's entirely intentional. In real life, magic doesn't necessarily come in the form of unicorns or wings or--

S: (BUT IT TOTALLY CAN.)

J: Yes, totally. :) But magic can also come in the form of an unexpected letter, or a beautiful smile, or a sudden realization or understanding that you never looked for before but realize was waiting for you all along.

S: Love comes when you least expect it. You have courage that you never knew was there. People love you that you didn't think especially did. Terrible things happen, but also wonderful, magical things in this lifetime. And you can't predict them and you can never expect them. And then somehow, they're there. Like love. Like kindness. Like a kiss.

J: One of our ultimate goals with Project Unicorn

was not only to give greater visibility to lesbian teens in young adult fiction and to normalize their presence in genre stories, but also to communicate a message of hope. Not all of our stories have happy endings, but the vast majority of them do.

S: I think that's because it's our greatest wish. No one deserves to be bullied or treated differently or mocked or hurt or ostracized. We've both been through all of that. It needs to stop. And it will. And it can. Every day, people are trying to *make* it better. It'll get there with enough action, with enough energy of change. And with enough stories.

J: People have always communicated through stories. It's how we learn about the world, each other and ourselves.

S: And I think it's how the world begins to change.

J: Our hope is that you, the reader, enjoy these stories and share them with other people who might enjoy them. Project Unicorn is our small, sincere attempt to broaden the scope of lesbian presence in young adult literature. We've put our whole hearts into these stories, and we deeply hope that they touch yours.

ABOUT PROJECT UNICORN

What is Project Unicorn?

Project Unicorn: A Lesbian YA Extravaganza! is a fiction project created by lesbian YA authors **S.E. Diemer** and **Jennifer Diemer**. It was created because of the obvious lack of lesbian heroines in the Young Adult genre, and the critical need for them.

Project Unicorn is updated **twice weekly** with **a free, original, never-before-published YA short story featuring a lesbian heroine**. Also, every story is a work of genre fiction (Fantasy, Sci-Fi, Dystopian, Post-apocalyptic, Historical, etc.).

Why Project "Unicorn?"

Because, like unicorns, lesbians in YA literature are almost mythical, nonexistent creatures. Our aim with this project is to simply bring greater visibility to girls who love girls in the YA genre. Also, we both just really love unicorns. :D

This is awesome! How can I support the project?

At the end of each month, Project Unicorn has eight new short stories that have been posted for free. We gather each month's set of short stories, and publish them in an eZine, available for purchase at Amazon, Barnes & Noble and Smashwords. Each eZine not only includes the previously published short stories, but two longer stories never before published and available only in the eZine. (Print volumes will come out quarterly–details on that coming soon!)

If you love what we're doing with Project Unicorn, the two greatest things you can do to support it is to talk about it on your social network, blog or web site, and purchase each eZine as it comes out. Project Unicorn is a very large undertaking, but we're deeply dedicated to giving queer-girls stories they can identify with. Thank you so much for being supportive, and please consider purchasing an eZine to help us continue with this project! <3 (You can also show your support by buying our other books, or simply donating to buy the authors a cup of tea. <3)

Find Project Unicorn at http://MuseRising.Wordpress.com

ABOUT THE AUTHORS

Jennifer Diemer and S.E. Diemer are the authors of several lesbian novels, novellas and short stories. They have been married for five years, and legally married for over one year (thank you, NY state!). They live, love and create together in their purple-doored cottage in the country, with their many magical and very furry children.

To find out more about their novels, novellas and short stories, please visit: **http://museisrising.wordpress.com**.

Find S.E. on Twitter at: **http://twitter.com/sediemer**

Find Jenn on Twitter at:
http://twitter.com/jenniferdiemer

Please sign up for Jennifer and S.E.'s newsletter— they will only contact you when they release a new novel, novella or short story, and you will be the first to know about the release! Sign up at http://www.oceanid.org.